Graham Dent had been interested in Tha
age of 10 and is currently treasurer of tl
Barge Research and Rear-Commodore of
Club. He worked for the Port of London A   . _ _ , ____,
including a spell dealing with barge traffic, and has recently
retired from HM Customs and Excise, where he spent the last
seven years of his career. He is married with two grown-up
children and lives in Leigh-on-Sea, Essex.

THE
THIRD HAND

Graham Dent

To John o Eve
Best Wishes
Graham Dent
19.10.02

ASHRIDGE PRESS

Published by:
Ashridge Press
41 Humberston Avenue, Humberston, nr Grimsby, Limcolnshire DN36 4SW

ISBN 1 901214 20 6

Printed in England by:
MFP Design and Print
Longford Trading Estate, Thomas Street, Stretford, Manchester M32 0JT

Colour origination in England by:
GA Graphics
Sheepmarket, Stamford, Lincolnshire PR9 2EB

CONTENTS

FOREWORD

This book, although fiction, is written as a tribute to the Thames Barge and the men who sailed her. The information on barges and the London docks is factual but some of the 'yarns' included are probably not, or at least have improved with the telling. It is up to the reader to decide which is which!

Similarly some of the barges, the owners and the places mentioned did – and in many cases still do exist. Again, its an interesting puzzle for the reader to solve.

Many people in the barge world have helped, although they might not have realised it at the time, with information for this book. They are too numerous to thank individually, but I would particularly like to mention the members of the Society for Sailing Barge Research. My thanks also to my son, Alex, Alan Murray and my cousins Simon and Tish Askins for assistance with computer work and especially to Sandy Threadgold who cheerfully undertook the horrible task of deciphering my handwriting and turning it into a manuscript. Joyce Haines rescued me from a problem with music, while Ray Chinn kindly read through the finished product and gave me a criticism. Thanks, to Nut and George Skidmore for kindly supplying the cover picture.

Finally, my heartfelt thanks to my family for suffering the trauma of dad writing a book.

G.E.D.

PROLOGUE

1964, Narrative of Jack Downing

Never in my 15 years as a journalist had I been an 'ambulance chaser'. Especially now that I was chief crime reporter (I was also television critic and obituary writer, but that was typical of a small town weekly). Nevertheless, I could not resist the tip-off that Detective Inspector Johnson of Mayfield CID gave me.

It was my habit whenever possible to meet 'Johnnie' for a pint once a week. He would then give me the gen on the latest criminal activities in the town. However this time he had only one thing to report – and it was not a crime.

"My lads have been following up a strange one," he said. "A chap was found washed up on the foreshore yesterday. Rushed to hospital, of course, with hypothermia, exposure and so on. Funny thing was his wife reported him missing four days ago and his yacht was towed in by the lifeboat the next morning. All the signs are that he was single-handed and went overboard trying to reef. Weather was rotten at the time.

"So we ask – where's he been the last three days? He can't tell us, not yet. Or perhaps won't, since he's asked to talk to you."

"Me?" I said, surprised.

"Yes, he claims you're an old friend, school or something."

"Hang on, Johnnie," I said. "What about the wife? Surely he's told her something?"

"Ah, no. All is not well there. You know the sort of thing - loves his boat more than he loves me. Silly fool will drown himself one day – and nearly did. And things didn't improve when he started muttering girls' names when he was coming round – Ellie, Daisy, Maud, some of them were. He she's one unhappy lady." He drained the rest of his pint and glanced at his watch. "Well, I'd love another one but I'm due in court this afternoon – don't want to upset the magistrates." He got up to go. "You'll do that, then, go and see this vanished yachtsman?"

"Oh yes, Johnnie, since he's asked, but what's his name?"

"William Furlong."

Bill Furlong, I thought as I drove to the hospital. We had been together at school, it was true, but in different forms, although we had been in the same cricket team. I would not have said that we close. Later our paths had crossed in sailing circles, but not often since he was not a member of my sailing club.

I had gone back to the office before leaving for the hospital and had gleaned some more information, mainly from our gossip columnist, Amanda Smyth. Furlong, it would appear, was a successful architect, practising in London. However, Mrs Furlong was much better known. She was a prominent socialite in her younger years and was now the owner of a chain of boutiques, her main interests, other than business, being the next man and the next bottle of gin.

Well, if she put it about, then so did her husband. Daisy, Maud, Ellie . . . but what sort of women had such old-fashioned names these days? I hadn't got any further with this line when I parked in a reserved space at the hospital – this wouldn't bother them as I had my press card on the windscreen. Before seeing Furlong, I had a word with his doctor, an old friend, Dr Murchison.

"How's crime?" he asked.

"Quiet at the moment," he replied, "but not if your man Furlong's been up to naughties."

"I doubt it," he replied. "Not the type, in my opinion. But something's worrying him very badly. He needs to get it off his chest – not to us doctors, not the police and certainly not to his wife."

9

I repeated what Inspector Johnson had told me.

"Well, he is certainly fit enough to talk now. If it's you he wants to confide in, I would say that it can do no harm – probably a lot of good."

"Wouldn't a psychiatrist be better?"

"We tried. Furlong told him to get out, he wasn't going to talk to a shrink."

"He sounds better."

"Physically a good deal better, but not mentally, so see whether you can get him to unburden himself."

Furlong seemed pleased to see me, and obviously remembered me a lot better than I remembered him.

"Why did you want to see me?" I asked after the preliminaries.

"Well you're a journalist," he said.

"There's several of those on my paper alone."

"But you know about such things."

"What things!" I persisted.

"Thames Barges," he almost whispered. I thought for a moment. True, at one time I had been a fan of these unique East Coast vessels, reading the literature about them, tramping across marshes to look at the remains of some and actually sailing on some of the more active ones. But my interest had waned when it became apparent that their trading days were over and the survivors only had a future as motor vessels. I had an inspiration.

"Ellie and Daisy and Maud. They're barges aren't they?"

He shook his head. "No. Daisy Maud's a barge. Ellie, she's…very special." He was silent for a while. "I'll have to tell you the whole story."

"Please do."

CHAPTER ONE
RESCUED

I was falling, down into the icy depths of the Thames Estuary. How foolish, I thought, not to use a safety harness when going for'rard in a blow like that. And then I knew no more . . .

When I came too, I was lying on a hard wooden deck, retching sea water.

Faraway, a voice said: "He's comin' round, skip."

"Don't call me that," an older voice snapped.

I drifted away again.

When I awoke, I was naked, under several blankets. A blue light was falling across my face. This puzzled me until I realised that the light was coming through blue curtains surrounding whatever bed I was in. After a while I raised one hand and, with what seemed like a great effort, pulled one of the curtains aside.

I was evidently in a ship's cabin, a fact borne out by the creaks and groans of a sailing vessel at sea. The bunk I was in was one of a pair as I could see its twin opposite, similarly shrouded by blue curtains. Underneath a skylight which let in some natural light, a highly polished oil lamp swung in bright brass gimbals between the bunks, reflecting on the surface of a large table below. Underneath the bunks and surrounding the table was a horse-shoe shaped settle covered with red leather, or a least imitation leather, cushions. I could tell there were lockers underneath the settle from the clasps and hinges I could see on the side opposite.

Against the forward bulkhead a pot-bellied coal stove supported a saucepan in which something, which smelled good, was heating. Above was a rack of hooks holding kitchen implements and several mugs.

On one side of the stove a companionway gave access to what must be the deck. While the other side was a cubby-hole for personal hygiene, as it contained a mirror and what appeared to be a foldaway washbasin. The only decoration was a calendar hanging above the mug rack. I could make out the legend "H.R. Fielder & Sons, Licensed Lightermen and Tug-Owners" on it, but not the dates.

Noises on deck seemed to indicate a change of course or shortening of sail and a few minutes later footsteps sounded on the companionway. A short, spare figure appeared and hung an ancient and damp raincoat on one of the hooks at the foot of the stairs, however he retained a disreputable trilby hat. Otherwise he was clad in a dark blue suit which had become baggy and shiny with age. Under it he wore a once white shirt held together with a collar-stud but bereft of its collar and a grey sweater which had also seen better days. His trousers were tucked into short Wellington boots.

He glanced in my direction and said: "You're awake, then." He took a ladle and a mug from above the stove and transferred some the contents of the saucepan to the mug.

"Get some o' this down yer lad. Do yer good," he said proffering me the mug. I pushed myself up in the bunk, and reaching out for the mug found myself looking into a pair of the bluest eyes I have seen, framed in a face with the colour and texture of a walnut. I took a sip from the mug, it was some kind of soup containing bits of meat and potato and was indeed very good.

"Thought I'd come and see 'ow yer were," my benefactor added. "Mate's got the wheel now things are a bit quieter."

I asked the classic question: "Where am I?"

"Why, you'm aboard the sailing barge Daisy Maud bound from West India Dock to 'er 'ome port Upshore in Essex with cattle cake, I'm Captain 'Appy Day, but yew can call me skipper or master, not skip like that scallywag Vic up there." He nodded at the deck-head.

"I'd better get back, we'll goin' inter Upshore directly." (Later I was to lean that the Essex term "directly" meant sometime in the indefinite future. Only the more positive "directly minnut" implied any degree of urgency.)

He donned his disreputable raincoat and disappeared on deck, leaving me with my soup. As I finished it, I reflected on Captain Day's words. Something was wrong. A sailing barge bound from London to Upshore with cattlecake. That could not be. But I could not think why. The soup had revived me and my body at last felt warm.

I decided to explore the cabin. Wrapping myself in one of my blankets, I scrambled out of the bunk and tottered towards the stove. I was drawn to the Fielder calendar. It was open at April. Someone had ringed the 16th and written, in a poor hand "Cattle-cake to Upshore". But it was the year that shocked me – 1939.

So the 16th April could well be the present voyage – in 1939? It again sounded wrong and again I couldn't think why. As I moved away from the calendar I could sight of my reflection in the mirror. I was looking at the features of a boy of 17 not a man of 47. This however seemed to be perfectly natural, but I did not have time to dwell on my reactions, as I heard someone opening the hatch at the top of the companionway.

This time my visitor was Vic, the barge's mate, who had come below to prepare a meal.

He was dressed similarly to the skipper, with the exception that his outside coat was a black oilskin, while a flat cap replaced the ancient trilby. His most prominent feature was a pair of large, protruding ears.

He promptly went to work at the table deftly chopping carrots and onions and peeling potatoes, talking incessantly while he did so, starting with his own life history. He was, he told me, 20 years old (although he looked older) and he had started on barges at the age of thirteen. A native of Rochester in Kent, he had begun on river barges on the Medway. Becoming bored with this he had hitch hiked to Upshore two years ago in the hopes of shipping on a coasting barge. He had not been immediately successful in this, and had worked for a while in an Upshore boat yard, but eventually he had secured a mate's berth and had served on several Upshore barges before joining Captain Day on the Daisy Maud only a month ago, when the previous mate, Tommy Dolby, obtained a skipper's berth.

Happy Day, he went on, was not only master, but also part owner of the Daisy Maud. The barge had been built around the turn of the century for Happy's father, but like all sailing vessels, ownership was vested in sixty four shares. Some of these had been sold to local tradesmen, but the majority remained with Day senior. Upon his demise he had willed his shares to Happy and his sister, Happy, by then mate on the barge, receiving the larger portion. The sister, however, had chosen to sell her shares to the barge's managers, Messrs Fowler & Dunn, who as barge-owners in their own right, were fast buying up all the barges in the Upshore area.

In fact, Vic went on, Fowler & Dunn were probably the third largest sailing barge owners on the East Coast after the Thames and Medway Barge Co. at Rochester and Goldsmith of Grays. The firm was run by the Fowler family, although there was a Mr. Dunn, whose interest was largely financial. He was a London shipbroker who found the firm's barges many of their cargoes. The other directors were Isaac Fowler and his two sons, John and Ernest, although there was also a daughter, Miss Ellie, who had just started learning the business from the office side. Ernest was a barge builder by profession, and had built a couple of the firm's barges in the 1920s. Now, with the recession, the barge-yard only did repair work and refitting and Mr. Ernest tended to bury himself in that and not interfere in other aspects of the enterprise.

"Now that Mr. John, 'e's the one you've got to watch", said Vic. "Crackshot young skipper 'e is. Got the firm's best barge an' 'e'd like to have this 'un an all "'cos she's a fast owld bit of wood when she's got the mind. Old Happy and Isaac sees eye to eye, 'cos they go back a long way, but John 'e'll be a proper bugger if 'e takes over."

He suddenly switched from barging politics to his great passion in life, gambling. If it moved, he would have a bet on it, he claimed.

"I'll tell you wot," he said darkly, "I'll 'ave a bet with you that we don't get to Upshore tonight, 'cos that winds a-droppin' and the tides nearly gorn." I replied that I had no money. Undeterred Vic said we'd imagine we had a bet and then reminisced for a while about racehorses and dogs that had done well for him in the past until Captain Day's stentorian whisper came from the skylight.

"Vic, get yerself on deck. That tides gorn an' we've got to bring-up."

Vic left and for a while I listened to the mysterious bangs, thumps and creaks of the barge being 'bought-up'. Some were readily identifiable, such as the roar of the anchor cable running out. There was a distinct absence of human conversation. Both men, I decided, must know exactly what they were doing. As the noises declined I drifted off to sleep again.

I was awoken by the thump of a boat coming alongside followed by voices on deck. Evidently we had visitors.

Shortly afterwards Happy Day came below with two other men. The skipper made no attempt to introduce me but it soon became evident that they were Captain Gascoigne of the Alicia and Happy's former mate Tommy Dolby, now skipper of the Silverfish. Both barges were owned by Fowler & Dunn and, like us, were anchored off Hibberts Island, awaiting the tide up to Upshore. From up for'rard the sound of an harmonica, indicated that the barges mates were making their own amusement.

Captain Day made tea for his guests and as it was being prepared the three men began to talk. Gascoigne was a large, florid man, who held positive opinions any subject upon which he was prepared to expound at length. Tommy, a much younger

15

man, was well aware of this, and it seemed to me, went out of his way to provoke Gascoigne. Once or twice he winked in my direction, which confirmed this belief.

He was a very different type, whose complexion and significant beer belly indicated, correctly, a distinct preference for ale. His wide slash of a mouth and twinkling eyes under heavy eyebrows, betrayed his sense of humour.

Captain Day, unlike his two guests, said very little and seemed to act as chairman of the meeting. This quietness was habitual to him and I had, already that day, heard one or more of his longer speeches. The conversation was not about the bigger issues of the day, even the possibility of war, receiving only a passing mention. Basically it was only about barges and matters relating to them. How such a barge was on the ways for a refit and how the shipwrights had found a bit of rot in her, how the mate of another had fallen overboard in West India Dock, how a third had gone aground on the Buxey and a fourth had broken her sprit in a Force 6 in the Swale, and so on.

Suddenly, however, the conversation came closer home and the subject was, of all things, Vic's oilskin.

"They're no good, them things," said Gascoigne. "Couldn't beat an old raincoat up there," he nodded at the deck head ,"yer goin' to get wet anyway, yer just want summat to keep the wind out. Anyways, what happens when one o' them oilies gets torn, can't repair it, no how."

"Oh, I dunno," said Tommy, "think I'll get one (a wink) when I can afford it. Fact is, I'll probably get Vic's when he wants some cash to put on a sure thing."

Gascoigne decided to change the subject "You goin' to enter this Barge Match then?" he said to Captain Day.

"Happen I will," replied Day enigmatically.

"You gotta," said Gascoigne emphatically. "She's a fast owld thing, this barge, when she gits a-goin'. An' you want to show them Fowlers a thing or two."

"An' what about Fowler & Dunn?" Day interrupted.

"Well ould Isaac won't like it much, but 'e's a fair man. Young

John, though, 'e'll be 'oppin mad, especially if you beat the Pride."

"Now 'ang on" said Day in one of his larger speeches. "The Pride of Upshore's a borsprit barge and we ain't."

That seemed to close the matter as far as he was concerned but Tommy rushed into the argument.

"Ah, but this barge 'ad a borsprit when your old dad 'ad her in the stacky trade 'an after you took over for a while. Another one can soon be rigged."

"Never did like the thing though," Day grumbled. "'Appen we'll see."

None of this, of course, meant anything to me at the time, but later I found out that Barge Matches or races were prestige events for both owners and crews and, in the past, had done much for barge design. The owner of a winning barge, quite apart from trophies and prize-money, could be sure of some lucrative business from impressed shippers.

The principal matches were held on the Thames and Medway, but the Upshore event had a good following and often attracted entries from the two major events. This year would be a very good one as both Medway and Thames events had already been cancelled owing to the possibility of war. However, the merchants of Upshore and district were determined that their match would go ahead, whatever.

'Borsprit' was the bargemens' name for the yachtsmen's 'bowsprit' and simply meant a spar extended from the vessels bows enabling it to set extra sails up for'rard, thereby being able to sail faster. Unlike the Thames & Medway events, which had several classes, the Upshore Barge Match was sailed in only two classes – those that had bowsprits and those that did not. Hence Captain Day's dilemma as Daisy Maud was currently among the 'have nots.'

Gascoigne, of course, had to have the last word.

"Yew put a borsprit on this one, she could beat anything, even that owld Pride. Never mind Fowler & Dunn, you enter 'er, you're the principal share holder after all." With this he went on deck, calling for his mate. Tommy shrugged and then followed him. Not at all disconcerted by the argument, Happy Day went on deck to bid his guests farewell. I went to sleep and knew no more.

I was woken by the distinctive clanking of a barge's anchor cable being wound in. This, however, was one of the other barges, as Captain Day and Vic were sat at the table hurriedly finishing huge portions of bacon and eggs. A third, smaller portion was being kept warm for me on the stove.

Vic brought it over to the table with the necessary cutlery, threw me an old jersey and trousers, muttered something about "Yew can wash up later on" and followed the skipper on deck.

When I had finished breakfast and dressed in my borrowed clothing, Captain Day called down that I could come on deck for the remainder of the voyage to Upshore. This was, of course, the first time I had been on deck since my rescue.

There was plenty to see. We were sailing up a river some two hundred yards wide. The land either side was evidently devoted to farming, probably grazing judging by the number of cows that had strayed on to the sea walls, which cut off our view of the actual lower land. Hills a mile or so away were patchworked with fields of crops. Occasional farmhouses and barns broke up this panorama.

The other two barges were ahead of us – Tommy easily recognisable at the wheel of his vessel, only a few yards ahead, but Gascoigne, who must have been the one I heard raising his anchor, was about half a mile away. With a fair wind and tide they had, like us, not set full sail, only topsail, foresail and a brailed up mainsail. The brails were handy devices, being wires which drew the mainsail in towards the mast like a theatre curtain and, as now, could control the amount of mainsail in use.

It was then that I met the third member of Daisy Maud's crew. Earlier I had now and again heard a dog barking, but evidently the animal was not allowed in the cabin. Now it rushed up to me as if I was a long lost friend, and give those parts of my body that were exposed a thorough licking.

"Soft ould thing," said Captain Day, "no good as a barge dog. 'Is name's Frank."

Frank. A funny name for a dog. Still, a lot of things in this world were odd.

"Time you learnt sommat lad," said the skipper and embarked on a speech which, for him, must have been the equivalent of Handels' Messiah for a singer. Starting with the windlass up for'rard which was used for raising the anchor he named every visible item of equipment on the barge. Much of this I immediately forgot, but I was impressed with the great wooden sprit which supported the mainsail diagonally – hence the name 'spritsail barge'. Also, the mainsheet block, large as a man's head, which travelled across the deck attached to a thick bar of wood called a 'horse'.

"Yew've gotta keep out of the way of that, lad," said the skipper, referring to the block.

The mate came aft.

"How much, Vic?" asked the skipper

"Not a lot, Skip."

"I tole yew . . . "

"Help if we could pass them two, though."

"Shouldn't be 'ard," said the skipper.

And it wasn't, for we were just going past Tommy, who waved and doffed his hat. I gathered from the previous exchange that Vic must have entered into a wager with the other barge mates as to which barge reached Upshore first.

Gascoigne proved no harder than Tommy to overtake. He had already dropped back, and a harder puff of wind took us past in fine style.

"Tole yew she was fast," shouted Gascoigne as we went past, while his dog and Frank exchanged friendly barks and growls.

"Moty-boat should be waitin' for us," Happy Day told Vic after we had passed Gascoigne. It was noticeable that Captain Day managed to convey contempt in his pronunciation of certain words – 'moty-boat', 'moty-car' and 'ingin', for example.

"That's where we're bound," said Vic "Upshore." Following his

19

gesture, I could see a church tower rising above a mass of trees.

"St. Michael's. The church," Vic went on, "stands on the only decent bit of high ground in the town. Lot of trees as yer comes up the river. Town Council likes 'em."

Indeed we were now coming up to signs of habitation. A few yachts lay at moorings off a yacht club. At a small wharf a crane was swinging bags of something into a single sailing barge and a large notice board advertised the existence of a ferry at that point on then narrowing river. Round the next bend, where no doubt the 'moty-boat' lurked, we should be able to see the whole of the town.

CHAPTER TWO
HOME PORT

Not one, but two, 'moty-boats' awaited us round the bend. One was crewed by a man whose shining bald pate reflected the sun and a young lad of about my own, apparent, age. This was evidently Fowler & Dunn's boat as it hustled up to take our line. The second boat was marked 'River Bailiff' and was manned by men in a semblance of uniform. There was nothing sinister in its presence, Vic assured me, as the bailiff was a member of the Fowler family and frequently assisted when there were several barges to moor. Frank treated both boats to an equal amount of barking.

As we towed up to our berth at the Town Quay, with Captain Day steering and Vic stowing the sails, the panorama of Upshore waterfront unfolded. Comments by both skipper and mate, then and later, filled in the blanks for me.

First we passed a buoy to which a group of empty sailing barges was moored. All flew, from their mastheads, the Fowler & Dunn houseflag or 'bob' as the bargemen called it. This consisted of the letters F & D in white on an orange background. I gathered that each barge-owner had his own distinctive flag.

Inshore was a row of fishing smacks, some of which had evidently preceded us up the river, as they were still taking their sails down or landing their catches. Beyond them, straddling the sea-wall was Fowler & Dunn's bargeyard, rather prettily set among the council trees. Two sailing barges were hauled up on the slipways outside the big shed that was the centrepiece of the yard. Inside the shed a large motor cruiser was under construction while several yachts and fishing boats waited attention on the saltings either side of the slipways. Evidently Mr. Ernest's shipwright empire was prepared to diversify.

Then we were up to the Town Quay. Although there was room alongside it's wooden piles for three or four barges, it was completely empty. I guessed the empty barges on the buoy had been moved away to make room for the new arrivals. Someone was busy organising ashore.

At the back of the quay stood two blocks of grim brick warehouses with a Georgian Town House sandwiched between them. At either end of the quay were two pubs – the rather plain King's Head and the ornate Jolly Fisherman which had baskets of flowers swinging from its veranda. Above all this soared the tower of the Church of St. Michael.

Vic was careful to inform me about the pubs: "Kings Head's the bargemens' pub – Jolly Fisherman's for yachtsmen and the like."

There was plenty of activity on the quay, despite the absence of barges. A number of lorries, one of them steam-driven, were loading from the warehouses. Two horses with carts were doing the same while, nearer at hand, a group of oil-smeared men were inspecting the workings of one of a pair of hydraulic cranes.

The Georgian building in contrast to the grimy warehouses was neatly decorated. It was, I gathered, the offices of Fowler & Dunn Ltd. Since the building was too big for their needs, parts of it were let to the River Bailiff and His Majesty's Customs and Excise.

On the opposite bank of the river and slightly upstream of the Town Quay was a timber wharf, piled high with sawn planks, where several barges and lighters were working. Notice boards proclaimed this to be the property of Fuller Bros.

Further upstream still was a mill, alongside which the masts and spars of two further barges reached for the sky. Opposite a gasometer proclaimed the existence of a gas-works, but no barges were present there.

Having manoeuvred us alongside the quay the motor-boat left us to moor up. She went downstream to collect Tommy, while the bailiffs boat pushed Gascoigne's craft in astern of us. When skipper and mate were satisfied with the mooring, Vic suddenly remembered the washing-up.

"I'll come and show you 'ow to do it," he said.

Vic evidently considered washing-up to be an art. Somewhere along the line he had remembered to fill a kettle and place it on the stove. It was now boiling. Vic transferred the contents to a bucket and added a little washing soda. Our task was not easy, as the plates were covered with congealed egg yolk and bacon rind from breakfast.

As we worked, Vic explained the sanitary arrangements for sailing barges. Each was issued with two domestic buckets. One was used for washing up and cleaning, the other as a toilet and woe betide the bargemate who mixed them up! No wonder Vic wished to supervise the washing-up. Finally we wiped the crockery dry with a tea towel marked "Property of London, Midland and Scottish Railway Co" and returned to the deck.

Captain Day had finished tidying up on deck and was awaiting our first visitor. This was the bald headed man from the motor-boat. It was only then that I realised that his left leg ceased at the knee and a wooden peg-leg had been substituted for the lower portion. As he hobbled towards us, Vic had time to explain that this was Ezekial Brown, formerly one of Fowler's top skippers, until one dark night a winch had run amok and so mangled his lower leg that the hospital had removed it. Now he was employed as ship's husband, making sure the barges had sufficient stores, dealing with manning problems and filling in with operating the 'moty-boat.'

"All right 'Appy" he said as he drew near, "want anything?"

"Oil for the lamps, o'course. Cabin coal. New mop wouldn't go amiss."

"See what I can do. See them barges on the buoy?"

"Yes. The Hubert. Put an ingin in 'er, ain't they?"

Ezekial lowered himself onto our cabin top and mopped his bald head. "Isaac's idea, but it ain't 'im, it's young John. Put ingins in the lot 'e would. 'E's pressin' for them two on the ways to be done while they're there, directly minnut."

"Everything all right, Captain Day?" asked another voice, female and without a trace of an Essex accent. I had been so intent on the one-legged man, I had not noticed the next visitor cross the quay from the office building. Perhaps I should have watched Vic's eyes, which definitely lit up. She was a girl of about eighteen and, although she wore spectacles, exceedingly pretty. Her dark hair was cut short and a crisp white blouse and tight black skirt accentuated her neat figure.

"Picked this lad up in the Thames, Miss Ellie," said Day. "Seems to 'ave lorst his memory. Dunno wot to do with 'im quite."

"I'll deal with him later," Miss Ellie replied. "I arranged for the other barges to drop down to the buoy, so that you three had a clear berth. The lumpers should be down shortly, but unloading may be slow as we've only got one crane, unless the other gets finished." She glowered prettily at the mechanics still struggling with the crane. "When you're ready, Zeke, I've got something for you to do."

"Got the other two barges to see, Miss Ellie." said Zeke.

"Very well, as soon as you can." She turned on her heel and strode back towards the office.

"Gettin' as worse'n big bad brother John, that one" Zeke said to her retreating back. "Runs the office now ol' Sid Oram's getting past it."

"Decent bloke 'ould sort 'er out," Vic ventured.

"An that won't be you" said Captain Day, "so don't go gettin' ideas." He took a puff on his pipe. "Anyway, 'ows things with you, Zeke?" Evidently Miss Ellie's instructions were low on the list of priorities.

"Isaac still won't 'ave me back on the barges," said Zeke sadly.

24

"'Taint fair. If I can nip around on the moty-boat I can do it on a barge. But it ain't 'im, it's John agin. 'Don't want no cripples on my barges,' I can just 'ere 'im saying it. Mind you, 'e puts ingins in 'em, crews'll be cripples. Must get on."

As if to demonstrate his agility he swung himself over the rail and stumped off down the quay. Shortly afterwards, Vic announced his intention to collect his winnings and, as he put it, "have a jaw" and disappeared down the quay. The dog Frank had departed some time previously on pressing business in the town.

The lumpers, as the local stevedores were known, arrived soon afterwards. After they had taken the hatches off, Captain Day expressed a desire to "go and see the ol' woman", by which I guessed he meant Mrs. Day.

"Look, young 'un, you can keep an eye on the lumpers. You can trust old Les, their foreman, but don't let 'em down the cabin". With this he departed.

I spent a pleasant afternoon sitting on the cabin top, watching the lumpers. They worked hard, much harder than the London dockers I later observed, but they had a passion for tea – much of which they brought with them in milk-bottles and drank cold. However, now and again they desired a hot cup which they offered to make themselves. Mindful of my instructions, I made it myself – on the primus which acted as back-up to the main cabin stove. From time to time I wondered what had become of Vic – and in the end decided that answer must lie at the King's Head.

There was only one interruption – the mate of Gascoigne's barge came forward and shouted, in a friendly tone - "Big booze-up in the King's 'Ead ternight." I could not decide whether this was to celebrate the return home or whether it was a device to relieve Vic of his winnings. Now and again I glanced over at the office in the hope Miss Ellie might appear, but there was no sign of her.

About five o'clock the lumpers began packing up and, as if by magic Captain Day reappeared. With Les, the foreman lumper, he inspected the two holds. Unloading had, as forecast, been slow. The second crane had sprung into life briefly but had soon expired again.

"Couple more days work there, Les," said Day.

"Might have to start the other barges," said Les.

"Suits me," said the skipper, "more time with the missus and kids." I was not really paying attention. A pony and trap had pulled up outside the office building. After a short delay, Miss Ellie appeared with an elderly gentleman who she assisted into the trap. The old man was dressed in the style of a bygone age with wing collar, cravat and a top hat. He also sported a set of bushy mutton-chop whiskers. Old Isaac, no doubt. Miss Ellie took the reins from the groom, who went to sit in the back, and drove the trap off at a brisk canter.

"Gentry off home" said Captain Day, a little sourly for him "an' so am I. Vic should be back directly."

This left me on my own and I was beginning to distrust 'directly'. But I soon made a friend. This was Jan, the boy who had been with Zeke on the motor-boat. He was Polish Jew whose family had fled to England in face of Herr Hitler's threats. They were now seeking to establish themselves in the Upshore area, for his father had been a doctor and his mother a university lecturer. But Jan's great passion was all things maritime. He spent his days hanging around the waterfront, making himself useful whenever possible for no wages, in the hopes of securing a mates berth on a barge. He spoke a form of fractured English, which I shall not attempt to reproduce here, interspersed with odd words of French and Polish. He must have been quite clever for he spoke at least these three languages.

I, however, seemed to have the knack of understanding him and we talked of many things, of Poland, of Hitler, of the Upshore barges, of the town of Upshore, the church of St. Michael and many more. Naturally the conversation was rather one sided, for my 'loss of memory' restricted my views on many topics. We were deep in conversation on the cabin top when a rather unsteady Vic appeared, clutching two newspaper parcels.

"Fish and chips," he announced, "compliments of Minstrel

Boy in the 2.30 at York. Saves washin'-up."

We split the fish and chips three ways and tucked in. Vic suddenly burst into verse:

"It was a dark and stormy night
A cargo of fish & chips we had embarked
When the skipper said to the mate,
Tell us a story, an' thus the mate began
It was a dark and stormy night
A cargo of fish and chips..."

And so on until Jan and I howled him down. Towards the end of the meal, I remarked, with a nod at Gascoigne's vessel: "He says there'll be a big booze-up at the King's Head tonight."

"Ah yes, 'ave ter be there. Mus' get me 'ead down for a while first." Vic crammed his remaining chips into his mouth and stumbled to the forecastle.

"He is happy, that one," said Jan.

"Very happy," I confirmed.

It was some while before a rather red-eyed Vic reappeared, by which time Jan and gone home.

"Come on lad, King's 'Ead," he said. "You're only 'avin shandies, mind."

The King's Head was a typical Victorian pub. I understood from Jan that there had been a King's Head on the site since Cromwell's time. The present building had replaced a much older one, which had burnt down during some drunken excess in 1898. It was renowned for the quality of its beer and the speed of bar service and therefore very popular with the bargemen.

It must be explained that there was a distinct 'pecking order' associated with the King's Head's three bars. The 'hierarchy' used the comparatively luxurious snug. This group roughly consisted of:- The River Bailiff, the Town Quay manager, Upshore's two Customs officers and senior employees of Fowler & Dunn, including their long serving skippers. The saloon bar was reserved for other barge skippers including visitors and local tradesmen. All others – barge mates, lumpers, yard hands,

27

fishermen, etc. - were restricted to the sparsely furnished public bar.

A smog of tobacco smoke drifted over the tables in the bar as most of the customers smoked, many of them favouring the more pungent varieties of pipe tobaccos.

The whole was presided over by the landlady Rosie Barnes, who ran the pub as a 'tight ship', with the assistance of two barmaids and a cellarman.

Rosie was the widow of the former landlord, who, indomitable lady that she was, had merely taken over the license after her husband died two years ago, recruited a good cellarman, and carried on running the pub that she loved.

The public bar tended to be the most crowded bar of the King's Head and tonight was certainly no exception. Word had gone round about the 'big booze up' and all available bargemen were present. This included some skippers, among them Tommy Dolby, whose recent promotion had not yet tempted him into the saloon bar. He and his mate Ike, a taciturn man from Colchester, had secured one of the few tables and Tommy waved me over to join them, while Vic went to the bar.

Ladies were rarely seen in any bar, apart from Saturday night, when available bargemen would take the 'missus' out for a drink.

"Drinkin' in pubs, young 'un," Tommy greeted me. "It'll be wimmen next." He winked at Ike and then drank mightily from his glass.

"'Appy decided about that borsprit yet?" he asked.

I replied that I had seen little of Captain Day since we berthed.

"'E'll think about it," said Tom, "Allus does, an' 'e'll make the right decision – yers plis Ned, old and mild." This last to Gascoigne's mate who had held up a glass suggestively. "Happen 'e gits that borsprit, I'll sail as mate for the Match. That Vic can be one of the others."

"How's that, Tom?" asked Ike. Ned returned with Tom's pint and my shandy plus a drink for Ike.

"That's on Vic" he said.

"Cheers, Vic," Tommy roared and then answered Ike's question. Five crew were allowed on a barge taking part in a match. "You could be in too, young Ike, if yer behaves yerself."

His pint supplied by Vic had disappeared with little discernible lapse of time.

"Your turn," he said, sliding his glass over to Ike who went off to the bar. Someone else placed another pint in front of Tommy.

"All the best," he said to the donor. He lit a cigarette, took a large swig from his glass, and then turned to my affairs.

"An' wot 'appens to you?" he asked. I said I believed Miss Ellie was making enquiries.

"Oh, she will," Tommy said, "Yew can be sure of that. Perlice an' all sorts. Too clever for 'er own good that one." Miss Ellie did not seem to be popular. Voices all round the bar were taking up the cry —

"On the Jo-anna, Ned!"

Ike and Vic returned with yet more beer, and with a show of great reluctance, Ned took his place at an ancient upright piano that stood in a corner of the bar. It was not a good piano. It was well out of tune and had one key not functioning, but Ned was a competent pianist and knew the sort of thing that his audience wanted.

We roared out A Long Way to Tipperary, Roll out the Barrel and several more. And then it was solo time. Ned played a selection of honkey-tonk jazz, then Florrie Hooker, one of the barmaids, came from behind the bar and sang The Boy In The Gallery in a clear soprano. She was a rather plain, blonde girl but she had a lovely voice and her audience listened, enthralled. Finally an unknown bargeman led us in a boisterous barge song – Stormy Weather, Boys. Then we were back to Daisy, Pack Up Your Troubles and other favourites.

And all the time, Rosie and her staff kept a tide of beer flowing with Rosie now and again protesting that "she didn't 'ave no singing licence". Even some of the snug customers had come through to join in, and I noticed Gascoigne and Zeke among them, but not Captain Day. No doubt he was at time with the ol' woman' and perhaps thinking of the 'borsprit'.

The fun went on until a number of loud rings on the old ship's bell behind the bar announced closing time. Tommy stood up and wiped his mouth.

"I'll 'ave a pee, then I'll be off to see the missus."

I hoped Mrs. Dolby would be glad to see him, since he had drunk at least a gallon, to my certain knowledge. But the beer had had little effect on him, apart from a reddening of his face.

"Yew an' Ike can walk back to the barges."

"But what about Vic? I asked.

Tommy guffawed. "Don't yew worry about Vic. 'E'll be busy trying to get inside Rosie's knickers."

"An' if that don't work, 'e'll try one of the barmaids." Ike added. They both laughed.

With that Ike and I went out into the night at the end of a memorable evening.

CHAPTER THREE
MISS ELLIE

Next morning as I prepared breakfast for myself and the still unconscious Vic, I mulled over the previous night's events. The most alarming thing had been Tommy's mention of the police. If Miss Ellie had contacted them I might be traced and returned to some dreary previous existence, or worse still something criminal might be found in my past – my next home could be prison. I thought of running away, but where to? I had no idea. Best wait sweat it out here and hope that the enquiries came to nothing. But then what? I was only still on the barge by Captain Day's charity and this could be withdrawn at any time. But, so long as I had a base of some sort, I could emulate Jan, help out on the waterfront and hope for a berth. And I hoped that I had made some friends who might be able to help.

Having thus reassured myself, I dished up the bacon and eggs and shook Vic awake. "Breakfast," I said loudly, waving his plate in front of him. Vic slowly came to.

"Ugh," he groaned, "you eat it, makes me feel sick." I should have explain here that, now I had recovered, I had been banished to the forecastle to join Vic. This compartment was largely used for the storage of sails, lamps and other spare items of equipment. It did however contain two cots and another stove, which were sufficient for sleeping and breakfast purposes. Captain Day evidently preferred to preserve the cabin aft for himself, apart from main meals. Vic was not the best of bedtime companions, as his conversation, apart from barging, was restricted to two topics – his gaming activities and (not altogether unrelated) his desire to marry a rich widow, preferably Rosie Barnes, who, he reckoned, was making a fortune out of the King's Head. He also snored loudly, which was probably one reason why Captain Day preferred him to sleep in the forecastle.

Now, he sat with his head in his hands for several minutes. Eventually he rallied.

"That," he said, "was the best booze up since the last Barge Match."

In his case, I thought, it had lasted most of the day .

"What happened after closing time?" I asked.

He seem to have a job remembering. After a while he said "Why me an' Rosie an' Florrie Hooker together. Three in a bed like. You wouldn't want to know the details though."

I didn't think this was true. For, if it was, how was it that he was in his own berth on the barge when I awoke? But it was not impossible.

Shortly after this Captain Day and the lumpers arrived, the captain shaking his head over the state of his mate. Discharging recommenced and the three of us went on deck. A general aura of hangover pervaded the waterside that morning. An exception was Tommy Dolby who called out cheerily as he went past on his way to his barge: "Good one larst night."

He looked at the wreck of Vic. "Get yer leg over, Vic?" Vic raised one thumb in affirmation.

"So did I," said Tommy, winking at me.

Later Jan arrived. When the tide made, Captain Day gave us permission to take the barge's boat away. This vessel was usually to be found hanging in davits on the barges starboard quarter but, while we were in port, had been dropped into the water, in case she was needed for some errand. She was about fourteen foot long and was equipped with oars and a small lugsail, obviously a cut-down barge sail, together with the mast, spars and rigging for sailing.

However we did not use the sail as there was very little wind this far up the river. At first we rowed and I found that, like riding a bicycle, this is an art that you don't forget.

But Jan said: "No, no. This is not how bargemen do it." He then demonstrated how to scull a boat with one oar in the stern crutch. Following his example I tried this as well and soon got the hang of it.

We explored the river as far as the area of the mill and gasworks, but could not go further as a low bridge, linking the two halves of the town, prevented much more navigation. Detecting a faint air from the west, we raised the lugsail and blew gently back to Daisy Maud.

After we had stowed the boat's equipment Captain Day announced his intention to have a pint in the snug of the King's Head and then spend the afternoon at home, working on his garden. So it was back to domestic chores and watching the lumpers. Vic had recovered sufficiently to do some painting. He was touching up the scroll-work on the barge's stern, standing up in the boat to reach it and swearing under his breath when his still unsteady hand caused him to make a mistake.

There was still no word from the office about my fate. I had made a point of watching the pony and trap, and especially Miss Ellie, arrive and depart and knew that she had put in a full day at the office. There had been other comings and goings at the office building but the only other person that I recognised was Zeke.

The evening was spent quietly. Neither the big booze-up nor the fish and chips were repeated as all those concerned, especially Vic, were short of money. Vic and I dined off tinned stew from the supplies kept in the cabin's lockers and turned in early.

The next day started miserably in many respects. It was raining hard and there was a fresh wind. We had run out of eggs and breakfast was therefore bacon and beans. Further discharging was impossible and neither Captain Day or the lumpers appeared. There was no sign of Jan or any other visitor and it looked as though I would have a boring day listening to Vic on the subjects of betting and widows.

But, shortly after nine, the expected summons to Miss Ellie

arrived. Borrowing Vic's oilskin, I ran across the quay to the office building.

Fowler & Dunn occupied the ground floor of the building. Presumably their tenants had the exercise of climbing the stairs to their offices. A large general office contained high desks and stools for Mr. Oram, the chief clerk, Bob, a spotty office boy, Miss Ellie and presumably Zeke when he was present. Other rooms led off this central one. A typist obviously occupied one for I could hear the clack of typewriter keys from behind a closed door. Another was littered with plans, half models of barges and other vessels and other paraphernalia. This, I guessed, must be the office of Mr. Ernie, the shipwright brother.

A small sandy-haired man, with spectacles pushed down his nose, dressed in a stained overall, appeared out of a door marked 'Isaac Fowler, Esq., Managing Director and Chairman' and went into the untidy office closing the door behind him. This must be the shipwright himself. Another closed office was marked 'John Fowler, Director'. There was no sign of Miss Ellie.

I was received instead by Mr. Oram, the chief clerk, who treated me with elaborate courtesy. "Please take a seat," he said. I sat down on what must usually be Zeke's stool, avoiding what must be Miss Ellie's place next to it.

Mr. Oram was a strange looking man. There was not a visible hair on his body and his skin was stretched tightly over his bones. This gave him the appearance of an animated skeleton. I thought that he was about ninety years old.

He seemed to feel the need to entertain me while we waited for Miss Ellie.

"I've been here a long time," he said. "I even worked for Mr. Isaac's father. I was his coachman. The family had two coaches then. Now they have only got a pony and . . . "

The street door flew open, An enormous man filled the door-frame. He was big in the best possible way. He stood about six feet or more tall and was broad in proportion, but without any trace of fat. Water dripped from his peaked cap, his oilskin and the small bag that he was carrying .

"Mr. John," said Oram obviously in awe.

John slammed the door, dropped the bag on the floor and strode towards Mr. Ernest's office.

"You in there, Ernie?" he shouted.

Ernest replied that he was.

Ignoring the rest of us the big man went into Ernest's office. As the door closed behind him, a shouted conversation started up. It sounded like a row. Mr. Oram and the office boy were obviously straining their ears to make out what it was about, but it was not possible to pick up the words.

Isaac Fowler, no doubt disturbed by the noise, came out of his office and went into Ernest's, leaving the door open. It immediately became quieter. We could not hear Isaac's words but we could hear the dutiful choruses of "Yes, father" and "No, father" from the two brothers.

Miss Ellie came out of the typist's room carrying a sheaf of papers. She was dressed as previously, but had substituted a cream blouse for the white one. She dropped her papers on her desk and sat down next to me, swinging her stool round to face me.

Without preamble she said, in her normal brisk manner. "I'm sorry, but our enquiries came to nothing. We couldn't find out anything about you. I did try to find you employment – my father wanted a lad up at the house. But he would need to know about horses, as he is to help the groom. You don't know about horses, do you? No, I thought not. So . . . "

A stentorian voice interrupted. "Who's this? Get rid of him."

"Why, it's dear brother John, returned from the sea," said Miss Ellie sweetly. "I've nearly finished, dear brother, so why don't you wait in your office and I will join you soon."

She smiled at him and my world lit up. John snorted and retreated into his office.

"As I was saying," she continued, "there's nothing we can do." She leant over and patted my knee. "Why don't you try the Salvation Army? They are really very good and their Citadel is only up in the High Street." She stood up. The interview was obviously over.

I must have blushed, for the office boy sniggered. He had been the messenger who had summoned me to the office. I now suspected that he had deliberately done this too early out of some malicious sense of mischief. I snatched Vic's oilskin from the peg where I had left it and went out into the rain.

I trudged across the quay with mixed feelings, half of me now agreed with a bargeman who I had heard call Miss Ellie "a bloody stuck up little cow". But the other half of me could still feel the imprint of her fingers on my knee.

"Sally Army!" Captain Day exploded later that day. "What can she be a-thinking of? That's for ould people and tramps, not a fit young lad like yew. Not that they don't do a good job mind. I'm not 'avin this, I'll 'ave ter think on it."

He retired to the cabin to think. The rain had eased off and our skipper had come down to the barge to see what was going on. The answer was not much, for the lumpers had not appeared and it was still too wet for Vic to do any painting.

Our skipper did not think for long. A quarter of an hour later he summoned me and Vic to the cabin. He had some documents spread on the table and his attitude suggested that some small ceremony was about to take place.

"As master and part owner of this 'ere vessel," he said looking steadily at me. "I am prepared to offer you the position of third 'and of the above vessel at a wage of two and sixpence per week plus grub. If yew agree I'll be gettin' yew ter sign articles directly minnut. Yer duties will be cookin', cleanin', and such an' me 'n Vic'll try an' learn yer some seamanship."

After this long speech he sat down and looked quizzically at me. I was a bit taken aback but readily gave my assent. A small document signing session followed.

"Need a third 'and when we get the borsprit," said Vic

"An' that's another thing." said Day. "I thort that one out the other night while yew two was playin' games ashore. Us'll do it. But it's about money, see. I got the entrance fee for the Match ter think of as well, and I ain't got enough for both. Can't expect no 'elp from Fowlers 'cos they're puttin' the Pride in, but I got some ideas, never yew mind".

36

After this even longer speech, he fell silent while we digested its contents. I felt guilty about accepting 2/6d per week, but assumed our good captain knew what he was doing.

"About the unloading," the skipper resumed. "Lumpers 'ave agreed to work termorrow, Saturday, ter make up fer terday. But they won't do the afternoon 'cos United's playin' at home. So what wiv orl that, we'll be clear of cargo sometime Monday 'an should sail on afternoon tide, 'cos there's another freight waitin' for us in Lunnon. Grain from Co-op Mills ter Ipswich, they tole me over the office."

We thought about this, too. I should be sorry to leave Upshore, Jan and the King's Head, but I now had employment and a home and must go where Daisy Maud went. I looked down at the knee Miss Ellie had patted – I would be sorry not to see the comings and goings of the pony and trap as well.

The weather had improved next day. Discharging recommenced and at a fast rate. No doubt the lumpers were inspired by the prospect of the football match and, by the time they marched off, only a few bags of cattle-cake remained in the holds.

In the afternoon just about everyone went off to watch Upshore United. There were, however, exceptions. Jan and I waited for the tide to make and then took the boat away for more sculling practice.

After Jan had gone home, an elated Vic returned to tell me that United had won by two goals to one. While we ate the evening meal he gave me a blow-by-blow description of the match. After we had washed up we pooled our available money and decided that we could afford the King's Head that evening. Captain Day had given me my first two and sixpence and Vic had evidently won a small wager on the result of the football match.

This financial business prompted Vic to embark on a fairly lengthy discourse on bargemen's wages. The vast majority were paid under what was called the "freight system".

This meant that the proceeds of each voyage less expenses, such as towage, pilotage and dock dues were divided up as follows:- owner one half, skipper two thirds of the remainder and mate one third. A simple example would be:-

120 tons of wheat at 2/-d per ton	£12.00.00
Less expenses	£ 2.00.00
	£10.00.00
Owner half	£ 5.00.00
Skipper two thirds	£ 3. 6. 8d
Mate one third	£ 1.13.4d
	£00.00.00.

No payment was made when sailing light, without cargo. The situation was more complicated in the case of Daisy Maud whose captain was also part owner and Fowler & Dunn the managing agent. Our skipper would receive a part owner's share and conversely Fowler's would receive a fee in return for their management. But the mate's share was still one third of one half.

"A third of sod-all is still sod-all," said Vic bitterly.

Third hands, who were comparatively rare by the 1930s, were the only ones to be paid a straight wage. But their money came direct from the barge skipper and had to be found by him. So Captain Day really was my benefactor.

Later we went over to the King's Head. We were served by Rosie Barnes herself, who told us that our drinks were being paid for and that we were to go through to that "holy of holies", the snug.

The drinks were on our skipper who was in the snug with Mrs. Day.

"Thought I'd buy yew two a drink. Gawd knows why," he said. I noticed that he had bought me lemonade rather than shandy.

Mrs. Day then took over. She was almost the exact opposite of her husband – a large, talkative woman with a liking for stout. She prattled on about a number of subjects – their two daughters, who were doing very well at the local grammar school, the garden on which Happy Day had been working so hard while we had been in port, the price of fish, what a nice girl that Miss

Ellie was (I glanced at the knee), how she was embroidering a new tablecloth for Daisy Maud and numerous others.

During all this, Vic took the opportunity to buy a round with our pooled money – pints for himself and Skipper Day, a stout for Mrs Day and a shandy for me – which caused the skipper to frown. Shortly afterwards the tinkling of piano keys announced that Ned was about to play for another sing-song. We went through to the public bar.

The sing-song followed the same lines as the previous one, but was somewhat subdued, possibly because of the number of wives present. When we arrived at the solo spot, which was evidently a regular feature, Florrie Hooker performed The Boy in the Gallery again. She was followed by Pat, the other barmaid, a dark-haired girl, vaguely reminiscent of Miss Ellie in looks. Her voice was not as good as Florrie's but she sang with enthusiasm and was well received.

After this we were back to the general sing-song and at this point the Days left. Since I realised that it was hopeless getting Vic out of the pub before closing time he and I joined Tommy, his wife and Ike, who were joining in the singing lustily. During a lull, Mrs. Dolby told me that she was Captain Day's (much younger) sister. This made Tommy our skipper's brother-in-law. Neither captain had made any reference to this and I assumed that they considered it a matter of small importance. Tommy was, I noticed, drinking considerably less – no doubt this was due to having the missus with him.

I left the pub just after closing time with Vic and Pat. But I lost them on the quay and went back on board Daisy Maud on my own.

Next morning Vic was not in his berth. No doubt Pat was accommodating him somewhere. As I made a breakfast for myself alone, I reflected that, if he was to be believed, Vic had worked his way through the female staff at the King's Head in double-quick time.

Since it was Sunday, the bells of St. Michael's were summoning the congregation. Most of the waterside population were churchgoers, although some preferred the Peculiar Peoples

Chapel or the Salvation Army to St. Michael's. There were, again, exceptions. One was Jan who was a Jew (albeit a non-practising one) and another myself, for I did not know what I was. A third was probably Vic, who did not strike me as a churchgoer, since at any given moment he was probably breaking at least one of the Ten Commandments.

I considered going up to St. Michael's, in case the pony and trap delivered its normal passengers there, but since I could not be sure that they went to this or any church, or, if they did, which service they attended, I elected to spend most of the day with Jan, chatting and drinking tea and then, when the tide made, more boating.

I felt guilty about Jan, for whereas I now had a job on the barges he, who had been trying for far longer, had not. I told him as much.

"Do not distress yourself, my friend," he said. "It is a berth of mate that I seek not third hand. And I have a feeling here," he touched himself in the area of his heart, "that I have not long to wait."

Vic did not return all day, neither was there any sign of Captain Day. I settled down to eat a lonely tea. I did not suspect that big drama was to come that evening.

After I had washed up, I was idly glancing at a discarded Daily Mirror when I heard someone land on deck from the quay ladder. Thinking Jan had returned, I went on deck. But it wasn't Jan. Of all people, it was Miss Ellie.

It was, for late April, a very warm evening. She was wearing, instead of her office uniform, a summer floral dress that left her arms bare. She was not wearing her glasses and was barefoot. The whole effect was to make her look younger and, if anything even prettier – and, strangely vulnerable.

She was hesitant, almost nervous.

"Er, is Captain Day aboard?" she asked.

I replied that I had not seen him all day and that he was probably at home.

"Oh," she said. "Then could I give you a message for him?"

"Yes, certainly", I replied.

"He should be able to sail tomorrow afternoon and there is another freight waiting for him in London."

Now, this was strange, Happy Day had told me and Vic all this on Friday. Nevertheless, I said I would tell him. There was a long silence. She made no attempt to go, and scraped at the hatch-coming with the bare toes of one foot.

"Would you like to go for a walk?" she asked suddenly, the words coming out in a rush.

"Yes, I would like that very much," I answered.

"Let's go, then," she said. She waited while I closed the forecastle scuttle (there never seemed any need to lock anything).

I made to help her on to the steel ladder let into the quayside, but she was up it as if she had been doing it all her life, seemingly unaware of the view she give me of her lovely legs. As I climbed the ladder she put on the court shoes that she had sensibly kicked off before coming down it.

"Let's walk down past the Jolly Fisherman," she suggested, "and through the trees to the boat-yard. I often drive over on fine evenings and walk there. It's nice and peaceful". I agreed, but there was still something troubling her.

As we set out along the quay, she said: "I owe you an apology. I should never have suggested the Salvation Army to you. I should have know that it wasn't suitable and that you would find something nautical." I told her that her apology was accepted, but she was obviously not entirely finished.

As we went into the trees beyond the inn, she said softly: "No-one knows what it is like to be me. Having to put on a front all the time. To pretend to be the efficient office-girl, the barge-owner's daughter who is a cut above everybody else. I'm not like that, not at all really. And it's so awful lately – with dad and Mr. Oram getting old, Ernie preoccupied with the barge-yard, and John away at sea most of the time. And it gets worse when John comes back, he thinks we're doing it all wrong and there's rows all the time, at home as well as at work." She was beginning to sound positively tearful. "It's never been the same since mum died. It's so unfair. I'm only fucking eighteen, for Christ's sake".

I was shocked and she sensed it but she recovered her composure. "I'm sorry about the language, but you don't work with bargemen and lumpers all the time without picking it up." She paused and I felt her hand creep into mine. "I'd love to be like other girls – to have boyfriends, go to dances, even a Saturday evening at the King's Head – they're good fun, I hear." She really was crying now. I swung her round to face me and she was instantly in my arms sobbing into my shoulder. I stroked her back to comfort her.

"I'll be your boyfriend," I said softly.

She took a step back. "Would you? Really? I'd like that. Very much."

For answer I kissed her full on the lips and was surprised by the fervour of her response. She suddenly became practical.

"We'll have to be careful, My brothers aren't goin' to like it an' my father will hardly give his blessin'. An' you'll be away a lot now."

"Never mind, we'll find a way." I said and kissed her again, only for longer.

We walked back to the Jolly Fisherman arm-in-arm and she told me something of her past life. When she was young, her family had been much less strict.

She had spent many happy days as an Upshore waterfront urchin, playing about boats, visiting the barges, and making friends with bargemen and lumpers (hence her agility on a ladder). But all this came to an end when she was eleven for her father sent her to a boarding school in Surrey. This nearly broke her heart at the time, but it was a good school. First they drove out her Essex accent and then they taught her to speak reasonable French, to sing fairly well and to play a competent game of hockey. But the subjects at which she excelled were mathematics and English.

When her mother died two years ago, her father brought her back to Upshore. Because of her English and maths he placed her in the office to learn the trade and also put her in charge of domestic arrangements at 'the house' two miles outside the town. This latter was a sinecure as the house was staffed by elderly servants who thoroughly knew their jobs. But, as she said earlier, the office work was becoming increasingly hard. It would be bearable if she had some outside social life, but her father and brothers felt that her place was at home. About her only entertainment was her occasional walks. But it would be different now, she said, snuggling up to me.

At the Jolly Fisherman we sprang apart as a stentorian voice shouted "Get out and don't come back!" The side door of the pub flew open and an irate landlord ejected Vic, who fell to the ground literally, at our feet. He pushed himself upright, glanced at us and lurched away.

"Oh! I hope he didn't see us," said Ellie (I could no longer think of her as Miss Ellie) "They're such shockin' ould gossips, them bargemen." It had been noticeable on the way back through the trees, that her Essex speech was returning. Was this something to do with me, I wondered.

I walked her to her vehicle. It was not the pony and trap but a neat red sports car. So she was a motorist as well! Was there no end to the talents of this wonderful girl?

She held up her face to be kissed again and slipped into the car, putting on her glasses to drive. As she drove off, she gave me a typical Essex farewell: "See yer termorrow!"

I watched the car until it disappeared round the bend at the top of the hill.

But I didn't see her on the morrow. At least, not properly. Of course, I saw the pony and trap arrive and deposit its occupants at the office and thought she managed a wave behind her father's back. But that was all for a long time.

Vic had not been in his berth again that morning, but arrived just before Captain Day, shortly after the lumpers started work. He looked surprisingly spruce and I wondered whether he had taken things easy after we saw him, since today we would sail. Either that, or Pat had worked some miracle on him. He made no reference to the previous evening or to what he was doing in the non-bargemen's pub or how he came to be chucked out. It was a fair guess that it was something to do with wagering, women, booze or any combination of the three. He did however give me a number of speculative glances, as though he was waiting for me to speak first. Perhaps, I hoped, he was suffering from some form of alcoholic memory loss and could vaguely remember seeing me but had forgotten the circumstances.

It did not take the lumpers long to remove the remaining cargo. And then we became very busy. The holds had to be thoroughly swept and all traces of cattle cake removed from the barge. Then all decks and rails were scrubbed, the hatch covers replaced, covered with their cloths and then the battens and chocks inserted to hold them tight at sea. Then the gear normally kept on top of the main hatch was replaced – the setting booms that were used to propel the barge in shallow water with no wind and no tug, a ladder, fenders, mops and brooms. The boat was tidied and hoisted up into its davits and sails loosened ready for setting.

All was finished by four o'clock and the "moty-boat", manned again by Zeke and Jan, was waiting to take our line. But there was still no sign of Ellie. I had noticed various comings and goings at the office building, but none of them involved Ellie. Perhaps she was being kept busy, or did not wish her brothers to see her taking too much interest in one particular barge.

Suddenly Captain Day remembered something. "Where's that useless dawg?" he asked. Frank had scarcely been seen while we had been in port. Now, at the last minute, he hurtled like a bullet across the quay, leapt on board and greeted us with a torrent of barks and yelps, wagging his tail frantically in pleasure.

We cast off, passed the motor boat our line and set off down river with Captain Day on the wheel, while Vic and I stowed the lines. She hadn't come, I thought bitterly. Then I saw her. She stood outside the Jolly Fisherman with a jacket over her blouse and her hair in a head-scarf, since it was a much colder day. As we drew level she blew a kiss and waved and waved and waved until I could see her no more.

CHAPTER 4
UP TO LONDON

I would like to be able to report that I spent the voyage to London idling on deck, perhaps with one had loosely holding the steering wheel, dreaming of Ellie – her brown eyes, the taste of her lips, the glimpse of her legs as she went up the ladder, the way she tamed Brother John in the office, her returning Essex accent and much more. But it was not like that at all.

It took us two tides to beat down river against fitful easterly winds, only to find that there was not sufficient water for us to pass through the Swin Spitway channel which led to the Thames. Together with several other barges we were forced to anchor to await more water.

But during those two tides I had been learning. Captain Day had certainly meant it when he said that he and Vic would teach me some seamanship. The skipper was a kindly and patient instructor, while Vic, now that he was removed from the flesh-pots of the shore, was a mine of information on matters nautical, rather inclined to pause and tell a suitable anecdote.

First I learnt to coil lines properly, then how to set the small mizzen sail aft of the helm. A bit of ropework followed – how to whip a rope's end, how to use a marlin-spike and some basic knots. Captain Day then introduced me to navigation – at least the version of it in use aboard Daisy Maud. No chart was ever in evidence and reference was only to navigation buoys, most of which the skipper referred to as though they were old friends. After all, he had been sailing these waters all his life, and could probably tell where we were at any given moment, to within a few yards. These principles applied aboard all Thames sailing barges and charts were only used for long, unusual voyages, such as down to the West Country or across the English Channel, he told me.

So I learnt navigation the Daisy Maud way, which consisted of taking several tricks at the brass-bound wooden steering wheel, under the skipper's eye and learning to steer a compass course, not of course necessary at the time, as we were within sight of land the whole time and there was no sign of fog. For this I had to keep an eye on the compass kept in a binnacle in front of the wheel. The skipper also did his best to "learn" me the points of the compass and the rule of the road at sea, but both of us realised that these two lessons would take some time for me to absorb.

The skipper also showed me how to fill, light and trim the barge's several oil lamps. Apart from the cabin lamps, there were the navigation and riding lights. He also showed me how to hoist the riding light, which was displayed when the barge was at anchor at night.

Vic's specialities were anchor work and the setting and furling of sails. He instructed me in the mysteries of the windlass up forrard. He showed me how to "fleet" the chain properly so that it would run out smoothly when we anchored. He and I, using a handle on each side of the windlass, would wind the chain, or cable as it is generally called, when raising the anchor and he showed me how to hold the cable with a stopper known as a "dog", while the chain was "surged" across the barrel of the windlass and how it was necessary to dampen the barrel with buckets of sea water while the cable was running out. He also instructed me in the use of "crab" winches to raise the great leeboards, one on each side of the barge, which reduced the sidewise drift of the almost completely flat bottomed vessel.

As far as the sails were concerned, I learnt from Vic how to tend the bowline which controlled the foresail, how to go aloft to stow the topsail and how to adjust the mainsail by use of the brails. He also did his best to teach me the names and positions of all the numerous halyards, brails, etc, which led down to various pinrails around the mast.

I learnt many strange names – the "stay-fall tackle" that was used to raise and lower the mast and gear on rare excursions above bridges – the "snotter" that connected the heel of the sprit to the mainmast – the "vangs" (pronounced wangs) that controlled the outboard end of the sprit and the "ceiling" which was the correct name for the floor of the holds.

Then there were the superstitions. Certain land animals must never be mentioned aboard, such as "fox" or "pig", although "dog" and "horse" could not be avoided as they were names of items of gear. It was bad luck to whistle as this could summon a strong wind. A hatch cover should never be left upside down – and this was sensible enough as the covers had a slight camber and could cause someone to lose their footing. But strangest of all was the affair of the milk.

Just before we reached the Swin Spitway, I was making tea in the cabin. Since fresh milk was rarely available most bargemen preferred condensed milk in their tea, so I had opened a tin ready to add to the cups once the tea had brewed.

Captain Day had come below to find something or the other and happened to glance at what I was doing. With a bellow of rage he seized the tin of milk, rushed on deck with it and hurled it over the side.

"Don't yew ever do that agen," he said on his return. I had never seen him so angry.

"Do what, skipper?" I asked baffled.

"Why yew'd opened it upside down," he replied, "shockin' bad luck that."

There was much else to learn on the domestic side. Vic explained that whereas Captain Day was prepared to accept scratch meals during the day, he preferred the evening meal, if conditions permitted, to be more formal with a table-cloth over the cabin table and places laid. Basically, at sea, we would eat in turn, possibly only two of us together and the third on his own unless he chose to eat on deck, at the wheel.

Food tended to be simple and sustaining and of the variety that could be virtually left to simmer while we got on with other things. Hence there were a lot of stews and suet puddings, spotted dick being a particular favourite.

Vic told me that the favourite meal on Ipswich barges was meat pudding followed by spotted dick. The crews would save the gravy from the meat dish and pour it over the pudding in lieu of custard. I commented that this must have been a fairly awful combination.

"Ah yes, but then they're a funny ol' lot, them Ipswichmen."

Fresh water needed to be conserved, Vic told me, particularly on a voyage to London, and washing up and personal hygiene performed with salt water, wherever possible. I asked him to explain this. It was easy enough to obtain water in smallish ports such as Upshore, he said. There was very often a tap on the quay and pubs would always oblige. But where we going – the London Docks – the PLA's water supply was geared to for bigger ships than Thames barges. Therefore, in the enclosed docks, it was necessary to wander about with a barrico, looking for a friendly office to supply a fill.

"Why, I've even 'ad to ask a bloke fillin' a cement mixer for a top-up," Vic said.

His attitude towards me at this point was peculiar. Something had reminded him of what he had seen outside the Jolly Fisherman the night that he had been thrown out, or maybe it was Ellie's kiss blowing and waving as we left. Although helpful enough as for a barging was concerned, he had started a series of catty remarks ranging from "Bit of 'orl right, that Miss Ellie" to "Goin' out with the little rich girl are we? Betcha dippin' yer wick there". I noticed, however, that he was careful not to make these comments when Captain Day was within earshot.

Once here was sufficient water in the Spitway, our little group of barges set out through the channel. It was now that Captain Day referred to as "yachtmen's weather" – fine and hot with a light breeze from just north of east. As a concession to this weather our skipper removed his trilby hat and replaced it with a knotted handkerchief – but otherwise remained dressed as usual.

With flood tide and wind behind them many other barges were coming up behind us and once we had passed the Swin Spitway buoy which marked the southern entrance to the channel and were headed across to the Swin which led to the Thames proper we were sailing in a positive armada of barges. They came from Ipswich and Mistley, Yarmouth and Lowestoft, Colchester and many other smaller east coast ports. All the big names in barging were represented - Paul, Cranfield, Horlock, Everard, Goldsmith and Francis and Gilders. There were barges of several variations of rig – borsprit barges, staysail barges and mulie rigged barges. A few were loaded with cargo for London but the majority were light, without cargo, sailing to the storehouse of England – the London Docks – for cargo for the towns of East Anglia.

A few struck a sour note – at least for Captain Day – these were those with engines, a box like wheelhouse taking the place of the small mizzen. Most still retained the remainder of their sailing gear – but there were a few that were completely powered with only a small pole-mast and a derrick. These were the lowest of the low in our skipper's opinion.

Looking astern there was a panorama of red-ochre sails, white head sails and black hulls, with the odd grey giving variety. One of the grey-hulled barges, with a bowsprit was overhauling us and was edging over to pass within hailing distance – painted large on her bows was the name Resolve and she was built of steel.

Eventually she drew level, and the enormously fat man who was steering her, sitting on an old packing case, raised a battered straw hat in salute.

"Gotcha agen, Arthur," he called to Captain Day. This was the first time I had heard anyone, even his own wife, call our skipper by his Christian name.

"Be a different story come the Matches," Skipper Day replied.

49

"Garn, yew ain't even entered any of 'em".

"Upshore one, you're on."

"Nah, yew ain't even got a borsprit. Need one to compete with me."

"Happen we'll 'ave one soon," our skipper replied.

"'Alf a dozen borsprits won't get yew up wiv us."

Who was this fat man, who was so ready to challenge us, I asked Vic.

"Why, that's Bully Briggs o' Mistley," Vic replied. "'Im an' the skipper 'as bin rivals for years. Not just the Matches either, race for turn whenever they get the chance."

Racing for turn occurred whenever two or more barges were due to deliver to the same port or load from the same ship and the masters fancied a competition, with or without a wager. Bully Briggs, Vic went on, despite his benign appearance, was a remorseless driver of barges and men, utterly ruthless and a great flouter of rules and regulations.

Resolve began to draw ahead, and further hailing became impossible. This did not deter Bully who held up a coil of rope, as if offering a tow.

"I'll 'ave 'im," muttered Captain Day, "just yew wait an' see."

Now we were getting into the Thames proper and, with the flood tide, a vast procession of shipping began to overtake us. Ships of all shapes and sizes were heading for the docks and wharves of the capital. There were tugs towing hoppers, which deposited dredged material further out at sea and 'gravy boats' which did the same for London's sewage. Dutch 'Schuits', or motor coasters and cranky Russian timber ships, mainly from the Baltic for Surrey Docks. There were tramp steamers of all nationalities, and ships of the regular lines, Harrisons from the West Indies, Blue Star from South America, Blue Funnel from the Far East and many others. Cargo passenger liners of the Royal Mail Line, Swedish Lloyd and Ellerman Lines bustled past. There were colliers bringing coal from the north east to London's power stations and gas works. Some of these were designed with low upperworks and collapsible funnels for going above the bridges in the centre of the capital. A solitary oil-tanker ploughed past on her way to the refinery at Thameshaven. Then queening it over all these, was a great white passenger liner of P & O Lines, probably the Strathnaver or Strathaird, making her stately progress to Tilbury.

This great ship reminded Vic of a story;

"There was this P & O liner lying at Tilbury landin' stage, see an' this ole sailin' barge was close alongside 'er when she run out o' wind, like an' she drifts dahn on the tide wiv the end of 'er sprit bangin' along the liner's boat-deck guard rails. Well, all these gold-braided officers came aht on the boat-deck an' a-starts tearing' their 'air – like the Royal Navy, P & O is, I 'ear - an the old skipper o' the barge, 'E's steering like, an' 'e calls aht ter the young mate up forrard – "Don't jus' stand there, boy. Do sommat".

"Like what, master?" sez the boy."

"Take yer coat orf, quick an' ang' it over the barge's name."

I laughed and the skipper, who had probably heard it before, managed a smile.

By now we were past Southend Pier, the longest pleasure pier in the world. and heading up towards the Chapman Lighthouse off Canvey. Our fleet of sailing barges was now scattered. A few had branched off towards the River Medway, others had fallen back and still more, like Resolve had drawn ahead of us. But groups of further barges could be seen over on the southern, Kent shore.

"Them's Kentishmen." said Skipper Day, grimly. "Yew gotta be careful of Kentishmen, son." He said no more at the time, but later from Vic and others, I found out there was a long-standing rivalry between the bargemen of Essex and Kent. The origins of this seemed to lie in seamanship. With the prevailing south west wind the Kent shore of the Thames was a weather shore, with the wind holding sailing vessels off the land. But the Essex shore was a lee shore with the wind holding vessels onto the land and much more difficult for sailing. Thus the Essex men claimed a higher degree of seamanship than their Kentish neighbours. This argument was the original one. But it had since been extended for the

Essex men claimed that they made the longer voyages up the east coast, whereas the Kentish men only indulged in 'ditch-crawling' around the rivers Medway and Swale. This, of course, was complete rubbish, as it ignored the many fine coasting barges, owned in Kent by owners such as the Thames & Medway Barge Co., Hutsons of Maidstone, and Daniels of Whitstable. Nevertheless an 'atmosphere' existed between bargemen of the two counties, to the extent that, only recently, an Essex barge on rounding Southend Pier Head had espied another barge in trouble, sailed over to render assistance, but withdrawn once it was realised that the stricken vessel came from Kent.

And now we were into Sea Reach proper with the roofs of houses on Canvey Island peeking over the island's sea walls on one side and a rather desolate Kent shore on the other. Here we encountered the Sea Reach dredger, not working at present, since it only operated on ebb tides. Groups of sailing barges were at anchor upstream of the dredger.

"Wot they do," said Vic, "is drag their anchors dahn on the ebb, till they catch in the dredger's moorin' chains, then they can swing alongside easy. An' they aint there for long 'cos the dredger can load 'em in a few minutes."

I asked what they were loading.

"Ballast. Goes into roads an' the like in them big new estates what's goin' up in Leigh and Southend."

"They've 'ad it, them barges," said the skipper. "Kicks 'ell aht of them, that trade. Unloadin' always by grab, see."

I could see that a huge metal grab weighing some hundred weights would do a lot more harm than the method that we had used at Upshore with cranes using slings to lift bags.

And so we went on, past the oil refinery at Shellhaven, the powder hulks at Mucking, then turned into the Lower Hope and finally into Gravesend Reach where we anchored for the night off the Ship and Lobster, a good bargemen's pub, with excellent holding ground offshore and clear of the wash of tugs and pilot boats that prevailed off the Town Pier.

However, after a short debate, we decided that we could not

afford an evening in the pub and turned in early.

The next morning we "mustered" at 6am to sail the rest of the way to the Royal Docks. There was not much wind about so we drifted most of the way on the tide. First we passed the town of Gravesend on the south shore and Tilbury landing stage on the north shore. Then the cement works of Northfleet and the entrance to Tilbury Docks. Then we were into Northfleet Hope up towards Grays, home of the big barge-owners E.W. Goldsmith.

We turned into St. Clement's Reach and passed Stoneness Light with the training ship Worcester moored off Greenhithe. Long Reach, the oddly named Erith Rands followed then Erith Reach and Halfway Reach with the Ford Motor Co. works and finally Galleon's Reach and the enormous Beckton gas works.

We locked into the Basin Entrance to Royal Docks with a crowd of tugs and lighters. Captain Day was very wary of the big steel lighters.

"They can do yew a power of damage," he said. "That's why we drop the anchor below water level and swing the boat inboard in dock. 'Appen a lighter 'its us the anchor can get set in ter the barge or the boat smashed while its in davits. Gotta do what yer can. Mind yew there's one or two quiet lay-bys where barges can go."

A uniformed PLA lock foreman came down the lock side distributing the docking notes that each crafts' guardian had to complete on entering the docks.

"Where you for, sailorman?" he asked while Captain Day filled up the form.

"Co-op Mills".

"There's an Occidental Lighterage tug and lighters up ahead. They're goin' there too. Send one of yer crew up to see the tug skipper. He'll probably give you a pluck up there."

"Remarkably 'elpful for a 'Please Leave Alone'," said Vic.

"They ain't all bad," replied the skipper.

So a tow was arranged. The tug and lighters waited for us in the basin and we hitched on to the stern of the last lighter.

"Lighters 'ave their uses, after all," said Vic. At the bridge at the West End of the basin we passed into the land of ships. To reach the C.W.S. Mill we had to tow through the length of the Royal Albert Dock and into the Royal Victoria Dock. Quay cranes dipped and swung removing their many cargoes. Masses of lighters, studded with the odd "sailorman", as sailing barges were known in the docks, were alongside many and sometimes swung out into the middle of the dock, impeding the progress of through traffic.

"They say there's a dockmaster up at the West (West India Dock) who wants all lighters moored fore and aft along the quays. 'E'll be lucky," said Vic.

Under tow he and I had nothing else to do but watch the view unfold. A tug towing a grain elevator passed in the opposite direction, followed by the PLA yacht St. Katharine with a party of sightseers aboard. A floating crane was lifting a railway loco-motive on to the deck of a heavy lift ship. A 'tosher', or small tug, went past with a Rochester sailing barge in tow. Her crew took no notice of us.

"Bloody Kentishmen," said Vic, forgetting his own origins.

Then we were through the last swing bridge and preparing to moor at the Mill. We moored up and exchanged a few words with the crews of two Colchester barges also due to load from the mill. Loading commenced after lunch with shoots propelling golden Canadian grain into the holds. The trimming was done by corn-porters who used large shovels to heave grain into the more awkward corners. They moved around on the grain with rags tied round their boots – this habit earned them the nickname of 'toerags' in the docks. When work ended for the day we were two thirds full. In the evening the crews of the Colchester barges came aboard and proved very sociable. While the skippers yarned in the cabin, one of the visiting mates produced a har-monica and the three mates and I had a musical evening sitting on the forehatch of Daisy Maud.

When I turned in that night, I felt that with any sort of luck we should sail the next day, ever nearer to our return to Upshore and Ellie.

CHAPTER 5
BORED IN IPSWICH

Sure enough we were able to leave the docks at lunch time next day. No tow this time. We set the topsail with a bit of mainsail and blew down the Royal Albert Dock. Sailing, I understood, was officially forbidden but generally winked at in the docks.

We locked out into the river and found we had just what was needed for a fast passage to Ipswich. A fresh south-westerly wind, although otherwise the weather was dull and depressing. It was decided that, if the wind held, we would press on all night for Ipswich. This suited all three of us – a fast passage and Skipper Day could return to his family and garden, Vic to his fun and games and me, of course, to Ellie.

There was only one incident of note on the way to Ipswich. Basically I was kept too busy to dream about Ellie, but about midnight we passed through the Swin Spitway and after finishing the washing up and tidying the cabin I went on deck. I stood up by the mainmast and gazed in the general direction of Upshore. Aft, Captain Day was handing the wheel over to Vic, before going below for a rest.

I caught a whiff of pipe tobacco and realised the skipper had come forward to join me.

"She's over there somewhere, ain't she, lad?" he asked quietly.

"She's a good 'un that girl. You stick wiv 'er, 'appen what may."
So he knew too.

He disappeared aft for a few hours sleep, but I stayed on deck, watching the odd spray slop aboard the deep-laden barge, for he had given me cause to think. I remembered his wife saying, in the King's Head a long while ago what a nice girl that Miss Ellie was. Could it be that the Days knew her in some other capacity than her office job? Could Skipper Day be one of the bargemen she had befriended as a child? Entirely possible. And what did he mean by "happen what may"? Was this some type of warning?

Still puzzling over all this I, too, went below and turned in.

I awoke next morning at 6am to prepare breakfast. By then we were gliding gently up the River Orwell, past the pretty village of Pin Mill, with its well-known pub the Butt & Oyster at the head of the hard where several sailing barges were drawn up.

By the time breakfast was cleared away, we were waiting to lock into Ipswich Wet Dock. Here we found many barges waiting to unload, nearly all of them locally owned, but they did include two of the fleet of the Thames & Medway Barge Co., and two of Piper's "Cockneys" from East Greenwich.

To my horror enquiries ashore showed that we were going to have to wait some time to discharge, as the barges in dock were all for the two great granaries of R.W. Paul and Cranfield Bros. and would be unloaded strictly in order of arrival.

And so we commenced a most boring few days. Almost to a man, the Ipswich crews spent every evening at home and often most of the day as well. The two Thames & Medway barges were Kentishmen of the variety who would have no truck with Essexmen such as ourselves, while the two Piper barges were moored too far away for much contact. Vic, who was not easily outdone, did a tour of nearby pubs and, finding the barmaids dull and ugly, invested his remaining money on horses, all of which lost.

We were driven more and more on our own devices for amusement. The skipper found plenty of small jobs on paintwork and rigging for us. But we could not spend all our time working and increasingly relied on conversation, even Captain Day becoming more voluable.

Thus we found ourselves talking about the possibility of war.

"'Appen there won't be one," said Captain Day. "If there is, I 'ope it's like the last 'un."

He meant what was then known as the Great War.

"Nah! That weren't no good," said Vic, "all them men killed in the trenches."

"Ah! But it was us in the barges what was supplyin' 'em. Regular fortune a lot of us made. I was mate with me ol' fella then. Cross Channel all the time we was. Why there was one ould skipper I knew, when 'e went below for a kip, 'e'd chuck 'is wallet on deck wiv mebbe seventy quid in it an' say to the mate, 'Anything 'appens while I'm below, 'ave a good time on that lot'."

"Wot about German subs?" asked Vic.

"Nah. They didn't bother wiv small fry like us. Royal Navy was a bloody nuisance, though."

I asked why this was, surely they were on the same side?

"Yew wouldn't think so sometimes, they knew nuffin' 'bout bargin'. They used ter send aht these young subbies and mid-shipmen in patrol boats to order us arahnd. No yew must sail here an' yew must sail there an' not at all at night. No bloody idea. There was one ould skipper I knew, 'oo when 'e came back 'cross Channel ter Dover, 'e'd 'ed straight fer a minefield 'cos 'e knew the Navy'd send a dirty great tug after 'im and once that 'ad got 'im in tow, 'e could ask to be dropped where 'e wanted ter anchor, not where the patrol boats wanted 'im ter go."

"This on'll be worse," said Vic. "Gas an' that."

"'Appen there won't be one," said the skipper again, closing the subject.

Another subject was the "stacky" trade. I remembered Gascoigne saying that Happy Day's father had the Daisy Maud in this trade.

"'Twas for London's 'orses," said Captain Day. "Fine lot of 'ay and straw they'd get through. We used to tek it from Upshore ter

Lunnon. Likely put root crops in the 'old and hurled a stack on top. Bales of 'ay some twelve foot 'igh. Course skipper couldn't see where'e was a-sailin'. So the mate would stand atop o' the stack an' give directions like. We'd rig ladders either end so as 'e could get up there and the sails 'ould be shortened to clear the stack. We'd leave an 'ole round the mast so as we would still reach the 'alliards and so on an 'appen we was goin' above bridges a slot to lower the mast inter. Borsprit was 'andy then 'cos we would set jibs on that to give more sail area, like. Funny thing was barges sailed just as fast wiv a stack as wiv aht."

I said that I thought that this was something to do with aerodymanics.

"Airy dammics," said the skipper. "I dunno where yew gits sich long words from, young fella."

But Vic was, once again, reminded of a story.

"There was this stacky barge, see, sailing the Medway thro' Sheerness where the Navy moors its ships. Anyway, the skipper misjudges the tide, like an' the barge fetches up aginst this Navy cruiser. As she drifts dahn the side of the ship, the barge leaves bits of 'ay 'angin' from everythin' what stick out – booms and such, I s'pose. Anyway the barge is nearly clear of the ship when a port 'ole flies open and this stoker sticks he 'ead out an' goes 'Baa!'," he said

On the third day of our wait in Ipswich Captain Day surprised us by buying a concertina from the mate of one of the Ipswich barges.

"Uster be a dab 'and on one o' these when I was a young mate," he said and then found Vic and I jobs to do on deck while he went down into the cabin to practice.

By evening he pronounced himself fit to play in public, as it were. So we had an impromptu concert on the forehatch. He had lost nothing of his old skill, but although the mate of one of the Piper barges was passing and joined in, attempts at a sing-song of the old favourites sounded a bit thin. So we settled for sitting and listening to the skipper playing. All things considered this showed our master in a new light and it was the first of several 'concerts'.

Needless to say this enforced idleness caused me to daydream of Ellie and our walk through the trees. Was I her boyfriend now? Had she really meant it? If not, why had she responded so passionately to my kiss? If only I could get back to Upshore. Was she waiting for me there or not? Sometimes I dreamed of her in her 'office' rig, sometimes in the summer dress and other times in nothing at all.

"Proper lil' dreamer you're becomin'," Vic commented once when he found me in a state of trance over the washing-up. If only he knew what I just been thinking! Fortunately his spiteful remarks about Ellie had now ceased. He had apparently become bored with this type of 'wit'. Which was just as well, since Jan had told me that murder had been committed on sailing barges over less.

The day finally came when we shifted into the unloading berth and commenced discharge. But Captain Day was summoned ashore to the office and came back with what, for me, was appalling news. When we had discharged the grain, we were to shift to a berth on the River Orwell and load machinery for delivery to a ship in Millwall Docks, London. No Upshore for a while yet.

So we moved to the riverside wharf where cranes lowered three large and mysterious machines into our holds. These had to be well lashed against movement at sea.

"Summat ter do wiv farmin' in the Middle East," was all that Captain Day could tell us. At least the wharf had a decent pub next door and this was where we had gone while the machinery was put aboard by experts. But we were not there for long as loading was completed by closing time and we were able to drop downriver that afternoon.

The voyage to London was unpleasant. The wind was from dead ahead once we were out at sea, and accompanied by rain squalls. We had to watch out for these, and drop the topsail in the worst of them. Nevertheless we made good progress and thirty six hours later we were locking into the India & Millwall Docks complex. There was a bit of delay until our ship was able to take the machinery, which was to be carried as deck cargo and therefore among the last items to go aboard.

"Got anuver freight," said Skipper Day gleefully after a visit ashore, "good 'un too. We move up into Indy Docks an' load canned goods – fer Upshore!" Thank God for that. All desires were met, the barge was continuing to earn good money – and there were many that weren't in the Thirties – which in turn improved the wages of skipper and mate and, above all, we were returning to our home port and Ellie!

So clear of machinery, we moved up to a ship at North Quay, West India Docks to load canned goods, mainly fruit, the skipper said. And here we met for the first time the true London dockers. They swarmed aboard, some time later than expected, when it was our turn to load, grumbling incessantly, with every other word a swear word. Much to my surprise Captain Day, who rarely swore, replied in similar language.

"Gotta do that, son," he told me. "Wouldn't get a thing done else."

Their main complaint was that they didn't like sailing barges, considering them pokey and hard to stow. This, of course, adversely affected their piecework rate and they infinitely preferred the big steel lighters, in turn loathed by bargemen. These were much easier for the dockers with little or no side-decks to stow under and only one large hatch.

"Fuckin' sailormen," one docker confided in me. "Burn the fuckin' lot, I say."

One afternoon and about fifteen delays for tea-breaks and disputes later, only a small pile of cases had built up in our main hold. On going below to make tea I found Vic and Skipper Day busily stowing cans of pears and peaches in the lockers round the table.

"Couple of cases got broke," said the skipper by way of explanation.

"Dockers broke a lot more for themselves, though," said Vic with a wink.

This was a near miss for half an hour later we had a visitor.

Until now, we had not encountered any other Upshore barges in our wanderings. But on the way to our berth we had passed the Pride of Upshore alongside a Palm Line ship. Our visitor was Mr. John. He went below to the cabin with Captain Day.

Vic hurriedly handed me a tin of Bluebell and some rags. "Brasswork on the wheel and binnacle needs a polish," he said. I'd done this chore that very morning. "See wot you can over'ear," he hissed.

I could hear John's loud voice plainly through the open skylight, but some of Skipper Day's replies were not so easy to pick up. The conversation when something like this:

John: "You thought about selling your shares in this barge yet?"

"Yus."

"And . . . "

"I'm still thinkin', give yer an answer directly."

"Well don't be too long about it, or you'll find freights hard to get."

Blackmail I thought.

"How's the third hand?".

"Good lad." I felt flattered.

"Unnecessary expense for you though. Still you know best. And this silly idea of entering the Upshore Match?"

"Still thinkin' on that."

"Well, if you can raise the money. But you're on your own. Pride's the firms official entry."

"'Appen we'll be there."

"Well I gotta go. Off to Upshore by train in the morning. Can't leave things there. Ellie's mooning about over something (This could be good news for me) and Old Oram's talking about retiring."

There were sounds of John getting to his feet. Evidently he had not been offered the normal courtesy of a cup of tea. I pursued my unnecessary work with vigour as he left. Captain Day seemed to assume that either Vic, or me or both had overheard the discussion.

"I'm not worried by 'im ," he said later. "Threatening ter cut off our freights. I got me own means of gettin' a freight. 'E can just bugger-off to Upshore".

John was lucky to have an elderly but experienced mate who could take over as skipper while John was away at Upshore or elsewhere. Pride, like us, was a three-handed barge and the third hand would move up to the mate's job. How this affected the division of freight money was unclear, but no doubt John came out on top.

Next morning loading suddenly speeded up, the dockers working almost with a will. What had happened? I asked. "Quite simple, really," said Vic. "There's a grapefruit ship due day arter termorrer – 'ighest piecework rate of the lot, they all want to be available for it."

So that evening we were finished and ready to sail for home. But this was to be another frustrating voyage. We sailed down to Southend Pier with no trouble and anchored at the Low-way anchorage to await a change of tide. The wind, which had been moderate north-easterly, soon freshened considerably and to-gether with a dozen other barges we were windbound in the anchorage, unable to move any further. The other barges in-cluded the giant Will Everard and the Pride of Upshore, under temporary command of her mate.

"John ain't goin' to like that," said Vic nodding in Pride's direction.

On the second day two barges braver than the rest perhaps, or foolhardy, set sail.

"They ain't goin' no where," said Skipper Day and, sure enough, they were soon back.

"This ain't good," said the skipper that evening. "I've known barges be stuck 'ere for weeks waitin' for that wind to change. Mind yew, 'appen it changes sudden, yew're in trouble less you can flit over the Yantlet quick, cos this'll be a lee shore."

Apparently there were two good anchorages in this, the lower part of Sea Reach, the Low-way just above Southend Pier for northerly winds and another off Yantlet Creek for winds with south in them.

However the wind eased off on the third day. We reached the Swin Spitway on a following wind and more or less drifted into an anchorage just inside the River Whitewater which led to Upshore. A glacial calm descended and persisted into the next day.

Next morning, after breakfast, I discovered both skipper and mate studying the shore.

"What d'yew reckon?" Happy Day asked Vic.

"Could be worth it".

"Shall us tek that useless dawg?"

"Give 'im a run."

Frank, the dog, had led a quiet life of eating, sleeping, and barking while we had been sailing. Admittedly he had disappeared while we had been in Ipswich, no doubt to sire a few puppies. Now apparently, he had a part to play in some enterprise.

"Better git the boat ready, then," said Captain Day. "Yew too, lad," he added to me. When the boat was launched and ready, Vic, I and the dog got aboard, Captain Day, before joining us, passed down a sack, a box of cartridges and a double-barrelled shotgun. I had not seen this weapon before and no doubt it had been well hidden somewhere aboard Daisy Maud. Vic sculled us ashore where we landed on a shingly beach. We pulled the boat up as far as we could and laid out an anchor since the tide was flooding.

Once over the seawall we found ourselves in a field of cabbages.

"They'll do fer a start," said Vic pulling up two cabbages and throwing them into the sack.

"We want summat decent," said the skipper. "Keep quiet, all o' yew." We all kept quiet, except the dog, who was scratching himself. Suddenly the skipper levelled the gun, and fired one barrel.

"Rabbit," he said. "Frank, fetch."

The dog urinated against a particularly large cabbage.

"Fetch," the skipper repeated, more urgently.

Frank scampered off to return in a few minutes with a lump of wood which, wagging his tail, he placed at the skipper's feet.

"Gawd," said Skipper Day. "Us'll 'ave ter find that ourselves."

Vic eventually found the dead rabbit which went into the sack with the cabbages. Later a second rabbit was dispatched and recovered without much help from Frank. The skipper, I decided, must be a very good shot.

"Let's try another field," Vic suggested as we walked back. We did, and a handful of young onions were added to the sack.

"Pity, there weren't no pheasant," said the skipper on the way back to the barge. That night we dined off rabbit stew, cabbage and onions, followed by tinned pears.

Next day the wind had filled in from the East and we had an easy sail up to Upshore. Again the 'moty boat' helped us up to the quay which contained only one other barge, the Hubert with her new 'ingin'. We had been away nearly three weeks.

CHAPTER SIX
UPSHORE AGAIN

Once again the motor boat was manned by Zeke and Jan. Both came aboard once we were moored up. Zeke to discuss stores and Jan to see me.

"For you, my friend," he said handing me a slip of paper, "From the little lady in the office."

Of course! Jan was the perfect go-between with his access to the barges. She must have seen us come up river and passed the note to Jan. I glanced at the note: "Tree walk. 7.30. E." She was obviously in the office, for, unusually, the red sports car was parked outside. But there was no sign of her.

My thoughts of Jan as a go-between were shattered by his next statement. "I have great news. At last I have the berth of mate. With Horace Carney on the Reed Warbler."

The Reed Warbler was by far the oldest barge in Fowler & Dunn's fleet. I had seen her skipper, generally known as Hoary, around the waterfront. He was probably the oldest skipper in the fleet, a long thin lathe of a man, and the only local bargeman with a beard. This was a long, straggly affair, often a repository for bits of dropped food, splashes of paint etc. No, Horace Carney was not impressive, especially from the perpetual dewdrop hanging from his nose. He nearly always had a cold.

"Ol' 'Oary Carney," said Zeke, wandering up. "I did one trip wiv 'im as mate, an' one only. That man's so mean, it ain't true. We jus' got clear of Upshore an' I found I ain't got no fags. I mentioned it ter 'Oary an' 'e sez, 'That's orl right, mate. There's a packet on me bunk, yew can 'ave 'em.' So I thinks 'good-oh', goes dahn an' gets 'em and lights one up. 'That'll be one an' sixpence' sez the ould skinflint. 'But they're only ninepence in the shops, skipper,' sez I. 'Teach yer ter bring yer own,' 'e sez. Nah! I wasn't doin' no more wiv 'im arter that."

But Jan was undeterred. "I have a mate's berth," he maintained. "That is all I require."

"Well, good luck, then," was all Zeke could say.

Later we received a visit from Miss Ellie. I saw her coming from the office, and I thrilled at the sight of her. A light blue blouse, this time, with the mandatory black skirt. I hadn't forgotten how pretty she was. But it was Captain Day she wanted to see, not me.

"An awful lot of breakages in your consignment, captain," she said.

"Oh. It's them London dockers, Miss Ellie," said Day. "Shockin' careless lot. Like a couple of cans of pears?"

"Oh yes please," she said visibly relaxing.

The skipper produced two cans from somewhere within his jacket.

"Decent drop of rabbit stew dahn below. 'Appen you'll stay to lunch." For once, he seemed in no hurry to go home.

"No, I'm sorry – I can't. Dad's not at all well and hasn't been in the last two days. So I'll have to stay in the office. But thank you, it sounds lovely."

So that was why the car was being used instead of the pony and trap.

"Bin to chapel, lately?" asked the skipper.

"Oh, yes. Most Sundays."

That was the connection, then. They were both Peculiar People. Ellie made her farewell and went back to the office. I gazed after her.

"She's a cool one," said Vic. "Didn't take no notice of yer." Oh

66

God, I thought, don't let him start up again. Why couldn't he have done like Frank, and gone ashore on the razzle as soon as we moored up. In fact if both he and the skipper had gone, I would have had Ellie all to myself, as the lumpers were busy with Hubert's cargo. But, realistically, she was probably taking no chances with her brothers and their possible informants.

I asked Jan what else had happened while we were away. Not much, he said. The two barges at the bargeyard had duly had auxiliary engines installed but Fowler & Dunn had no plans to convert any more, either because of shortage of finance or the imminence of war or both. We had just missed Tommy Dolby who had sailed for London the previous day.

Soon it became apparent that both skipper and mate had stayed on board to finish the rabbit stew and I had to go below and prepare the lunch. We sat round the table and had a really good feed. When it was finished Captain Day announced that he was going home. He had, I noticed, prepared a sack full of canned goods for his family. Vic, too, disappeared ashore and at last I had the barge to myself as the lumpers were not starting until the next day.

But Captain Day had left me a long list of tasks to perform and I was busy for the rest of the day. But, of course, I was on deck about the time Ellie was due to depart for home. She was late by about half an hour. No doubt kept on office matters. She was wearing an outdoor coat and a headscarf. She paused by the car, looked around, and then hurried towards Daisy Maud. I went up the quay ladder to meet her.

She flew into my arms and kissed me full on the mouth. "Sorry, couldn't wait," she said, when we came up for air. "You will be there tonight, though?"

Of course I would, I said.

"I'd better go and see how father is," she said. "See you later." I noticed she was back to her private school mode of speaking. I gave her another peck and she jumped into her little car and roared off.

Somehow I passed the time until just before seven thirty. I

made my way past the Jolly Fisherman and into the trees. And there she was, waiting for me. This time, as it was a chilly evening, she was wearing a white sweater and blue slacks. As we walked, hand in hand, through the trees she wanted to know about our voyaging. When I explained about our boredom in Ipswich, she said: "If only I had known, I could have made some excuse to drive up there." This possibility had never occurred to me.

When I told her of John's visit in West India Dock, she pulled a face. "He worries me. Sometimes I think he would do anything to get his own way. I do hope that Captain Day knows what he is doing. John's not stupid and it wouldn't pay to cross him."

The poaching incident amused her. "He's a lovely man, Captain Day. I've known him since I was a little girl on the waterfront. He's long since realised that I know all about his poaching and thieving from cargoes. But all of them do it, to varying degrees."

I told her that she was not popular with all of the bargemen.

"Oh! I know that. O' course I'm not. Owner's daughter, first point of contact with them in the office. Little 'ould rich girl. I wouldn't expect to be popular. But one day soon I'll show 'em." I wondered what she meant by this.

We had turned round and were nearly back at the quay. She looked at her watch.

"I don't want to go home yet, but it's too chilly to say out here. I know. Let's go in the Jolly Fisherman.

Wasn't this risky? I asked.

She said that it shouldn't be as the landlord was fairly new and was unlikely to know us. It was not likely there would be any bargemen in the inn.

"What about Vic?" I asked remembering our first walk.

"Well, he already knows doesn't he? But I shouldn't think he'll go back."

We went in. The Jolly Fisherman was much better furnished than the King's Head. It catered for a 'better type of customer' – yachtsmen, the town's professional men and so on. I was rather embarrassed, for I had not yet had that week's pay and Ellie paid for the drinks. We sat in an alcove where we could be alone. Ellie raised the subject of the Barge Match.

"It will be a good race if Captain Day gets his borsprit. It'll be between him, Brother John and Bully Briggs, unless Thames & Medway send up some of their flyers from Kent. Did you know they would like to take us over?" This was a surprise.

She nodded. "Yes, it's a fact. Father's already had discussions with them. The only thing that seems to be holding them back is the possibility of war."

I asked what John felt. "Oh, he's against it, o'course an' Ernie's not sayin' anythin'."

"And you?"

"I don't know. It depends on the terms. If they'd let us carry on as we are, I think I'd be for it."

She changed the subject. "About the borsprit. I could help. I've a little money of my own." I thought this a very generous offer, but said that Captain Day had his own ideas.

"So've I," she said, brushing her lips against my ear.

Not wishing to embarrass the other customers we went outside. It was a good twenty minutes before Ellie got into her car and drove away calling "See you tomorrow" as she went.

Next morning there was a conference about the borsprit in Daisy Maud's cabin. Apart from Captain Day, Zeke was present and two men I had not met before. Vic was nowhere to be seen and I was deputed to make an endless supply of tea.

The two visitors were Mr. Bliss, Mr. Ernie's foreman shipwright at the barge yard, and Wilfred Hooker, the local sailmaker and father of the King's Head barmaid. Mr. Bliss was never to be seen without his bowler hat, which he regarded as a badge of office. As it was during working hours he was also in overalls. I took an instant dislike to Mr. Hooker. He looked rather like an overgrown ferret and wore an eyepatch, which must have handicapped him in cutting sails.

"It's like this 'ere," said Captain Day. "It's abaht money see, I gotta raise some finance. That reminds me, I gotta ring ould Dunn." What on earth did he want with Fowler & Dunn's sleeping partner?

"Happen I could save yer money," said Mr. Bliss, rubbing his bushy moustache. "Must 'ave some ould borsprits round the yard. Might even find this barge's ould 'un."

"Nah, yew wont find that," said Captain Day. "Vicar 'ad it. Wanted a flagpost or such."

"Still, what yew reckon? Shall I look for one?" persisted Bliss.

"Yew wait an' see. I'd rather 'ave a new 'un. Might not be able to trust an ould un."

"Mek yew up a new un sure. Jus' giv' the word."

"New sails," said Captain Day turning to Hooker. "Can yew make up a quote fer a topmast staysail an' a jib an' all the riggin' ter go wiv this lot? An' it don't finish there 'cos us'll need a new topsail, present one's jus' abaht 'ad it."

Hooker scribbled away in a notebook

"Tidy ould sum, that'll be," he said.

"Never yew mind. Jus' get me the quote an' I'll deal wiv it".

After some more detailed discussion which I did not follow well, Bliss and Hooker departed. Zeke stayed on.

"Bliss'll see yer orl right," he said. "Jus' 'ope 'Ooker gets one of 'is 'ands ter cut yer sails. 'E'll mess it up, for sure, 'appen 'e does it 'imself."

"That ould eyepatch ain't doin' 'im no good," said Skipper Day, "'E's oright on quotes an sich, but 'e aughter let someone else cut the sails."

"'Ow abaht goin' elsewhere?"

"Ony add ter the cost. Anyway's 'ow does I know I trust a foreign sailmaker?"

"'Ooker it is then."

"'Ooker it is."

"Captain Day," I said, plucking up courage, "Miss Ellie could let you have some money."

Both men stared at me.

"I dessay she could, young fella," said Captain Day, "but I durst tek it. That 'ould reely do it wiv the Fowlers. Yew thank her very much when you see 'er though."

That was the end of the meeting.

"He won't accept your money," I told Ellie on that evening's walk.

"I didn't think he would for a moment," she said. "He's a proud man. Wants to do it all himself."

"He's obviously got a plan," I said "But he's not saying what it is. "Nevertheless he's very grateful for your offer."

The next day was Saturday and we were obviously in for a spell of hot weather. Ellie was already back in a summer dress and we discussed plans for the weekend.

"We could go for a picnic on Saturday afternoon," Ellie suggested. "I'll provide the food and I know a nice quiet place for it."

I liked this idea and we agreed to meet at half past two.

"I don't know when else I'll see you though. I won't be able to get away on Saturday night and Sunday morning will be chapel. Sunday afternoon, perhaps or a walk in the evening."

I suggested that we discuss this on the picnic and asked her about her chapel going.

"Well, I'm not really that religious," she said, "but father likes to go to the chapel and there's some nice people there, like Captain and Mrs. Day."

And how was her father?

"A lot better, thank you. He should be back in the office on Monday. It would ease the load a lot. I just hope John isn't around to stir up trouble." John had left that day to rejoin the Pride in Great Yarmouth.

We were back at the Jolly Fisherman. "Can't go in there to-night." said Ellie. "Father expects me back soon. But we've got somthin' ter do for a while, haven't we?" We had...

When I returned to Daisy Maud, Vic was on board in a vile mood.

"'Spose yew've been wiv that little cow," he greeted me.

"Careful, Vic," I said quietly.

He calmed down a bit and explained. He had been to a meeting of Fowler & Dunn's bargemen, held in the saloon bar of the

King's Head, obviously in a beery atmosphere. The meeting had not been well attended since so many barges were away. Neither had it been supported by the older men, who tended to be more loyal.

The meeting lacked both chairman and agenda and descended into criticism of the Fowler family with Ellie running John a close second in unpopularity. It broke up with those present vowing to pass on their views to the men absent.

Vic evidently expected more from the meeting and, I think, would have liked to say more about Ellie. Eventually realising that he had not got a sympathetic audience he went off to drown his frustrations in the public bar.

The next day I couldn't wait for two-thirty to arrive. I kept looking at the clock on St. Michael's tower and its hands hardly seemed to move. A picnic with Ellie! And what a picnic it would turn out to be!

"What's up wiv that boy?" Captain Day asked Vic, when he came down to the barge.

"Gotta date wiv yew-know-who," said Vic darkly. Skipper Day refrained from comment.

Our cargo was not considered urgent enough for the lumpers to work on Saturday, which made time go by even more slowly. Jan appeared but, realising I was preoccupied, did not stay long. Upshore United had finished their season so there was no football match, but Vic announced his intention of having a lunch time pint and then getting his head down for the afternoon. Captain Day was obviously off home, so there would be no awkward questions when I left. By the time the church clock said at last, twenty-five past two, I was on my own and set off to meet Ellie.

As usual she was waiting for me just inside the trees. The weather was now brilliant with the sun beating down out of a cloudless sky with a light easterly breeze. Ellie was sensibly dressed in sandals, shirt and shorts which did everything for her legs.

"We've got rather a long walk, I'm afraid," she said, "but it'll be worth it."

She was carrying a picnic-basket which I took from her,

We followed the path through the trees, past the now silent bargeyard and into open country beyond. On the way we passed a few other couples out walking, but no-one that we knew.

Then we found ourselves confronted by a gate and stile and notices that said: "Private land, keep out."

"It's all right," said Ellie, "my father owns the land."

As she clambered over the stile, I saw her nipples outlined against the taut material of her shirt. She was obviously not wearing a brassière. I began to feel sick with anticipation of what she had planned.

We walked across the field to the seawall. Here there was a small, sandy beach. It was around high-water on a spring tide and the water was well up the beach. We sat on the sea-wall and, after a kiss or two, investigated the contents of the basket – there were sandwiches, chicken legs and slices of various pies. We ate a few items and lay back in the grass on the sea-wall. A solitary barge was dropping down river.

"What gives barge sails that particular shade of red?" Ellie asked.

"Skipper Day says the mixture is red ochre, linseed oil and Ingredient 'X', which is a secret."

"What do you think it is?"

"Sea water, I think".

She sat up, as if reminded of something, and started unbuttoning her shirt. "I know, let's go for a swim." She stood up, dropped her shirt to the ground, and started to push her lower clothing over her hips.

"But we haven't got any costumes" I protested.

"We didn't worry about 'em when I was a kid on the waterfront." She was naked.

"But..." I was about to point out that we were adults. But with a twinkling of bare buttocks she ran into the water. She stopped when she was up to her shoulders in the water and watched me finishing undressing with interest.

I plunged into the water and tried to grab her, but she had

73

gone. I fell flat on my face. She was giggling at me from a safe distance.

"Plenty of time for that later. Let's swim."

She was, as I might have expected, a good swimmer, far better than I, although I must admit the shape of her naked body under the water was putting me off.

We swam for about a quarter of an hour, until she suddenly swam inshore and stood up with the water half way up her thighs.

"There you are then," she said, thrusting her chest out. I took in her perfectly formed breasts with their jutting pink nipples, her flat stomach, the abundant black hair between her legs.

We splashed ashore, hand in hand, kissing as we went.

"We'll dry off in the sun," said Ellie, "but first I must do something about THAT." She lunged for my manhood. And so we lay nude in the sun, doing to each other the things that lovers usually do, but stopping short of actual sex, as we had no precautions and Ellie did not consider the time of the month right to do it unprotected.

I spent that evening in a state of euphoria. Somehow I found myself floating across to the King's Head in the company of Vic and Hubert's crew.

"Like a cat what's got the cream." was Vic's only comment. For a Saturday night it was quiet in the King's Head. The many men who were away included Gascoigne and Ned, so there was no pianist. One of the lumpers stood in with an accordion. Both barmaids were available to do the solo singing, but somehow the evening lacked something compared with its predecessors. Fortunately, there was no sign of Captain and Mrs. Day as I would have been embarrassed had they talked about Ellie. We spent more time talking than was usual on a Saturday night.

Hubert's skipper was a youngish man as befitted his position as master of the firm's experimental motorised barge. Like Tommy he was newly promoted and preferred the company in the public bar to that in the saloon. As was to be expected he was enthusiastic about his new toy.

74

"It's the thing of the future," he said. "Happen one day all barges'll have engines, probably be made of steel too, 'cos that don't rot like wood."

His mate, an older man, was not so enthusiastic.

"We was up at East Mills, Colchester 'fore we 'ad the ingin," he said, "an' there was two of Thames & Medway's motey-barges there. They was a-messin' around wiv blow-torches and sich, tryin' ter start their injins an' one of the skippers 'e sez 'Ony one thing worsen this an' that's them bleddy ol' red sails we uster 'ave."

"War wont help," said the skipper. "Companies won't want to spend money then. I hear Fowler & Dunn ain't doin' any more engines."

"Good job, too, " said Vic, loyal to sail. "Yew weren't at the meeting, yisterday, then."

"No. No point with so many away. An' what you got to go on anyway? John's a loud mouthed bully and Ellie highty-toighty. That's all. You wait till you got more'n that."

Like the Thames & Medway takeover, I thought, but said nothing.

At closing time Vic announced that he had important business to attend to.

"Like yew did this arternoon," he added.

I gathered that he meant Rosie, Florrie, Pat or any combination of the three, so I walked back to the barges with the other two.

The weather next morning was threatening. All morning the skies were leaden and by midday I could hear rumbles of thunder. It did not look good for an afternoon with Ellie and any thoughts I had of finishing what we had started the previous afternoon seemed dashed.

We had agreed to meet at two thirty again in our usual spot. A picnic had not been mentioned but, Ellie being willing, any opportunity would do as far as I was concerned. At two o'clock the deluge began. Thunder, lightning and, worst of all, torrential rain, which even fell as hail at times. Frank the dog, scampered on board and joined Vic in snoring in the foc's'le. I sat dejectedly on the foc's'le companionway, my world at an end.

Suddenly I became aware of a different sound among the claps of thunder and drumming of rain on the decks. I borrowed Vic's oilskin and went on deck to investigate. The little red sports car was alongside on the quay with its hood up and Ellie sounding the horn repeatedly. I scrambled up the ladder and threw myself into the car on the passenger side.

"Best I could do," Ellie said when we pulled apart. "You're making me all wet."

"You might have to take your dress off," I said hopefully. She let that pass.

"We'll have to get away from here before someone sees us."

She drove past the Jolly Fisherman and up the hill, then onto the road that led into the country beyond Upshore.

"It can't keep raining like this for long, can it?" she asked rhetorically.

We passed a big house set back from the road in its own grounds. With the rain I was unable to see much of it.

"That's where I live," said Ellie, "but I can't take you there. Too many people prowling around."

"Where shall we go?" I asked. Dashing round the countryside in a cramped and damp sports car in a thunderstorm was beginning to lose its appeal, even with her. I half thought of suggesting going back to the barge and using the after cabin, but decided that this was too risky, with Vic aboard.

"Don't worry, we'll find somewhere," said Ellie.

Somewhere eventually turned out to be a tearoom in a village some miles outside Upshore. Ellie bought us tea and toast which we consumed under the eagle eye of a forbidding waitress.

"A pity its turned out like this, " she said and squeezed my hand under the table to the indignation of the waitress. "Did you know you're due to sail again tomorrow if discharge is finished?" Her ankle was rubbing against mine under the table. "To pick up another freight in London?"

I felt mutinous. I did not want to go. I wanted to stay with her. She sensed my feelings.

"Still," she said philosophically, "think how much hotter

things will be when you come back."

The rain was easing off. We finished our snack and went out to the car. On the way, just to give the waitress full value, I gave Ellie a very passionate kiss. She responded in kind pressing her body against mine.

"That will give the old cow something to talk about." she laughed as she started the car. On the way back we pulled up in a leafy lay-by.

"Too damp to get out," said Ellie as she flung her arms round my neck.

"I don't think anyone will see us here," she whispered as she undid my trouser buttons. She eventually managed to wriggle out of most of her clothes which was more than I could do. But, within the confines of the small, damp car we managed a passable repeat of the happenings of the previous afternoon.

"If only that waitress could have seen what we were up to," she giggled as we drove back to Upshore.

She dropped me in the High Street and I walked back to the quay through the wet and dripping town.

When I returned on board Daisy Maud I found Vic gazing despondently into a mug of tea.

His only comment was: "Bin dashin' abaht in fast cars then." So he must have heard us drive away. He did not even make any comment about my borrowing his oilskin without permission. It occurred to me that I had not heard anything lately about 'winnins' and that maybe he was having a run of bad luck.

Not that bad, though, for he still seemed to have the money for visiting the pub.

We had a meal, prepared and eaten almost in silence, apart from a few remarks about the weather.

"Did you know that we sail again tomorrow?" I asked him.

"Nah. Seems likely though. 'Eart-renderin' for some that'll be."

There seemed to be no pleasing him in this mood and I was relieved when he took himself off to the pub early, leaving me with the washing up.

77

"I'll see you off when you go tomorrow," she had said when we parted. "Honest I will."

And that was the best I could hope for, as once again she was not available in the evening.

After washing up I curled up on my bunk, not really intending to go to sleep, but I must have dozed off. Sometime later I was woken by a rough hand shaking me awake. It was Vic.

"Wanna word wiv you," he said thickly. He seemed, of all things, rather embarrassed.

"Look, this ain't the beer talkin'. I'm tellin' yer this fer yer own good, so don't take it the wrong way. You can't see it, can yer? Luv is blind, someone once said. That cunnin' little minx, Miss Ellie, she'll stop at nuffin to get 'er own way. She's usin' yer to git at her brothers. Ter cause trouble. 'Er old man's gettin' past it an' she wants ter be runnin' the firm an' they can either work wiv 'er or git out, as she sees it. Nah, us bargemen we knows, 'cos we've know 'er a lot longer than yew, see. An' don't take no notice of 'Appy Day, 'cos 'e's fond of 'er, in a father-like way, see. Yew think on, an' yew'll see I'm right."

He paused and patted my shoulder.

"No 'ard feelings, like."

And he was gone as quickly as he had appeared, no doubt back to the pub and his lady loves. I laid awake , thinking furiously for a long time.

I had felt that Vic was jealous of my relationship with Ellie for some time, but his advice had seemed well meant in his rough way. But was Vic influenced by the current dissension among some of the bargemen, of which he appeared to be a ringleader? As for his claim that she wished to run the firm of Fowler & Dunn, surely this would be affected by the (admittedly) possible take-over by Thames & Medway?

And Ellie's own attitude. When I though about it, she had made all the running in our relationship, especially in sexual matters. Even the tears on our first walk could have been an act to gain my sympathy. She had declined the ultimate sex act, when I would have thought that she would have been only too

78

ready for it. True she was promising it, but events since the picnic had prevented it. But, there again, she was dictating when and where we met, a really determined girl, in love, should be prepared to take chances, to miss routine Sunday chapel, just to be with her man. Also, I had seldom heard her utter an endearment, which was strange.

But all this could be quite simply explained by her nature. She was in love, true, but determined to control events. She would go to chapel because that was what *she* wanted to do. She would stay at home on Sunday night because *she* wanted to. We would have sex at a time of *her* choosing.

She might well be manipulating her brothers, with or without my help. But she could still be in love with me.

CHAPTER 7

INDUSTRIAL UNREST

Ellie's prediction proved correct. We finished discharging in time to sail in the late afternoon. The only good thing about this, at least in my view, was that we were not likely to be away long. Captain Day told us that we had a freight arranged which was to pick up a cargo of timber from the Surrey Commercial Docks for Fuller's timber yard at Upshore. This was not the freight he had been hoping for, but he was sure that Mr. Dunn would have it for us soon.

So that was why he was in touch with the director/shipbroker. A special freight – but what possible bearing could it have on the Barge Match and borsprit money? But I had someone much more important to worry about – Ellie. I had had a bad night of lurid dreams – one of which featured Vic as the Big Bad Wolf threatening Ellie as Little Red Riding Hood.

I still could not decide - she loves me, she loves me not. I now felt that a good test would be whether she saw us off this time – surely a girl who waved her man away as passionately as last time – could not be false, or could she?

The moment of departure came. The motor-boat had our tow-rope, the shorelines were being let go – and she came out of the office. She ran to the quayside. She was dressed not in her office "uniform" but one of her summer dresses. Neither was she wearing glasses – she seldom did now – except for driving.

This time she didn't care who saw her – she stood on the quay waving frantically as we towed away down river. Hubert's crew and several lumpers watched with interest. But perhaps it didn't matter. John was away and Ernie probably at the bargeyard and Vic and Happy Day knew roughly what was going on. I stared astern until she dwindled to a still-waving dot.

"Remember wot I tole yew," Vic hissed as he dropped one of the fenders on to the main-hatch. "It ain't as it seems."

"Yew two in luv or what?" said Captain Day, looking at the dirty rim of his tea mug. "Two of yew ter do the chores, an' yer both gettin' thin's wrong. Want me ter wash-up an' shew yer 'ow ter do it?"

We were anchored at the mouth of the river, having run out of tide. The skipper had been finding fault ever since we dropped the tow-line and although I thought some of his criticisms justified some definitely were not. I certainly had a lot on my mind and kept going over the arguments for and against Ellie and I knew I was letting the barge's domestic arrangements slip. Vic, I thought, was worried both about his speech the previous night and his poor performance with gambling recently. Several times the skipper had made a rare comment about him being slow with the bowline as we tacked down river.

"Yew both better sharpen up termorrow," the skipper went on, "'cos that's a-goin' sou'west an'll freshen." He had this uncanny aptitude for forecasting the next day's weather and was generally right.

He was exactly right about the next day. We had an exhilarating sail down to the Thames and there were no further complaints about the performance of Vic or myself. We anchored for the night at the lonely Yantlet anchorage and sat on deck as darkness fell watching the lights of Southend and its pier came on and the twinkling and winking of a myriad of navigation buoys. These Captain Day tried to explain but, being somewhat tired, I became confused about "flashing" and "occulting" and we decided to turn in for the night.

The next day we made it up to the Surrey Docks. These docks were the home of London's timber trade, although some other cargoes were handled there. Timber was everywhere. It was piled high on quays, on ships waiting to discharge and the numerous barges and lighters collecting from the docks. Here the specialist deal-porters plied their trade, often performing balancing feats with a particularly long plank on their shoulders. The smell was like a huge sawmill.

But there was an additional disadvantage for sailing barges. If the other dock systems suffered from drifting lighters, the "Surreys" were ten times worse. Since the Surrey Docks was really a number of small docks joined together by "cuttings", the lighters would often block an entire area. A sailing barge's only hope of movement was by taking a wire ashore to a fixed point and then winding in on the wire on the small "dolly" winch above the windlass. This could be backbreaking work and all the time there was the danger of damage from the great steel lighters.

We took our cargo of timber, not from one of the cranky Russian timber carriers which we had seen downriver on my first voyage, but from a smart Norwegian motor ship, that looked brand new. Loading went on until we had timber on deck to a height of about five feet. This was chained into manageable bundles.

"Good old cargo, timber", said Vic. He, despite our differences over Ellie, was as informative as ever. "Nice an' clean ter work wiv an' gives us a small stack. Not as big as 'ay stackies, mind. But 'elps keep us dry at sea. What yew got ter watch out fer, though, is splinters when yew goes muckin' around on top of the stack."

I said that I would be careful of this. A lighter banged into Daisy Maud aft.

"Pesky lighters," said Captain Day. "When I was a young mate, me ol' fella got right fed-up wiv 'em. There was one lighterman allus seemed ter be runnin' inter us, so one early mornin', 'e's a-'angin' abaht near us an' me ol' fella gets me an' the third 'and to lay some white jibs aht on the fore'atch and 'ide under them. Sure enough, up comes this lighter. 'An we rise up all clad in these jibs, see an' makin' ghostly noises an' a-clankin' bits of chain, like. Yew should 'ave seen that lighterman's face. Didn't see 'im no more.".

I had one shore excursion while we were in Surrey Docks. The oil for the lamps was low and Captain Day sent me ashore to purchase some more.

"There's a chandlers in Plough Way," he said and gave me some money. "Mind yew git a receipt though." So I went off and found the chandlers. They let me have a jar of oil for a very small amount and also gave me a receipt. This I dropped in a pocket of my jacket and promptly forgot, as Captain Day must have done, since he didn't ask me for it when I gave him his change.

We were soon done with the Surrey Docks and dropped down river to the Ship and Lobster below Gravesend. Here there were several barges anchored including Gascoigne's Alicia and Bully Briggs' Resolve.

"Might be worth a visit ter the pub ternight," our skipper observed.

When we arrived at the Ship and Lobster, Gascoigne and Ned, Bully and his mate, plus several others were already there.

"Where's that borsprit, then?" asked Bully as soon as we walked in.

"That's a-comin' directly," said Captain Day.

"Yew'll be racin' staysail, yet," said Bully.

"'Appen".

Bully Briggs generously bought all three of us a drink plus one for himself. His capacity for beer exceeded even that of Tommy Dolby. It was equalled by his appetite for food, as was evident when a huge helping of pie and potatoes was placed before him.

"Makes that stew we 'ad on the barge look like a snack," he said to his mate.

Gascoigne coughed as though he was about to make an announcement.

"I was loadin' over in Tilbury Dock yesterday," he said. "An' there was a Thames & Medway barge at the same ship. 'Er skipper reckoned they was after taken' over Fowler & Dunn."

"Cor! That'd do it," roared Bully thro' a mouthful of pie. "Kentishmen takin' over an Essex firm. Yus, that'd do it."

Vic had put on his shop steward's face. "An' there'd be a strike yew'd never see the end of. Lad's are upset ennuf as it is."

"Who'd go on an ould strike?" said Skipper Day.

"Any Essexman."

"Garn! Yew're all talk, yew an' the other barflies in the King's 'Ead."

"I'm all fer a strike," claimed Bully. "More work for us Mistleymen." He took an enormous swig from his glass.

"You're from Essex, too." said Gascoigne.

"Only jus', only jus'," Bully mumbled through a mouthful of pie. "Yew knows full-well us Mistleymen's a law to usselfs. Comes o' bein' on the border 'tween Essex and Suffolk."

"Yew wait till I tell the rest of the lads," said Vic.

"Yew'll do no such thing," said Happy Day. "'Tis a rumour , no more. Yew wait 'til we get the word official-like."

"An' if we do?"

"Still ain't worth no strike. Yew ain't in any union. What will yew do fer money?"

"Spend it on beer for me." Bully held out an empty glass.

This raised a laugh and the subject of Thames & Medway was dropped, although Vic still simmered.

Next day we set sail for Upshore. This time I was not looking forward to our return. I would have to say something to Ellie and I would not like to forecast her reaction. She might want nothing further to do with me. But I had dreamed up another, more optimistic theory. If she was only using me, would she have gone as far as she did? It would not have been necessary, just being seen in my company would have been sufficient. And, anyway, if her brothers were the target, why did she go to such lengths to avoid them and their associates? Hopefully she was genuinely my girl.

For part of the voyage we had Alicia and Resolve as company. For a while we were leaving both of them behind, but then Bully clapped on his extra jibs that he carried on his bowsprit and slowly began to overhaul.

"Now, that's got 'im worried," said Captain Day. "No borsprit, less sails and 'e's 'aving a job to catch up."

By the time we parted company at the Wallet Spitway, Bully was within waving distance, but Alicia was a dot on the horizon behind us.

The wind was southerly and fairly light, but now began to freshen.

"That keeps a-goin', we'll be Upshore this evening," Skipper Day observed.

"When's highwater?" asked Vic.

"'Bout half-past-seven."

"Good," said Vic. "Should be able to 'ave a chat in the King's 'Ead."

"Not still on about a strike, are yew?"

"No, but we gotta talk tactics."

The skipper shook his head. "Ony ever bin one bargemen's strike. At Sittingbourne, Kentishmen." He spat over the side. "They 'ad a union of sorts. Got real vicious it did. Even chained barges together across Milton Creek to stop non-strikers a-gettin' in. Course guv'nors won in the end. Allus do."

But my mind was elsewhere. Half-past-seven. She said she walked among the trees on fine evenings. Perhaps we could make it into Upshore in time for me to meet her.

The wind held all right and the clock on St. Michael's tower read a quarter to seven as we approached the timber wharf. We sailed right into our berth, reducing sail as we went for no motor-boat was on duty. When we were moored up Captain Day said: "Well, its orl-right fer me, I can walk 'ome from 'ere, easier than the quay. What yew two goin' ter do?"

It was a long way round from the timber wharf, across the bridge and up to the Jolly Fisherman I was worried that Ellie would have been and gone by the time I got there.

"King's 'Ead, me" said Vic. "See the lads. Tommy's here for once."

"Take the boat." said Happy Day. "Easiest way. Don't get drunk though."

"As if I'd do that."

"Take the lad wiv yew. That way boat'll come back orl right."

Good. That would save me a lot of time. Vic and I got the boat into the water, ready to cross the river to the Town Quay. But another delay occurred. One of Goldsmith's barges, deep laden with coal, was blowing up to the gasworks, under topsail only, on the last of the flood tide. We had to wait and let her pass. This delay was to have a considerable effect on future events.

I sculled Vic over to the Town Quay, waited until he had disappeared in the direction of the King's Head, (I'd told him I would see him there later) moored the boat up to Tommy's barge Silverfish, and set off in the opposite direction.

The little sports car was parked, as usual, behind the Jolly Fisherman, so she must already have set out on her evening walk. I hurried through the trees, expecting to meet her at any moment. Suddenly I heard a muffled scream from a thicket at one side of the avenue of trees.

I ran into the thicket. Ellie, almost naked to the waist was struggling with Bob, the spotty office-boy. I ran forward, swung Bob round and hit him with all my might. He reeled back and fell into a patch of nettles. Ellie fell into my arms.

"Oh! Bill. He said he was going to fuck me," she sobbed into my shoulder.

Bob got to his feet, rubbing at nettle stings. He glared at me then fled.

"Piss off, you little cunt!" Ellie screeched after him. And then resumed sobbing.

"How did it happen?" I asked.

"I . . . I was just walking among the trees an' he jumped out on me an' dragged me in here. Then he... started ripping my clothes, You came just in time! Oh, Bill . . . " There was a long pause.

She raised her tear-stained face to mine

"Take me. Take me, now."

She slipped out of what was left of her clothes and lay back on

86

the grass, her legs apart. I quickly shed my clothes and then I was kissing her – her lips, her breasts, her nipples, her navel, and finally her pubic hair. Then I was on top of her, plunging deeper and deeper until we both climaxed together.

Later we wondered what to do about her torn clothing.

"My brothers will go mad if they see me like this," she said, trying to pull the top of her dress together. I loaned her my jacket which, although too big for her, hid the damage when buttoned up. She twirled round in it.

"Perhaps I'll set a new fashion," she said. She seemed to be taking her experiences with both Bob and me very calmly, especially considering that she had been a virgin.

She must have read my thoughts.

"You learn a lot about sex in a private girls school," she said. "Even if you don't get the chance to practice it."

"Do you think we ought to tell the police?" I asked, referring to Bob.

"About what you did, no fear," she laughed.

"No, Bob."

"Don't worry about him. I'll deal with him. He's been asking for trouble, anyway. Nasty little boy."

"How about your brothers?" She immediately became business like.

"John's at home, unfortunately, But I know a way into the house, I've used lots of times before, which should avoid him and the servants. So I'll drive home soon and you better go to the King's Head. Act as though nothing happened (that will be difficult, I thought.) I'll return your jacket tomorrow."

And so we walked back to the car. As we finished kissing she murmured. "Thank you, thank you, Bill darling. I do love you." Was there an emphasis on the "do?" I thought there was.

She drove away with a cry of "See you tomorrow" and I watched the little car until it disappeared.

I walked to the King's Head very slowly. A number of my theories had fallen down. We had had sex at last and she had called me 'darling'. And yet there had been that slight emphasis

I thought I detected on the word 'do'. Did this mean that my theory that she was in love with me, but determined to do things her way, was correct? It was also looking as though Vic had got the situation entirely wrong. Sooner or later I was going to have to get the truth out of her.

I went aboard Silverfish to check that our boat was still all right. There would be sufficient water to cross the river until at least three hours after high water, which was roughly closing time. So I should be able to get Vic back aboard in time.

I approached the pub with some trepidation. Vic must have realised that I was meeting Ellie, and might create a scene in front of the whole public bar. But I need not have worried. The bar was buzzing with the Thames and Medway situation, coupled with the usual grumbles about John and Ellie. Practically all the Fowler & Dunn bargemen were in port, with the notable exceptions of Hoary and Jan, who were waiting for cargo at Woolwich and Gascoigne and Ned, waiting for the tide to change down river, but due to arrive on the next flood tide. In the general hubbub my presence went almost un-noticed.

Tommy Dolby bought me a drink as Vic was in the thick of it arguing, cajoling and encouraging, according to the attitudes of the men he was talking to.

"Only a rumour, Vic," Tommy called.

"Rumour. Then Fowlers 'ave got to confirm or deny it," Vic said. "I say we form a delegation ter see 'em."

"An' yew know what their answer 'll be," someone in the crowd called out. It struck me that Vic's rabble rousing was not going well. Ike, Tommy's mate, who normally did not say much, climbed onto a chair and addressed the bar.

"Listen to 'im," he gestured to Vic. "Just listen to 'im and 'e's a Kentishman hisself. A stirring up trouble. Why yew'd think Thames & Medway 'ad sent 'im 'ere ter do it."

And that was effectively the end of Vic's crusade. Some men laughed at Ike's words, others became angry. Vic crept away into the saloon bar to talk exclusively with Pat, the barmaid.

"Good wheeze that, Ike," said Tommy when the three of us

were seated. "'E was gettin' too big for 'is boots."

"Yus," said Ike, "But if the rumours are true, there'll be 'ell to pay. Essex an' Kent all over agen."

"Where did Vic git it from?" Tommy asked me.

I explained about Gascoigne and the Thames & Medway skipper he had talked to.

"Gascoigne? He'd do an' say anythink to increase 'is sense of 'is own importance."

"That Medway skipper could of bin stirrin' 'im up," said Ike.

"Well, young Ike, this jist ain't good enough," said Tommy. "Get the beer in."

Later I sat aboard Silverfish with Ike, drinking a mug of coffee that he had made me and worrying that Vic might arrive too late for us to cross the river in the boat.

"Don't yew worry abaht 'im," was Ike's advice. "Yew just go when you're ready. 'E's likely shacked up with that Pat."

But Vic did eventually arrive, somewhat befuddled and obviously still smarting over his treatment in the public bar. He totally ignored Ike who he obviously considered the architect of his downfall and I sculled him back to our barge in silence. At least, he hasn't noticed that I'm no longer wearing a jacket, I thought.

INTERLUDE — 1964

"What do you think, so far?" asked Bill

His tale had taken a long time to tell. It was, necessarily, in instalments, for I could not be at his bedside often, with the demands of work. He was now out of hospital and recovering at home. He and his wife were considering a divorce.

I took a deep breath before I replied:

"It's certainly a very detailed tale."

"But what else? What is it?"

"Well, there's no story for me in it, if that's what you mean."

"No, what is it? Is it a dream?"

"No, I don't think so, dreams are not usually remembered in such detail."

"Is it true?"

"Well, I think we both know that the places are real. And I tell you that many of the firms are too, especially the shipping lines you mention in the Thames. Some of the barges, also, Will Everard for one. But the people – I don't know."

"Can we find out?"

"Oh, yes. I've already got a researcher with a better knowledge than mine – someone who really knows the Thames barge scene. But, in the meantime, I'd like to hear the rest of your tale - it may contain some clues and, anyway, you've got me hooked on it."

And so, he continued.

CHAPTER 8

A SUDDEN DEATH

The discharge of our timber continued next day. Captain Day called in at lunchtime and admitted that we had no further cargoes in prospect.

"Happen I'll ring ould Dunn see if that special 'un turned up yet."

That evening he was back again. Vic and I were clearing up after our evening meal when he clumped down into the foc's'le, something he rarely did unless fetching an item of gear. He sat down heavily on Vic's bunk.

"Isaac's dead," he said bluntly.

"Dead?" we chorused.

"Yus, dead. Didn't you see all the hoo-ha over at the office?"

We hadn't, partly because we had been busy, and partly because our view across the quay was obstructed by other barges and cargo piled on the quay. Slowly we got the whole story out of the skipper.

While Captain Day had been talking to Ellie about his mysterious freight, which was now available, a furious row had broken out in Isaac's office between him and John. The subject had been Zeke. John maintained that a ship's husband was an unnecessary luxury and that his duties could be carried out by one of the office staff. This, presumably meant Mr. Oram, Ellie or the typist, since Bob, the office boy, had suddenly resigned for no apparent reason and had not come in. Isaac was vigorously opposed to this. Zeke had served the company for a long time, first as mate, then a skipper and a good one, too and finally as ship's husband. The least the company could do was offer him employment as long as he wanted it and Isaac was only sorry it was not possible to take him back on barges. But John was adamant that Zeke must go. Isaac then lost his temper and told John that Ellie, Ernie or even old Oram were worth two of him and that he only wished John would stick to skippering the Pride and stay out of the firm's business. John, in return, accused Isaac of being senile and of having no idea of how to run a modern business. Isaac yelled at John to be quiet then clutched his chest and fell to the floor, banging his head on his desk as he went.

"That Miss Ellie was marvellous," said our skipper. "It was 'er what tried ter bring the ould man round an' 'er what sent for an ambulance. That John 'e jus' set with 'is 'ead in 'is 'ands."

Isaac was taken to hospital but it was too late to save him. We sat in silence for a while.

Vic was the first to speak: "S'pose we'll 'ave ter deal with that bastard John now."

Captain Day ignored this.

"Vic," he said, "'ave we got any light blue paint?"

"Don't think so," said the mate, glancing at the chest which held our paint supplies.

The skipper felt in his pocket and produced a few coins which he gave to Vic.

"'Appen we ain't, git some in the mornin'. Light blue, mind, not dark. Brushes as well if need be. Don't go spendin' it all on booze or 'orses, neither."

"What's if for, skip?"

Captain Day sniffed at the use of his shortened title.

"Mournin'. Traditional-like. 'Appen yew git some, yew an' the lad paint our quarter-boards blue in the mornin'."

The quarter-boards were the low wooden rails round the stern

92

of the barge, normally painted white. Evidently they were repainted blue if someone important to the barge died.

"Dunno 'ow this affects our next freight," the skipper went on. "'Appen I'll find out in the mornin', one-way or t'other."

Shortly after that he left. Vic and I completed our clearing up in silence. My thoughts were with Ellie. I had never really met her father, but despite her remarks about the rows at home, she obviously respected and even loved him. She must have felt his sudden death terribly. It was possibly a selfish thought, but I doubted whether I would see her again before we sailed.

Later Vic and I visited the King's Head. It was quieter than usual in the public bar, but not unduly so. Old Isaac had been a remote figure to most of the mates and younger skippers, and they had no particular reason to regret his passing. The atmosphere was more speculative than anything. The consensus of opinion was that John would now run Fowler & Dunn and this was dreaded by most. There was also some speculation about the effect that Isaac's death would have on the possible Thames & Medway takeover.

"That John, 'e wouldn't 'esitate ter sell us out if it was worth 'is while," said Tommy.

"Could be Thames & Medway wanted Isaac's know-'ow," said Hubert's skipper. "I 'eard as their directors is all solicitors, accountants and the like. Don't know nothing about bargin'"

"P'raps Vic knows what they've got in mind." added Ike, who was fast becoming Vic's chief tormentor. But Vic was leaning on the bar talking to Florrie and didn't hear.

Captain Day visited us during the next morning while we were turning the quarter boards from white to blue.

"We're orl right," he said. "We can sail as soon as timber's out. Tomorrer morning that'll be." He went on to say that Isaac's funeral would not be till the following Monday and that he would like to be there. As we should be in London then he would travel back for it.

I asked who was in the office. He said that he didn't have to call there as he was dealing direct with Mr. Dunn by phone. But, with what was almost a wink, he said he did not have change for a call

93

box and had called in and used one of the office phones. Mr. Oram had been there and Miss Ellie.

"Bearin' up wunerful well, she is," he said. I was tempted to go rushing round to the office. But since the skipper and Vic were off ashore, I had to stay and keep an eye on the unloading.

A little later, after they had gone, I had two mysterious visitors. One was a big man who looked and probably had been, a prize-fighter, the other was minute and had a furtive look to him. It was this second man who did the talking.

"His Mister Halliday haboard, please?" he asked politely.

I was so unusual to hear Vic's surname that I had to think for a moment. No he was not, I replied truthfully, and I had no idea where he was.

"Then would you hask him to call on Mr. Pocock, the book-maker, please?" asked the furtive man, who I was now begin-ning to think of as 'The Ferret.'

"Hat his hearliest convenience," he added. The prize-fighter cracked his knuckles. Then they turned and went away. This all sounded rather ominous to me.

When Vic returned later, obviously after a few pints, I relayed the message. He went a shade paler under his sun-tan.

"Well we're sailin', ain't we?" he said defensively, "Pocock will 'ave ter wait till we're back."

And so, next morning, we did sail. Just beforehand one of the waterside urchins delivered a parcel containing the coat I had loaned Ellie. With it was a note which read: 'Thanks for the loan. All my love. E.' With a sigh I thought that this would be my last contact with Ellie for a good while.

But there I was wrong. She was on the quay to wave us away. She was wearing a black outfit and dark glasses, no doubt as mourning for her father. But she waved as enthusiastically as ever, much to the amusement of Tommy and Ike who were both aboard Silverfish. And I watched until I could see her no more.

Again we had a pleasant easterly and fine weather for the passage up to London. This triggered off the following conver-sation:

94

Vic: "You ain't arf lucky, young fella. You've jus' done summer sailin'. Different in winter."

Captain Day: "Jus' wait till you spend a few weeks waitin' for a fair wind at Southend or in the Jenkin."

Vic: "An' when you go to loose the brails on the mains the snow falls out o' the sail an' turns yew inter a little snowman."

Day: "An' yew 'ave to chip the ice orf the windlass 'fore yew can git the anchor up."

Vic: "An' you git a gale like the one larst year when some barges ended up in Holland."

Yes, I reflected, I had all this to come.

When we got down into the Thames we were once again in company with several other barges. A number of their crews were intrigued by our blue quarter boards. Some had not heard of this tradition while others enquired as to who had died. The news did not seem to have spread this far south..

Finally we sailed into the oddly named Erith Rands. Captain Day revealed the nature of our mystery cargo. It was, rather mundanely, bagged grain from a ship in King George V Dock, part of the Royals group of docks. It was to be delivered to a place called Nether Rushbrook, which neither Vic nor I had ever heard of.

"Yew'll like it there," said our skipper.

The only other information he would give us was that Nether Rushbrook was a village on the River Rush, a tributary of the River Colne. He said that he would tell us the rest later.

So, once again, we locked into the Royal Docks and found the ship that we were to load from. To my delight the Reed Warbler, with Jan and old Hoary, was loading from the ship ahead of ours and in the evening Jan sculled over for a chat. They had just heard of Isaac's death from another Fowler barge which had arrived just before us.

"My captain, he is very upset," said Jan. "He has known Mr. Isaac a very long time. But he will not paint the quarter-boards blue, as you have, for he says he cannot afford the paint."

I asked him how he found the mate's job.

95

"Oh, I am learning very well. My captain is good seaman, but pity he is so mean. Yesterday he sends me ashore on an errand and asks me to buy two cream cakes for tea. When we have eaten them, he asks me how much they were and I say "eightpence". 'Not worth it' he says and gives me sixpence."

I thought that Jan's English was improving well. The next day Captain Day travelled back to Upshore by train and bus, for the funeral was the day after. At about the time of the funeral Vic and I, with Hoary and Jan, joined the crews of two other Fowler & Dunn barges, also loading at the Royals, in the Roundhouse pub just outside the dock gates. Here, when everybody had got a drink (Hoary, I noticed, let one of the other skippers buy his), one of the captains proposed a toast to the memory of Isaac.

To our surprise Captain Day did not return that day or the next. By then we had finished loading and moved, together with Reed Warbler, to a quiet berth away from rampaging steel lighters. There were plenty of odd jobs to do including, now that the funeral was over, repainting the quarter-boards white. Needless to say, Captain Day, on his return, found us easily enough.

For once, our normally reticent skipper was bursting with information.

"I didn't come back yesterday," he said almost as soon as he put his case down, "'cos I 'ad ter go ter the readin' of ould Isaac's will, what was yesterday. I was a benny – benny – benny fishery in the will."

"You was what?" asked Vic. The skipper gave up.

"I 'ad some'at ter come in the will. But that ain't the point. Ould Isaac sewed things up proper in the will."

To keep us in suspense he launched into a description of the funeral and the setting of the will-reading in the oak panelled offices of the Fowler family solicitor, who presided over the proceedings, dressed as the traditional family solicitor complete with wing collar and pince-nez. The family were all there, plus their senior servants and a few of the older barge skippers, who were, no doubt also beneficiaries. But now we wanted to hear what was in the will. Eventually he put us out of our misery.

Isaac apparently had much more faith in Ellie than in John. So although John, as eldest son, received the bulk of Isaac's estate, the majority of his shares in Fowler & Dunn went to Ellie. Isaac had also appointed John his successor as chairman of the company, but Ellie was to become managing director when she was twenty-one, and, in the meantime, was to become manager, with sole responsibility for the day-to-day running of the firm. For the time being Mr. Dunn would be managing director.

"That won't make no difference," said the skipper. "'E's too busy in Lunnon ter interfere much. As fer John, 'appen Ellie's got any sense she'll keep 'im at sea as much as she can."

"You done orl right, there," said Vic to me, "yer girl friend really is the guv'nor now."

I had decided that one word should suffice to keep Vic in order now, so I used it.

"Pocock." I said.

"Nah then, yew two," said the skipper placatingly. "Any more questions?"

We asked about Mr. Ernie's position. "Oh 'e'll be 'appy he gets the barge-yard an' all that goes wiv it. It'll be a separate concern now with 'im as the guv'nor."

Vic asked what our master received under the will.

"Well, t'was an ould model of this ould barge when she was new-like, 'cos she was built by Fowlers' an' it must 'ave bin kicking round their office, somewhere. Still, Isaac must a-thought I was best person to 'ave it. Give the missus some 'at else to dust, keep 'er out of mischief. By the way, ould Isaac put a cody-some'at at end of 'is will – 'e said on no account should Fowler & Dunn 'ave anythin' ter do wiv Thames & Medway. Can't see as that makes a lot o' difference 'cos one of their directors was at the funeral and 'e was puttin' it abaht that they wouldn't make no takeover 'cos of the war what might 'appen."

"So that's that," said Vic.

"'Appen. Nah we're orl ready ter sail, are we? Right we will soon as tide serves. Nah, I'm goin' ter git me 'ead dahn. All this talkin' makes me tired."

I went on deck and reflected on this news, especially on how it affected Ellie and my relationship with her.

Unfortunately things were no clearer. On our first meeting she had protested about her lot in virtually running the firms affairs. Did she really mean this? If so the conditions of the will had not exactly improved her position. Or, as Vic had suggested, was she merely using me? Certainly, Captain Day had not said that she had refused the additional responsibility, so perhaps she was happier now that her position had been made clearer and John pushed more into the background. I *had* to see her and sort all this out, but could see no hope of doing so in the immediate future.

CHAPTER 9
THE MILLER OF NETHER RUSHBROOK

So, in the late afternoon, we sailed. The wind was still Easterly, but fresh, and despite a hard thrash to windward we made good progress.

As the evening drew on, I went to relieve Vic in tending the bowline so that he could go below for a meal. He seemed in a good humour again, no doubt he had been thinking how the Thames & Medway affair seemed over and the risk of John running the firm considerably reduced.

"This 'ere reminds me of a story," he said, nodding at the white horses on the waves running up the estuary. He was, in fact, quite wet from spray. "There's this barge on its way to Ipswich, beating down Sea Reach an' it's like this on'y worse an' it's raining an' all. The mate's up forrard tendin' the bowline and 'e's gettin'' well wet and fed up. After a while 'e goes aft an' says to the skipper. 'Can't we bring up, skipper?' Now the old skipper 'e wants ter press on for Ipswich. 'Nah!' he says, 'we got ter get ter Ipswich. Yew go back ter your end of the barge.' So the mate goes back an' 'e tends the bowline an' gets even wetter, then ''e goes aft agin an' sez 'Skipper, yew got ter bring up. I can't stand

99

this no more'. 'No,' sez the skipper, 'We're a-goin' ter Ipswich. Yew get back to yer end of the barge.' Bit after this skipper 'ears the anchor cable runnin' aht. 'What's a-goin' on?' 'e asks. 'I've anchored my end of the barge,' sez the mate, 'Yew can do what yew bloody like with your end!'" He guffawed and went below.

Next morning found us at anchor in the River Colne, off the entrance to the River Rush, the seawalls surrounding which could be seen winding away across the marshes towards a cluster of buildings which must be Nether Rushbrook. The marshes were used as grazing land, as several cows had strayed over the seawall. But the higher land around the buildings was substantially wooded. Occasionally the sounds of agriculture drifted to us through the still morning – the lowing of cattle, the roar of a tractor, the report of a gun used either by a gamekeeper or poacher.

"Moty-boat'll be aht directly the tide serves," observed Captain Day.

A Colchester barge drifted past, on her way to her home port.

"Yew a-goin' in there?" asked her skipper as he drew level with a nod towards Rushbrook.

"'Appen, directly," said Captain Day.

"Good luck," said the other skipper, sarcastically.

High water came and went with no sign of the expected 'moty-boat'.

"That's Barney for yew," said Captain Day. "Don't know what 'e's a-thinkin' of. 'E must be able ter see us, aht here."

"Who's Barney?" asked Vic.

"Barney Thornton, o'course. Richest man in Essex, 'e is."

Vic and I were none the wiser. The skipper went on "'Appen 'e don't come aht termorrer, we'll 'ave ter use the settin' booms ter pole up."

"Bugger that," Vic muttered to me. "That's bloody 'ard work, that is."

But he need not have worried. For next day a motor boat, of sorts, appeared. It must have started life as a ship's lifeboat but now, instead of its original white, was a dirty grey. This colour was probably due, at least in part, to the billowing clouds of black smoke which its exhaust emitted. In the stern a small dumpy figure could be made out clutching the tiller.

"That's ould Barney," said Captain Day. "Knew 'e wouldn't let us dahn."

"Mornin', Arthur," said the figure. "Us'd better git a-movin' 'fore this auld girl packs up. Git yer crew ter shorten up on the anchor an' I'll take yer line."

Hectic activity, then, for me an Vic for a while and then we were able to sit back as Barney towed us up the winding River Rush. A typical Essex scene went past of seawalls beyond marshes where sea lavender grew, and skylarks fluttered overhead.

"Wouldn't like ter try ter sail up 'ere," said Vic. "Though I s'pose the ould boys musta' done at one time. Reminds me of the barge beating up a river like this an' the master sez ter the young lad what's mate, 'Is that gull a-swimmin'?' Coupla minutes later he sez: 'That's a walkin' an' the skipper sez 'Ready abaht then.'"

Once we were moored up to the ramshackle mill at the bend of the river, Barney came aboard. The 'richest man in Essex' was not an impressive figure. His hair was thinning and he also wore extremely strong glasses, repaired in places with bits of wire and even sticking plaster. He was dressed in a shirt which, long ago, had been white and was now partially covered by a pullover of greenish blue which was more holes than wool. His trousers also showed signs of having once been green and were held in at the ankles by bicycle clips. His feet were tucked into a pair of muddy plimsols. The whole was covered with a liberal coating of grime, partially from the motor-boat exhaust, but also from other activities which could only be guessed at.

He flashed a yellow grin at Vic and I, then shook hands with Captain Day.

"Long time, no see, Arthur," he said "'ow's things?"

"Come below, an' I tell you," said the skipper.

They retired to the cabin, and shortly afterwards we heard the clink of bottle on glass. I knew that Captain Day kept a bottle of whisky on board but, like the gun, it was rarely seen. Barney must be a very special guest for it to be produced. Vic had come to the same conclusion.

"An' all the trouble skip went to ter get this cargo. Whats 'e up ter?"

As usual we endeavoured to eavesdrop at the skylight but could not make out any words as both men were talking quietly.

After about half an hour they emerged.

"Enjoyed that, Arthur," said Barney. "Thank'ee." He turned his attention to me and Vic. "Now, time I showed yer young fellahs arahnd. Yew commin' along too, Arthur?"

Captain Day said he would. "Like ter see the ould place, agen."

We climbed on to the quay and stood in a group as Barney waved his arms around.

"This 'ere's me mill," he said. It seemed to be largely built of corrugated iron, some sections of which were loose and clanged around in the breeze that had sprung up.

"Replaces the ould windmill what uster be 'ere," said Barney. "But that won't interest you lads much, yew'll want ter see the pub." The four of us , plus Frank the dog, who was finding a lot of new smells, set off up the hill to the village.

Hamlet might have been a better description, for it consisted of a small green surrounded by rows of cottages. There was no sign of life as most of the residents, as Barney explained, worked on the surrounding farms. There was, however, a post office-cum-general-store and a public house called, appropriately, The Miller's Arms. There was also a church which stood some way outside the main habitation.

We went into the pub. As I ducked down under the low door lintel I noticed the legend above it which read 'B. Thornton, licensed to sell Beers and Spirits.' Vic too had seen it and gave me a nudge.

The only people in the pub were a group of old men playing dominoes at a table in one corner.

"It'll liven up this evenin'," said Barney. "Me tenants are due ter pay me their rent. They'll all be in."

102

A very pretty girl, with flaxen hair tied up behind her neck, appeared out of a room at the back of the bar. Vic's eyes lit up.

"This is me daughter, April," said Barney. "Four pints of mild, luv. On the 'ouse."

Thanking Barney for the beer we sat down at a table. "She's a good girl, April," Barney went on after a swig of his beer. "She's a-goin' ter marry the right one, though. I ain't 'avin' 'er foolin' arahnd wiv jus' any ould bloke. Same goes fer me other daughter, May." Perhaps he'd already got the measure of Vic.

"Still, Arthur," Barney went on. "Anytime you lads want a beer, jus' come up 'ere. 'Appen pubs meant ter be shut, jus, go rahnd the back an' tap on the winder. Girls'll pass it out ter yer and you can drink it on the bench rahnd there. Settle up later. Any stores go an' see the missus over the post office. 'Appen she ain't got it, she can go off on 'er bike an' get it from next village."

He paused for a drink of his beer.

"Yew still got that gun, Arthur?" he asked.

Captain Day said that he certainly had.

"Yew feel free to 'unt anywhere rahnd 'ere. All my land anyway. Mind yew, 'appen yew want ter go further on ter the land of that ould bastard up at the 'all, what gives 'imself airs an'graces. I shan't object."

I was furiously calculating. Motor boat, mill, pub, post office, land, some of which was obviously rented out to tenant farmers, all were Barney's and all operated by his family and tenants. That was how this unimpressive little man had come to be 'the richest man in Essex.' The only thing in Nether Rushbrook that he did not appear to control was the church but I wouldn't have been surprised to see him in a (no doubt grimy) surplice ready to take the service on Sunday.

Vic too was thinking, but I was sure that his calculations had to do more with the fair April and her, as yet unseen, sister May.

"Drink up, I'll git yer another," said Barney. He certainly didn't get his reputation by being miserly.

And so it went on until well after normal closing time. We did not go hungry for at some stage enormous pasties appeared on the bar, with an invitation from Barney to help ourselves. Eventually Barney announced that it was time for his afternoon nap. Since there seemed no hope of our discharge commencing, we took the hint and returned to the barge and turned in ourselves.

In the evening we returned to the Miller's Arms. It was indeed crowded, most of the customers being farmers or their employees. Barney was sat at a table in a corner with a cash box open in front of him. He had had a wash which had removed at least some layers of dirt and was now dressed in a crumpled brown suit. Now and again a farmer would hand him some money which he would count and add to the contents of the cash box and then make meticulous entries in a ledger. Both daughters were serving behind the bar, May proving as pretty as her sister April, but brunette instead of blonde. A gleam came into Vic's eye as he recognised a happy hunting ground.

Although we were not, geographically, far from the sea in Nether Rushbrook, we were treated as objects of curiosity by the farmers and began to feel that we were many miles inland. The talk in the bar was of crops and sheep and cattle and market prices. Captain Day was quite at ease with much of this for as he said later, barges carried the farmers' produce and many men came into barging only because they could not find work on the land. Vic and I fared less well, Vic because he had always lived in towns and I because I had no long-term history, agricultural or otherwise. Vic was also possessed with a desire to investigate the two beauties behind the bar and I was beginning to miss Ellie badly.

A distraction arrived in the form of roast potatoes. These were placed in bowls on the bar, for the clientele to devour, by a comely lady who must be Mrs. Barney. A conversation then started between her, several farmers and myself, about the merits of different brands of potato and the best way of preparing them. Vic, for his part, was able to ask the daughters what part they had played in arranging the repast on the bar, thus gaining an opening.

The evening then passed quickly enough and we left fairly

early, expecting a busy day's discharge to begin early in the morning.

"Be down early termorrer an' git yew started," was Barney's farewell remark.

And he was down early in the morning.

"Right, cloths and 'atch covers off, lads," he said to Vic and I. We duly obliged, but by the time we had finished Barney was staring up at the sky.

"Nah!" he said, "not worth it. Might rain. Put 'em back." So back went the hatches and covers.

Barney wandered off on some other business.

"'E wont do nuffin terday," said Captain Day. "I know 'im of old. We might as well tek the gun an' that useless dawg an' get some grub."

And so began an idyllic ten days. Every day Barney would come down to the mill and lift a few bags out of the holds with the ancient hand propelled crane attached to the mill. Or maybe not, if he did not fancy the weather or had a pressing engagement. Most of our time was spent hunting across Barney's land with the gun and Frank the dog, who distinguished himself by actually retrieving a dead rabbit. More of our time was spent at the Miller's Arms drinking pints of mild and eating Mrs. Thornton's excellent snacks. Both beer and eats were heavily subsidised by Barney, so we had no money problems. With the hunting, the standard of food aboard the barge had gone up, for we had a continuous supply of game and vegetables.

I wondered why Captain Day did not go home as we were only twelve miles from Upshore as the crow flies. I assumed this was due to lack of transport or, more likely, a desire not to let Barney out of his sight for too long. The two men had several sessions of negotiations in the barge's cabin, sometimes over whisky and sometimes over tea.

"I reckon I know wot that's arl abaht," Vic said one day. "Skipper's tryin' ter get money out of Barney for the borsprit an' entrance fee fer the Barge Match."

"Well don't do anything to spoil it," I said, for Vic was evidently making good progress with the Thornton girls. Whether anything physical had happened I was not quite sure, but I rather felt that Vic was being held back, probably because of indecision about choosing between April or May, or possibly out of fear of the parents reaction.

The only black spot in our sojourn at Nether Rushbrook was the continued, and sometimes unnecessary, removal of hatch covers and cloths. Then one day we had a visitor.

I was just leaving the post office after buying a packet of tea when I heard the rare sound of a motor vehicle approaching the village. I stopped just as a familiar red sports car appeared. It was Ellie. She saw me and pulled to a halt alongside the green. As I ran up to the car she was taking off her headscarf and glasses.

"What are you doing here?" I asked.

I was immediately confronted by the efficient business-woman Ellie.

"Officially I'm here as representative of the managing owners to find out what's happened to their barge," she said and alighted from the car. "We haven't heard from Captain Day for weeks." She grinned. "But unofficially I'm here to see you." I knew everything was all right.

"Can we walk up there?" she asked, nodding at the trees above the mill. I said yes, it was all Barney's land.

"Good," she said, slipping her hand in mine. "Actually I've got some rather alarming news."

She said no more for a while for we were too busy kissing.

"What's this news?" I asked eventually.

"John's found the torn dress and the receipt." I was puzzled.

"I thought you were going to throw the dress away."

"I was, but I decided it was repairable and put it with my sewing. But I don't seem to find much time for sewing and John found it when he was looking for a shirt that I was going to mend for him. Still I told him I had caught it on something and that seemed to satisfy him. But then there's the receipt."

"The receipt."

"Yes, for lamp oil from a chandler in Rotherhithe."

I remembered dropping the receipt in a pocket of the jacket I had loaned her. Captain Day had never asked for it and I had forgotten about it. But how had John found it, I asked.

"It must have fallen out of your pocket. John found it behind a settee. It's made out in the barge's name. At the moment he doesn't associate it with the dress but he's wonderin' how it got in our house. If anything he's suspicious of Vic not you."

I was relieved and kissed her again. She was wearing a black dress, presumably still in mourning for her father, and as she clung to me it felt as though she wore nothing underneath. Behind us was a leafy dell similar to the one at Upshore.

"That looks suitable," she said and led me over to it.

I started to undo her dress. She was, indeed, naked underneath it.

"I stopped in a field on my way and took off my underthings," she said. Now that, I thought, would have been an interesting sight for a passing farm labourer.

"There's nothing like being prepared," she added as her dress fell to the ground.

Later, as we lay relaxing, still without clothes, in the sunshine that filtered through the trees, Ellie again did the unexpected. She pulled her handbag over, rummaged inside and produced a packet of cigarettes and a lighter. Then she lit a cigarette.

"You don't, do you?" she asked.

"No, and neither did you."

"Put it down to the strain of having sex," she giggled.

"You'll be drinking in pubs next." We both laughed.

I judged the moment right to ask her about our relationship.

"Of course I love you, silly," she said when I had finished. "I wouldn't have done that if I didn't." She thought for a minute. "But I know what you're thinkin'. It wasn't always that way. When you first appeared I desperately needed to do something to prove my independence to my father and brothers. I had decided that a boyfriend would be a good answer. You were ideal, no past, not local." I was beginning to feel vaguely angry. "So that first evening when I came to the barge was a sham and the display I gave on that beach was to keep you interested. But then I began to miss you when you were away and, when you rescued me from Bob, I suddenly knew, you were the one. I really did fall in love with you." I felt relieved.

As she finished speaking she had been studying my loins. She stubbed out her cigarette.

"You look as if yer ready ter go agen." she said, Essex returning. I began to get to my feet.

"No," she said softly. "Stay there. My turn on top."

Later, fully dressed, even to Ellie's underwear, which she had kept in her capacious bag, we walked down to the mill. I took the opportunity to ask her how things were at Upshore.

She said that Zeke's sacking still stood. John refused, as chairman of the company and head of the family, to take him back on.

"You heard all about the Will, didn't you? I asked Captain Day to tell you and the mate."

"He did," I said. "Congratulations."

"Nothing's really changed. John still tries to throw his weight about. I just try to keep the Pride away from Upshore as much as possible and he hasn't so much reason to pop home now. I'll do the same with Daisy Maud in case John gets any silly ideas. So far as the others are concerned you're urgently needed in London. But you may have to wait for a freight there. John's being very sticky about Captain Day having cargoes because of his attitude about his shares. But me and Mr. Dunn will do our best for you."

Her only other news was that the office boy, Bob, had at least had the grace not to reappear. To strengthen the office staff she had taken on a Mrs. Murphy, who had worked for a local bank, but she was still looking for an office boy.

"You don't fancy the job do you?" she asked.

But on reflection, I didn't. Although it meant that I would see a lot more of her, I felt that I owed it to Captain Day to remain with Daisy Maud.

When we reached the mill both it and the barge were deserted, although the hatch covers were still off. Presumably Barney either intended to do some more work or the covers were off simply because Vic and I were not there to replace them. Ellie was quite pleased because it gave her the chance to inspect the remaining cargo. While she did this I took a somewhat crumpled packet of tea down to the for'c'sle.

"She's still about a third full," she said when I came back up. "I dunno. Where are Mr. Thornton and Captain Day?" I told her that, to the best of my knowledge, Happy Day and Vic had gone shooting on the marshes, while Barney was probably on business elsewhere.

"What's the time?" I asked her.

She looked at her watch and told me.

"They're probably up at the pub by now," I guessed.

"Then I must go up there and see them. You follow me in a little while – no, sod it, we'll go together, hand in hand."

So we set off for the Miller's Arms . . . together.

As I had expected, Captain Day, Vic and Barney were sitting with their pints on the bench outside the pub. It had obviously been a successful shoot, for Frank the dog and a brace of ducks lay at their feet.

"Here come the love-birds," said Vic. The red sports car parked alongside the green had not gone un-noticed. Ellie looked levelly at Vic.

"Yes, love-birds, Mr. Halliday, and we don't care who knows it."

Barney and Captain Day muttered something that sounded like congratulations and Barney then offered us drinks. These were soon passed out through the window, a pint of mild for me and a half-pint for Ellie.

"I told you about drinking in pubs," I said to Ellie.

"This is outside a pub, silly."

Ellie thanked Barney for the drink and took a sip.

"Now, business," she said with an abrupt change of mood. "Mr. Thornton, why's Daisy Maud still one third full?"

"Take's time to discharge an ould barge, Miss."

"Who's doing it?"

"Why, I am."

"On your own?"

"Yus."

"Well, if you can't cope, then the crew will have to help."

"We do the 'atch covers an' that," said Vic.

"Oh, yes. Crew's responsibility that. No, I mean slinging the bags and working the crane. Crews often did it at one time. I expect you and Bill and Captain Day, if need be, to start doing it tomorrow. The barge is urgently needed in London."

"Was I too hard on them?" she asked as I walked her back to her car. It was not like her to have doubts. No, I said, they had had a marvellous time lately, and so had I.

"Let's treat them like we did that 'orrible ould waitress," she said and we had a passionate kiss in full view of the three miscreants.

CHAPTER 10

STARVATION BUOYS

The next three days were hard as Vic and I struggled to unload the rest of the cargo, with some help from Barney and Skipper Day. It was not an easy job – at least for us. We had trouble with the rickety crane and with passing strops round each bundle of bags. Fortunately Skipper Day had acquired, somewhere along the line, one of those useful tools – the docker's hook, with which we were able to spike and then drag individual bags over to make up a 'sett' of bags ready for lifting. Vic told me incessantly that this was not bargemen's work and should be done by lumpers or similar.

The two older men also did their fair share of grumbling. Barney felt that Ellie had interfered with what was properly his domain, while Captain Day, like Vic, felt this was not bargemen's work, not these days anyway.

"We use ter do a lot of our own discharge," he said, "on open beaches an' little ould places. Use ter rig our own tackle ter do it, an' all."

He had other doubts, too. "She ain't got no cargo in Lunnon. She jis wants us outa the way. Can't stand seein' us 'ave a good ould time. Anyways me an' Barney ain't finished our business."

The drinking in the Miller's Arms continued on a reduced

scale. It was now less for enjoyment and more for replacing lost sweat and easing tired limbs and muscles. Hunting, of course, was out of the question.

On our last day the skipper and Barney completed their 'business', apparently in an impasse. "Stubborn ould fool", said Barney as he left the barge.

"Stubborn ould fool", said Captain Day as he came on deck.

Also on our last day, to my delight, Ellie came again to see how we were progressing. She expressed her satisfaction and then said to the Skipper. "I'm afraid your cargo at London is running a little late. You'll have to lay at Woolwich and await instructions."

"Oh, yus," said the skipper, disbelievingly.

"You'll sail tomorrow, then," she said with an air of finality.

Unfortunately it was a day of heavy showers so Ellie and I were not able to repeat our walk of the previous occasion and all that went with it. A kiss and a cuddle at the back of the mill had to suffice.

"Just think," she said as I held her in my arms. "I'll be nineteen when I see you again." Her birthday was in a few days time. I did not know when mine was or even exactly how old I was, so I said nothing on this subject.

"I hope we're not away too long," I said.

"Oh it won't be too long, darling," she said. "You've got to come back to Upshore to prepare for the Barge Match if nothing else."

I brightened up. "I'll bring you a birthday present. A parrot, perhaps."

She laughed. "Just bring yourself. That's present enough. See yer then," and she was gone.

We sailed next morning in a cloud of black exhaust smoke from the old life-boat.

"We'll not be a-goin far," said Captain Day gloomily, "That's a-goin ter blow."

Barney dropped the tow off the river's mouth and circled us in his disreputable boat, while we made sail.

"Don't yew forget," he called to Happy Day, "the offers allus there, 'appen yew want it."

He opened his throttle and disappeared into the river.

"What 'appened wiv 'im?" Vic asked the skipper as soon as we settled down.

"Stubborn ould fool," said Captain Day again. "Wanted ter giv me the money an' all I wanted was a loan. I ain't no more prepared to tek 'is money nor Miss Ellie's. I pays me way, see?"

"I'd've teken it," said Vic, "reckon 'e can afford it."

"You ain't me," said Captain Day and that was the end of the matter.

Our skipper was, as usual, right about the weather. We spent two days anchored under the lee of Colne Point, riding out a north-easterly gale. With us were several of Samuel West's barges which took ballast sand from Colne Point and two of Goldsmith's barges also headed for Woolwich to await orders. With the weather fine, apart from the wind, we did not lack company from the other barges, for in the lee of the Point it was calm enough to move around in the barges' boats.

There were several gatherings aboard one barge or the other for tea, conversation and music, even Captain Day's concertina being pressed into service, although Frank had developed a habit of howling dismally while it was being played.

On the third day the wind dropped and, in company of the two Goldsmith's barges and one of West's we set out for Woolwich. It did not take us long to leave the others behind, for the West barge was deep-laden with ballast and as Captain Day said: "Them two Goldsmith iron-pots is round chiners, never as fast as the 'ard-chiners."

I was mystified by this remark, but Captain Day and Vic began to talk about Goldsmith's barges and I was able to work out some kind of answer. Apparently the firm of Goldsmith was sometimes referred to as 'The Pickford's of the North Sea' for the quantity and variety of cargo that its vessels carried.

In the late eighteen-nineties Goldsmith had ordered a total of thirty-eight steel barges, the largest group consisting of twenty of 150 tons burthen. This twenty was variously built at Deptford and Southampton, the Southampton craft all having round chines and the Deptford ones hard or square chines. All were nicknamed 'ironpots' together with any other barges built of iron or steel. The Deptford craft were definitely considered superior to their Southampton sisters, they were reckoned to be faster, easier to handle and had more comfortable cabins.

No-one was too sure, forty years later, why Goldsmith had ordered so many barges, but it was generally thought that the firm had connections with the cement industry and obtained the contract for delivering cement for building the National Harbour at Dover.

"Mind yew," said Captain Day, "this 'ere barge is a fast ould bit o' wood. We'd probably 'ave left 'em be'ind anyways."

So we had another fast passage to London anyway and by late afternoon were preparing to moor at Woolwich. Sailing barges would lay at a number of buoys at Woolwich waiting for orders. This was very convenient for the Royal Docks, only a few hundred yards away, and not too far from the other dock systems and the wharves around the Pool of London.

But with the slump in the nineteen-thirties, cargoes became scarcer and scarcer and barges could spend weeks on the buoys and, of course, no cargo meant no money. Although the better firms paid their skippers a small retainer and mates could claim some tiny form of Social Security, times were extremely hard on the buoys and for this reason they were known as Starvation Buoys.

With Fowler & Dunn's good contracts and their connection to the shipping world through Mr. Dunn, it was unusual for their barges to be on the buoys. So we were pleasantly surprised to see Tommy Dolby's Silverfish lying on the outside of the third tier of barges on the buoys. We were able to moor alongside her and Tommy and Ike were on hand to help with our lines.

Sometime later Vic and I sat with Tommy and Ike on the mainhatch of Silverfish. Captain Day had retired for a snooze while Frank was barking at a dog on a barge some three or four away from us on the tier.

"So 'ow's yer belly auf fer spots, Vic?" asked Tommy.

"Oh! I ain't bin doin' much," said Vic. "'cept unload the soddin' barge at Rushbrook. Nah, young Bill 'ere 'e's got a nice bit o' leg . . . "

"Pocock," I said and Vic halted. But Tommy joined in.

"Oh Miss Ellie! Guessed that way back. She weren't a-wavin' to yew Vic, nor ould 'Appy eether." He winked, I felt as though my face had gone the colour of beetroot. But worse was to come.

"She a decent lay, lad?" asked Tommy. If possible, I went an even deeper red. But I felt I could talk to Tommy. She was, I assured him, extremely good.

"That's the ticket, young'un," said Tommy. "Do you realise," he went on addressing the two mates, "when they're wed, young Bill 'ere will be a-bossin' the likes o' us arahnd?"

"Third 'and ter manager." Ike whistled. "That wouldn't be at all bad."

I realised my leg was being pulled, so I took a leaf out of Captain Day's book.

"'Appen we'll see," I said.

But Tommy had raised a serious subject. Thoughts of marriage and its implications had not occurred to me, or to Ellie, I was sure. And with my lack of background, any such idea, however desirable, was going to be extremely difficult.

Tommy and Ike were somewhat short of food, but we were still well stocked from Rushbrook, so, since the weather was still fine, we had a communal breakfast next morning, this time on our main-hatch.

"Cargoes are a bit 'ard ter come by," Tommy remarked. "We bin 'ere some days already."

"Thought the slump was over," said Vic.

"Shippers probably cautious 'cos there might be war."

"'Appen there's war," said Captain Day, "There'll be more ter do. Military cargoes an' the like. 'Appen there ain't, things'll pick up anyroad."

"Don't get us aht of this 'ole, though," said Tommy.

This was the start of several days on the buoys, with only

maintenance to do, but without the wherewithal to go ashore, apart from taking Frank for a run. Spare time was again spent in making and drinking tea, yarning with the crews of surrounding barges and, now and again, making music.

Communication between owners and brokers and the barges on Starvation Buoys was via a Mrs. Bax. This lady, who lived in a house adjacent to the Woolwich waterfront, possessed a rare luxury for those days, a telephone. On receiving a call, Mrs. Bax would shuffle her twenty-two stone to the foreshore and bellow the name of the barge required. The message would be passed from craft to craft until it reached the right barge. All of this took some time, so Mrs. Bax kept a supply of pennies to 'loan' bargemen to ring their callers back. For this service she was paid a retainer by most of the larger barge-owners and brokers which helped supplement her earnings from taking in washing and Mr. Bax's wages as a foreman stevedore in the docks.

Thus it was that two days later a Bax roar of "Daisy Maud" was heard on the first tier by the mate of Calluna who was whipping a rope's end. He passed it on to the skipper of Trilby on the second tier, who was taking a pipe on deck, and in turn, he passed it on to Tommy who was doing nothing on Silverfish on the third tier. Tommy jumped aboard Daisy Maud and shouted down into the cabin where we were having a cup of tea.

A few minutes later I sculled Captain Day ashore in the boat.

"Yew come along o' me," he said, "leave the boat on an anchor."

As we walked the short distance to Mrs. Bax's he explained that the phone call was probably from Ellie and that he thought that I might like a word with her when he rang back. But, much to my disappointment, when Mrs. Bax ushered us into her parlour where the phone was kept, we found the call was not from Ellie but Mr. Dunn's office. Captain Day dialled the number and Mrs. Bax settled down, unashamedly, on the sofa to listen to his side of the conversation. No doubt, with her husband working in the Docks, all information was useful. I, too listened, but did so leaning on the doorpost.

116

But the skipper gave nothing away, just saying "Yus" and "No" in the right places. As we went back to the barge, I pressed him for information but he just said:

"Wait till we git back aboard an' I'll tell the lot o' yer."

Back on board Daisy Maud he rounded up Vic, Tommy and Ike and made his announcement.

"Well, we've both got freights, Tom," he said. "Cattle cake to Upshore, agen. Ship in King George V. Reed Warbler'll be loadin' too, but she's already in the dock wiv export cargo."

Reed Warbler. Now that was good news, for she was Jan's barge. But why had Ellie routed us straight back to Upshore, after she had promised to keep us away for a while? But that, too, was good news for it meant that I would see her soon. And, since the news had come from Mr. Dunn's office, it could be that he, as the new Managing Director, thought differently or perhaps a mistake had been made. No matter, I would soon be with Ellie.

"I dunno abaht yew, Tommy," the skipper was saying, "but soon as that ebb starts, I'm droppin' dahn ter the lock entrance. Might as well git locked in 'cos the ship's already there."

Tommy agreed and on the first of the ebb both barges followed Captain Day's suggestion.

King George V Dock was unusual in that each berth had a permanent pontoon off the quay. The ships would lie on these pontoons, which would leave a strip of clear water next to the actual quay. Here barges and lighters could lie and take overside cargo, but these passages were not of much use to sailing barges as their masts and spars would not clear the lines holding the ship to the quay. Nevertheless this arrangement did reduce the number of dumb lighters that were around.

Thus, as we approached the Panamanian tramp steamer from which we were to load, there was only one barge alongside her – the Resolve. On the opposite side of the dock Reed Warbler was discharging iron pipes into a Russian ship. Jan saw us and waved.

As we moored up astern of Resolve, Bully came aft to greet us. He was eating a sandwich which looked as though it had been made from a complete loaf.

117

"Wotcher, Arthur," he said, "looks like we might be loadin' together. They ain't started us yet."

"Two other ter come."

"More the merrier, like."

"'Ere's one of 'em".

Tommy was nosing in astern of us and we rushed round to take his lines and moor the Silverfish alongside us.

"All Upshore craft, then?" Bully said when we'd finished.

"Thas right," said Captain Day.

"Mebbe I'll give yew a thrashin', 'appen we leave together."

"Yew're all talk," Captain Day said.

"Serious I am, lets talk abaht it when the other barge gits 'ere."

He'd finished the sandwich and waddled off, no doubt in search of further food.

Bully, in order to slake his insatiable thirst for beer, went ashore to the Roundhouse with his mate in the evening. Shortage of funds kept the rest of us aboard and that suited me as Jan sculled over from Reed Warbler.

Barge life was doing him good. He seemed broader and more muscular than before. His English had also improved and he was even picking up some of the Essex idiom, no doubt from close association with Hoary. I told him of me and Ellie.

"I am very pleased for you, my friend," he said. "She is a most ... delightful girl when she is not being – er – hoighty-toighty in the office."

But Jan was brimming with stories of Reed Warbler and Hoary so I let him have his head.

"She is a terrible old barge, that one," he said. "One day we are at anchor, deep-laden and we are in the cabin, drinking tea. But there is no cushions on the lockers and when I go to get up, I cannot, for my trousers they are held between the bunk boards. The barge, she has moved so much in the sea that is running, that she do this to me. Hoary and I, we cannot remove the trousers, so I have to leave them there and wriggle out of them. Then Old Hoary, he lend me a pair but they are too big and keep falling down. This is all right on the barge, but when we get to Upshore,

I have to send my mother a note to bring down another pair.

"Also we have bed-bugs and they are driving me crazy, so I wish to kill them. I ask Old Hoary and he say put pepper down for them. 'Will this kill them?' I ask and he say 'Yes. It make them sneeze and then they break their backs'."

I laughed. Jan went on to tell me that barge crews were now being issued with gas masks when they returned to Upshore. He and Hoary had already got theirs and he had gone below to find the old man trying to put his on with a lighted cigarette in his mouth.

"Got ter try it," Hoary said. "Don't want to get caught aht like them poor buggers in the trenches last time."

We talked for a long time of our various adventures, although some of my exploits with Ellie I would not even tell Jan. He was interested in Nether Rushbrook and said it sounded like a bargemen's heaven and hoped that Reed Warbler would go there one day. Eventually Vic came and broke us up because he wanted to get some sleep.

Loading commenced next day and by knocking off time for the dockers, both Resolve and Daisy Maud were finished, while Silverfish was partly full and Reed Warbler had finished discharging her pipes and come over to join us. All four barges, however, remained alongside the Panamanian ship so that the four skippers could have a conference.

This had already started when I was summoned aft to make the tea. As I entered the cabin, Bully was speaking.

"So that's agreed then. When we leave 'ere we 'ave a race for turn."

"It won't be a race fer turn," said Tommy, "we ain't even goin' ter the same place."

"First ter the Swin Spitway buoy, then," said Bully, not to be outdone.

"I ain't gettin' involved in no wagers," said Hoary.

"Yew needn't, 'appen yew don't want to. But we won't go mad. Skippers five bob, mates two and a tanner."

Bully glanced at me. "Third 'ands wot they can afford."

119

"We might be able ter git some other barges in," said Tommy. "Gascoigne's arahnd somewhere. Thought I could smell 'im earlier." This got a laugh.

"Any others we see, we rope in,"Bully decided. "'Appen they're willin'."

So far, my skipper, had said nothing. Now he raised an objection.

"Wot abaht your borsprit?" he asked Bully.

"I'll leave it steeved up," said Bully. "Then I'll be staysail, same us the rest o' yer. Worse, 'cos of windage on the borsprit, but I gotta giv yew a chance."

Bully had, on entering the Docks, raised Resolve's borsprit to avoid damage to it. This process was knowing as 'steeving-up'.

"Nah, wot abaht this tea, young man?" Bully said. "Meetin' closed. Got any grub?"

CHAPTER 11
RACING FOR TURN?

By the next evening all four barges had completed loading. When we had moored them in a quiet spot just by the lock entrance, we adjourned to the Round House to sort out the wagers. Vic, since he had some little experience in such things, was appointed to hold the money or IOUs, since some of us were short of cash. With the exception of Hoary, all the skippers and mates contributed, whilst my stake was sixpence.

"'Oo'ever wins decides 'oo gets what on 'is barge," Bully decided. "'Appens it's me, as it will be, yer can let me 'ave me winnin's next time yer sees me."

Bully was again bound for Mistley, but us other three for Upshore.

"What do yer reckon on the wind?" Ike asked.

"Light westerly, could go easterly," Captain Day said without hesitation. "Dunno when, though. Fine weather breeze, see."

"'Ope it does go easterly, make it more interestin', beatin' ter windward."

"Good idea, this," said Tommy a pint or so later. "Giv us some practice for the Upshore Match."

"Yew'll need it," said Bully, "Now what Arthur reely wants is some practice with a borsprit."

"Can't see me way clear ter gettin' one o' them," said Captain Day. "The money, yer know."

"Case yew can't go up agin me in the Match," Bully suggested, "Yew an' me'll 'ave a side bet on thissun."

"Like what?" Captain Day wanted to know.

"Loser buys winner a new 'at."

Early next morning the four barges locked out together. While the lock water was being adjusted to the river level, Bully strolled down to the Pierhead. When he returned he went to each barge in turn saying: "Tide's still a-floodin' a little. Winds light westerly. Nah, there's a tug hangin' on ter the Pierhead waitin' for a ship. When 'e thinks we're ready ter go, 'e'll blow 'is whistle as a five minit warnin, then 'e'll blow agen at the start. That cost me the price o' a pint. Startin' line's the Pier 'ead."

A small lighterage tug was locking out with us and, with a great effort, was able to pull the four barges out into the middle of the river while we set topsails, foresails and mizzens. Then after the tug had let go, we separated and set the rest of our sails. While this was going on, a hoot from the tug at the pierhead warned us that there was five minutes to go. All four of us were almost standing still as the flood tide, although easing off, was about counterbalancing the wind in our sails.

Bully seemed to be having trouble as Resolve's steeved up bowsprit was hindering the setting of his headsails. We could hear him roaring at his mate to sort things out. But us other three were staying up, with Reed Warbler catching a stronger zephyr of wind and surging ahead just as the tug blew the starting hoot.

It had been agreed aboard Daisy Maud, that Captain Day would steer and look after the mainsheet and vangs, Vic would tend the headsails and me the leeboards, but I was to hold myself ready for other duties as they arose (largely tea making, I suspected). But I was in a good position to hear the skipper's running commentary on events.

"Goin' ter be a mite tedious 'til the ebb starts. 'Tis nearly 'igh water. I'm goin' to take Margaret Ness as close as I can. Might even pick up a back-eddy."

Tommy called across. He was, if anything, slightly ahead of us. "'E ain't doin' bad fer an ould one!" He gestured at Reed Warbler.

"'E ain't no slouch, old 'Oary," Captain Day shouted. "Keep 'im talkin'," he muttered to me.

So I chattered to Tommy about the weather and how I would be glad to see Ellie, and all the time Captain Day was easing us over towards Margaret Ness, the steep-to point of land between Gallions and Barking reaches. Eventually Tommy could no longer hear me, and realised what we were doing. But, too late, we already had the advantage at the Ness. Bully had now sorted his troubles out and was coming up astern on a breath of wind, while Reed Warbler was still finding private breezes in the middle of the river.

"I want yew ter do a coupla things, young Bill," said the skipper. "First drop the boat's stern on the after fall and pull up her bow on the forrard fall, then find all the ould buckets on the barge an' fill 'em up with salt water."

By the time I had done all this, we were out in the middle of Barking Reach, looking for the first of the ebb. The order was Reed Warbler, Daisy Maud, Silverfish and then Resolve. But Bully was fast overhauling Silverfish, now that he had got his barge sailing properly.

Captain Day felt he owed me an explanation for my recent activity. "The idea o' lettin' the boats stern dahn, is so as it acts like a little wind-scoop. Could make a difference 'cept them others are all doin' the same. The water's fer chuckin' on the mainsail if need-be. Mek's it 'old more wind."

He paused, then went on. "That ebb's a-runnin' now. Nuffin' won't 'appen for a while. We'll jist a-drift dahn on it. Nah, yew go an' make me an Vic a nice cuppa tea. Feed that dawg, too, while yew're abaht it."

Frank had been totally unmoved by the opening stages of the race and had been curled up asleep on the main hatch. Now he was looking around expectantly. I took him to the focs'le and fed him a bowl of scraps from our meal the previous evening.

By the time I had done this and made the tea, the light westerly and the young ebb had borne us out of Barking Reach and into Halfway Reach. The order was still the same but with the four barges more closely bunched.

"We'll 'ave ter do summat ter git clear," said the skipper as he drank his tea. "We'll try the water. Git Vic aft to 'elp."

So Vic and I threw the buckets of water onto the mainsail.

"'Ow's it goin', skipper?" Vic asked. He had been forrard the whole time and bereft of human conversation.

"Not bad, so far. Just 'ope no bloody steamships nor tugs and lighters git in the way."

The water did seem to make a difference. The race was now in two pairs, us and Reed Warbler, Tommy and Bully as we turned into Erith Reach which brought the strengthening breeze more abeam. This was evidently not a good point of sailing for Reed Warbler and we were fast overhauling her. But ahead was Erith Rands which turned more to the North East, and I could appreciate that we might have to gybe there and then gybe back for the aptly named Long Reach which followed.

"Watch, 'Oary," said the skipper to me as we entered the Rands, "tell us when 'e gybes."

Halfway through the Rands, Hoary gybed over.

"He's gone," I shouted to Captain Day. Coming up astern of Reed Warbler we were sailing faster and taking her wind.

"'Appen I go ter windward," the skipper was saying half to himself. "'E might luff an' force me ter gybe. 'Appen I go ter lew'ward 'e'll tek our wind, but then 'e's got ter gybe back an' I'll be past. Go to leeward an' 'ope we don't gybe oursel's."

In a louder tone he said to me: "Nip forrard an' tell Vic we'll be goin' well to loo'ard of Reed Warbler." We pulled over to give Reed Warbler a wide berth and managed to hold the same gybe. At the end of the reach Reed Warbler gybed back rather untidily and lost a few yards, sufficient to give us the lead.

Not much happened in Long Reach, except that Bully finally went past Silverfish. I took the opportunity to make tea and sandwiches, which we ate with relish. As we came to the end of this reach, Captain Day called me and Vic together and said: "We'll be stayin' well clear o' Stone Ness point, too shallow ter go close in there, an' there might be a back eddy. We'll haul well over an' go straight for Broadness at the end o' Fiddlers Reach. Might even git away wivout a gybe agen."

This tactic worked well, especially since Silverfish elected to go much closer in on Stone Ness and then lost even more ground. Then we were reaching down Northfleet Hope, our best point of sailing and not Silverfish's strong point. Our lead increased again but Resolve was now catching up well. As we reached the end of the Hope Vic called from forrard.

"Skipper. There's a bleedin' great ship comin' outa Tilbury Dock."

"Gawd! So there is an' she's got tugs on 'er. Time she swings ter go dahn river she'll tek up most o' the room. We'll 'ave to git right over on the Gravesend shore." He altered course to do this.

"Sod it!" he said, half to himself. "Tide runs fastest on the Tilbury side. Fastest bit o' tide on the river an' we've gotta miss it. Them other three won't though. Ship an' tugs'll be clear o' them.

We shot past the swinging ship, which was a Brocklebank liner, well over on the Gravesend shore. There was a hail from the ship's stern tug.

"In an 'urry, aintcher, mate?"

"Too right, mate," the skipper called back.

We were now in a bad position. The liner had straightened up and was about to set off downriver with the assistance of her bow tug. We dare not cross her bows to regain the Tilbury side of the river, where the tide ran more strongly and we were fast approaching the congested moorings below Gravesend Town Pier, where tugs, pilot boats and other small vessels were constantly on the move. The other three barges had all managed to pass between the liner and her tugs and the Tilbury Dock pierhead and were in a far better position.

"The penalties o' bein' in the lead," said Captain Day rather poetically for him.

125

So, by the end of Gravesend Reach, we were a rather poor last.

Through the Lower Hope and into Sea Reach there was little change. Bully now appeared to be leading our little fleet. But the breeze was getting lighter and lighter.

Off the Chapman Lighthouse we passed close to a shrimp boat out of Leigh.

"That'll go easterly, soon," her skipper called.

"Sooner the better," said Captain Day. We were now almost wallowing with only the remains of the ebb tide and the wash of passing ships to give any movement. The other barges were no better off and their headsails were hanging lifelessly.

"Better try the water, agen," said Captain Day.

Vic and I filled the buckets again and threw the water on to the mainsail, but to no avail.

"Might as well 'ave some tea," said the skipper. There was no change after I had made the tea, except that the weather was getting warmer. We were halfway through our mugs of tea, when Vic shouted. "Look at that, skipper."

A dark line was spreading across the water from the east.

"That's wind," said Captain Day, "quite a bit o' it. Trouble is them other three'll git it first. Let's git ready fer it."

He put Daisy Maud, as best he could, on a course towards the Kentish shore, while Vic and I trimmed the sheets ready for a beat to windward.

"'Ere we go," said the skipper, as the first zephyr began to move us through the water. Soon we were tramping along heading toward the Yantlet mudflats on the Kentish shore.

"'Appen this 'olds," said Captain Day, "we'll make Upshore ternight, let alone the Swin Spitway."

We tacked and were off on a new heading towards Thorpe Bay, just below Southend Pier.

"What about the race, skipper?" I asked.

"Nah! Don't think we got much chance now. Too much bad luck, still yew never know."

The other barges were now hard to distinguish, as several others had joined us from both Thames & Medway and all were tacking right across the river. Only Resolve, with her steeved-up bowsprit and light grey paint was easy to pick out and she seemed well ahead.

We tacked again off Thorpe Bay, and again off Minster on the Isle of Sheppey and a third time near a buoy called Blacktail Spit on the Essex side. Only a short tack followed and then we were set up for a long board through the Swin Channel and took in turns to go below to prepare and then eat a meal.

Captain Day ate last and by the time he came up to relieve Vic on the wheel we were off the Whittaker beacon.

"We can bear orf a li'l fer the Swin Spitway," said the skipper as he took over the wheel. A few barge sails could be seen around the horizon, but only one was anywhere near us, charging up the Swin behind us.

"Ain't that Bully?" asked Vic.

"So that is," said the skipper. "'Ow the 'ell did 'e git back there?"

"Must've gone past 'im on the wind," said Vic.

"Yus, Reed Warbler, I'd expect to, mebbe Tommy an' all, but not Bully. 'E must 'ave 'ad some bad luck. Broken sommat, mebbe."

"Well, 'e's gettin' a move on now orl right."

"Yus, we might 'ave a race o' it yet. Let's get 'er goin'"

Daisy Maud certainly "got goin'", but so to did Resolve

"Gawd," said the skipper after a while. "Would you believe it. That wind's a-'eading of us."

"We ain't layin' the buoy. Nuffin' like," Vic called from forrard. We could now clearly see the Swin Spitway.

"We'll 'ave ter tack for it. 'Gainst the flood too."

"Should be the same for Resolve," I said. I had been commissioned to keep a look-out aft and watch Resolve.

"Not yet it ain't an' 'e's got more room ter play wiv."

I saw Resolve's headsails begin to flutter.

"He's being headed now."

"Right then, we're both a-beatin' up for the buoy then."

And so we went tack for tack with Resolve, with her closing the distance all the time.

"Remember yer rule o' the road, son?" Captain Day said after a while. "Wot tack are we on?"

"Starboard"

"An' Bully?"

"Port. We've got right of way."

"Good lad. Now yew git forrard with Vic an' git ready to holler at Bully when 'e gits close.

Resolve was getting alarmingly close, her bows chucking clouds of spray aside.

"Now!" Captain Day yelled

"Starboard!" Vic and I cried in unison.

Bully did not appear to hear. Resolve's steeved-up bowsprit looked due to hit us abreast the mainmast.

"Starboard!" we roared again.

This time Bully did hear and threw Resolve up into the wind. We shot between him and the Swin Spitway Buoy.

"That's the way ter do it," said Vic triumphantly. "We beat 'im by abaht ten foot, skip!"

For once Captain Day ignored the shortening of his title.

"Let the jib flap, Vic. I want ter 'ave a word wiv 'im."

As we spilt the wind from our foremost headsail, Resolve surged alongside within hailing distance.

"Yew ould bugger," Bully cried, "I could of done wiv a new 'at." He seized the remains of his straw hat from his head and threw them into Resolve's wake.

"'Appen there'll be another time, Bully!" Captain Day shouted.

"Yeah! Like the Upshore Match! We'll settle up, directly. See yer then."

He and his mate hardened their sheets in, and he charged off up the Swin Spitway channel. We followed more sedately.

"I reckon I know wot 'appened to 'im," Captain Day said when we had all gathered aft. "Bully likes 'is vittles, see. So 'e sends the mate below to mek a meal and 'e manages the barge on 'is own. When the meals ready an' the mates 'ad 'is, it's Bully's turn. 'E wants ter mek a proper job o' it, no snacks on deck for 'im. So

128

'e goes below an' leaves the mate on deck on 'is own. Now that mate o' Bully's 'e's a good lad at sail-'andlin' an' that but 'e ain't no 'elmsman an' 'e starts wanderin' all over the ocean. Same time we're tackin' over on the other shore an' we seen none o' this. Reckon that's 'ow we got past."

"Wot abaht them other two?" Vic asked.

"Well, they ain't ahead of us, that's fer sure." A group of barges was sailing over for the Swin Spitway. The wind had gone back to its original direction and they were laying it easily. "Reckon they're in that lot."

At the Wallet Spitway buoy, Bully hardened his sheets some more for Mistley and we bore away for the River Whitewater and Upshore. We saw a wave from Resolve before we parted.

"Talking abaht grub, young Bill," said Captain Day, "ain't it time yew got us sommat?"

But we did not make Upshore that night and anchored off Hibberts Island, as we had on that first voyage when we had also been carrying cattle-cake. This suited me, as by the time we arrived at Upshore in the morning, Ellie would be at work, and I could see her straight away.

CHAPTER 12
THE BATTLE OF UPSHORE QUAY

As we came within sight of Upshore Quay we had our first surprise. Waiting for us was not Fowler & Dunn's smart varnished 'motyboat' but the river bailiff's launch, with Zeke in a navy Guernsey with "River Bailiff" picked out in white on its chest. He offered no explanation and simply took our line for the tow up to the quay.

As we came in sight of the quay, there was Ellie waiting. I guessed someone at the TB hospital on Hibbert's Island must be keeping her informed of her barge's movements. As soon as I could jump ashore, I did so and took her in my arms in full view of the quay's population.

"Did you win?" she asked, when I gave her a chance. I wondered how she knew of the race.

"Of course. No parrot though."

"You brought yourself. That's what you promised."

"A promise is a promise."

"Nice chatting to you darling, but I've got an office to open up. Why don't you come over later for a proper talk?"

"I'll do that." Now this was different, invitations to the office. It couldn't have happened in Isaac's time.

By the time I was back aboard the barge, Zeke had arrived and was explaining his good fortune.

"... so Miss Ellie, she went an' saw the council committee what controls the bailiff an' sez the cover ain't good enough, wiv the bailiff an' 'is assistant both goin' off at five o'clock, unless they wants overtime. What 'e needs she sez is another assistant so as there's a bailiff's man around everytime the tide's in. So she persuades the committee, an' I'm sittin' arahn' unemployed, used ter handlin' moty-boats an' with a first-class recommend from Ellie. So they gives me the job an' 'ere I am, assistant river bailiff."

"I'm puttin' it abaht, what a good thing she did fer me but she still ain't liked by a lot. There's them what still think she's a stuck-up little cow, and there's them what say a nineteen year old girl shouldn't be manager an' agen there's them what don't believe Thames an' Medway 'ave backed off. But she's orl right in my estimation."

"She allus was, in mine," said Captain Day.

"They might be right 'bout Thames & Medway," said Vic.

"'Ow do we git on abaht stores an' that now, Zeke?" asked Captain Day. "We need quite a bit."

"Yer tells Ellie or that new woman."

"I'll send Bill over wiv a note directly minnut. Be good fer 'im, 'es a-courtin' Miss Ellie, see."

"Good for 'im."

So later I went over to the office with a note requesting the usual lamp oil, and several other things. Ellie was at her normal desk. She had not, as yet anyway, moved into one of the private offices. There was no sign of Mr. Oram, and a dumpy, but not unattractive, woman occupied Bob's former seat. This, I guessed, must be the new recruit, Mrs. Murphy.

"That will be all right," said Ellie after a quick glance at the stores list. She was wearing one of her floral summer dresses. I wondered if the 'office uniform' was a thing of the past. She must have guessed what I was thinking.

"New policy," she said, "we come to work in what we feel is comfortable." I raised my eyebrows significantly.

"Oh no!" she laughed, "I wouldn't do that. There are limits."

"Why did you bring us back to Upshore so soon?"

"Because I couldn't live without you, my love," she giggled, and then went on in a more serious tone, "but there is another reason. Ernest wants Daisy Maud on the yard to get the bowsprit fitted and other jobs ready for the Match. He's got to fit you into his schedule, see."

I said I didn't think Captain Day could afford it.

"I know," she said, "but I've asked Ernest not to send his bill in for a good while. That will give Captain Day more time to raise the money. Caroline, here" – Mrs. Murphy smiled at me – "used to work for father's bank, she thinks the manager would grant a loan, if I recommend it."

Ex-employees being found jobs, extended credit, loans recommended, no office dress code, no arguments about stores, things had changed. I asked after Mr. Oram.

"He's gone sick, again. His lumbago's bad. He'll really have to retire in the autumn. There'll be an opening for a bright lad in the office, then." I wished she'd stop trying to lure me into office work. I wanted to stay at sea now, but I let the remark go without comment. Instead I asked whether she'd be going for a walk later.

"No," she said, with a grin, "but you'll be coming home with me this evening. No excuses, it's your last chance for a while. John's due back tomorrow."

The home we had so studiously avoided before! She must feel confident of her position now. But John was obviously still a force to be reckoned with. She said that she doubted whether she would get a proper lunch-hour and I would probably be busy with the barge. But she would call for me at the close of business for the day.

It was not until about five-thirty that I saw her locking the office building and strolled over to meet her. Daisy Maud was deserted as Captain Day had gone home and Vic and Frank had disappeared. The red sports car was parked nearby, and after a little while we drove off.

Ellie explained that she generally used the car for work now.

"It's handy if I have to go out somewhere." I was worried about my clothing for I was wearing a jacket, trousers and shirt that were other people's cast-offs. "Don't worry about that," she said. "We just sit down to dinner in whatever we happen to be wearing." So I was being taken to dinner. I felt highly honoured. We turned into the drive leading to the Fowler residence.

We entered the house through the kitchens where Ellie introduced me to the elderly couple who looked after the family's needs. Ellie asked for tea to be brought through to the drawing room as soon as possible. We made our way there next.

It was a large room containing comfortable armchairs and sofas. Pictures of past Fowlers looked down from the walls and a number of potted plants lined the walls. French doors looked out on a large garden.

Ernest was sitting in one of the armchairs, reading a copy of The Times. He was surrounded, as usual, by a number of plans and textbooks spread out on the floor. As we entered he put down the paper and got to his feet.

"You must be Eleanor's young man," he said and shook hands. "Pleased to meet you."

He frowned at me over his spectacles.

"I've seen you around the quay."

I explained that I was the third hand on Daisy Maud.

"Ah, yes, with Captain Day. You'll be coming on the yard soon." He sat down again and resumed his reading. Ellie and I sat on a sofa and I told her the story of the race to the Swin Spitway. She was rather intrigued with Captain Day's theory that food had got the better of Bully Briggs.

"I've never heard of a race being won like that," she said. "By the way, the other two barges made Upshore on this tide. There's no room for them on the quay, so they're lying on the buoy."

We had our tea, and then Ellie suggested that we visit the stables.

"Dinner wont be long, Eleanor," said Ernest, "and don't forget we've got another guest."

"Why does he call you Eleanor?" I asked as we went over to the stables.

133

"It's my proper name, really," she answered, "but everybody else calls me Ellie. Have done, since I was about two."

She showed me round the stables, and introduced me to the groom and horses. Evidently horsemanship was yet another of her accomplishments and she sometimes rode with the local hunt.

By the time we had finished at the stables a Bentley saloon had joined the sports car outside the house. No doubt it belonged to the mysterious dinner guest.

We arrived back in the drawing room just in time for me to be introduced to the guest before we went through to the dining-room for dinner. He was Rupert Dunn, the shipbroker, now managing director of Fowler & Dunn and he was staying over-night for discussions with Ellie and John the next day. With his monocle, clipped moustache and tweed suit with bow-tie he looked more like a retired army colonel than a successful shipbroker.

Dinner was not the complicated affair that I had been dread-ing. It was quite a simple meal. Roast beef with all the trimmings followed a leek and potato soup, while the sweet was that old barge favourite, spotted dick. A claret, which Ellie declined, accompanied the meal.

During the meal Rupert Dunn said to me "I understand you're with Captain Day on Daisy Maud." I confirmed this and he went on: "Was that freight I arranged for Nether Rushbrook any help?"

I had to think about this. In the end I said that it certainly had been, but Barney and Happy Day had disagreed over money.

"Yes," said Mr. Dunn, "he's a very obstinate man, your skip-per. He wants to do everything by his own efforts and won't consider what he believes is charity. Ellie would help him out, Mr. Thornton would give him the money out of friendship and so, for that matter, would I. But he'll have none of it. I don't believe he really likes the idea of a loan either. The sensible thing for him to do now is to sell his shares in the barge."

I was horrified and it must have showed.

"It makes sense," he said. "It might seem hard, but in this day and age it's the right thing to do. The days of the skipper-owned or even part-owned barges are gone. It's only the big owners like ourselves, Thames & Medway, Goldsmiths or Francis and Gilders that can survive in this economic climate. No sailing barge has been built for eight years now and look at the numbers being sold for houseboats or yachts the last few years."

Ellie interrupted him to say that these were mainly in the Kentish cement trade. But he was not to be deterred.

"And it will spread, that's just the start. The war, if it comes, might make a difference but I forecast that in ten, twenty years all coastal carriage will be in motor vessels, with only the bigger owners having the capital to finance them. And if we don't do it, then the Dutch will. Their motor coasters, 'Schuits' they call them, are already making big inroads into the British coastal trade. No, that is the sensible answer for Captain Day, sell his shares, but not to your brother John, Ellie, that would be asking for trouble. Either the company or Ellie or me. Now that's enough of that, let's talk about something happier."

So we talked about my voyaging on Daisy Maud. As we finished our coffee, it became evident that Ernest was bursting to discuss some technical point with Rupert Dunn.

"Were you going to the King's Head tonight?" Ellie asked me

I wasn't, but she was obviously looking for an excuse, so I said I was.

"I'll come with you," she said. "We'll leave these two to look at their old plans."

So we boarded the sports car and set off. Of course, we stopped on the way and it was quite late when we reached the King's Head. We had discussed Rupert Dunn's remarks on the way and Ellie said: "I dunno. Mr. Dunn's right, I reckon. But I'll try your skipper on a bank loan."

At the pub Ellie made a bee-line for the snug. I protested.

"I'm Fowler & Dunn's manager, silly, and you're with me," she said, "of course we can drink in the snug. This whole class system is stupid, anyway."

The snug was almost empty, but the skipper and Mrs. Day were there, no doubt celebrating his return after several weeks. As soon as he saw us, Captain Day went up to the bar.

"Still drinkin' mild?" he asked. We said we were and he came back with a pint for me and a half for Ellie. Since Nether Rushbrook, the skipper seemed to have dropped his disapproval of me drinking alcohol. When we were all seated, Ellie lit one of her occasional cigarettes.

"Stunt yer growth, they will," said the skipper, lighting his pipe.

"In which direction?" Ellie asked and we all laughed.

Mrs. Day was full of Ellie and my relationship and they quickly lapsed into girls' talk.

"She'll 'ave yer weddin' arranged 'fore yew know," said Captain Day. I sounded him out about a bank loan.

"Don't 'old wiv no banks," he said, rather as I expected.

Ellie, I thought, had gone rather pink and I thought that I had better rescue her. But she did this for herself by getting up and ordering another round of drinks. The river bailiff was leaning on the bar and she paused to speak to him, no doubt about how Zeke was shaping up.

When she returned, Captain Day was talking about the race.

"'Spect ould Bully'll send me a postal order for a new 'at," he said.

"What sort of hat will you get?" his wife asked.

"'Nother trilby, I 'spect. Don't like bowlers an' them."

He went on to say that my share of the winnings should be about five bob.

"'Appen Vic don't spend it all. 'E's rahn the public now. Fancies 'is chances wiv Rosie agin, daresay."

Shortly after this Ellie and I said goodnight and left.

"Can I drive you home?" she asked.

Daisy Maud was the only home I knew. I laughed. "It's less than a hundred yards."

"But you could ask me aboard for coffee or something.

"What about Vic?"

136

"Oh! He'll be busy for a while yet. Rosie will see to that. I had a word with her when I ordered the drinks." She paused, "I've got to have you inside me tonight," she whispered.

So we went aboard Daisy Maud. I suggested that we went to the after cabin just in case Vic came back, but that, obviously we avoided Captain Day's bunk. While I made tea, since there was no coffee, she did a strip-tease for me.

"Tea in the nude, lovely," she said, as I handed her a mug.

It was a splendid end to a super evening.

"I dunno, dinner with the nobs, dashin' abaht in a sports car, drinkin' in the snug, no doubt a bit o' how's-yer-father thrown in. Whatever next?" This was Vic the next morning. Ellie had left about half past twelve, but he had returned just in time for breakfast, looking decidedly the worse for wear.

"Oh Gawd. 'Ave I gotta eat that bacon?"

I told him it was that or nothing, so he left me alone and ate.

Ellie had said "come over to the office any time." So in the middle of the morning I went over there, leaving Vic to keep an eye on the lumpers who had started on our cargo.

Caroline Murphy was in the office on her own. I had forgotten the meeting between Ellie, John and Mr. Dunn which was going on in Isaac's old office. But Mrs. Murphy said that it wouldn't be much longer and made me a cup of coffee. The meeting broke up while I was drinking it. John was the first out.

"What's he doing here?" he demanded, meaning me.

"He's my boyfriend and he'll come here whenever he likes," said Ellie from behind him.

"As long as it doesn't disrupt the work."

"I'm the manager and I'll be the judge of that."

John was just framing an answer to that when Rupert Dunn appeared.

"Come on, John," he said, "leave them alone. I'll stand you lunch up in the town."

John took the hint and they left.

"You can expect a visit from John later," said Ellie. "One of the things he's worked up about is Captain Day's shares. Anyway,

137

did you enjoy it last night?"

"Enjoy what?"

"You know."

"Oh! The meal. Yes, it was very good."

She threw a ball of screwed up paper at me.

Sure enough we did receive a visit from John. Unusually all three of us were aboard. Vic and I were idly watching the lumpers from the foredeck and Captain Day aft in the cabin. John, who appeared to have dined well, went straight aft to the cabin, from which Ellie and I had carefully removed all trace of occupancy the night before.

"I'm keepin' out of 'is way," said Vic and disappeared down into the fo'c'sle. "See wot you can find out," he hissed from down there. Once again it was not hard to follow John's side of the conversation. Mainly he seemed to be making a last ditch attempt to obtain the skipper's shares in the barge. At one point he asked about a certain receipt for lamp oil. I did not hear the skipper's reply but whatever it was it seemed to satisfy John for the moment. In any case, I thought, the receipt was not so important as I was now legitimately visiting Ellie's home.

Suddenly I looked up and saw Pocock the bookmaker's men approaching along the quay.

"Pocock's men," I said to Vic down the fo'c'sle scuttle.

"I'm not 'ere," he hissed back.

The two men halted at the head of the ladder.

"His Mr. Halliday here?" asked the ferret man.

I was about to say no when John appeared and began to walk forrard along the side-deck, still saying something angrily over his shoulder to the skipper. I suddenly thought that the two bookies men probably didn't know Vic by sight.

"That's him," I said on impulse.

John climbed the ladder, without acknowledging my presence. When he was two or three rungs from the top the big man reached over and pulled him the rest of the way by the front of his clothing, then tripped him so that he fell to the surface of the quay. The bruiser then planted an enormous foot on John's chest.

Several lumpers stopped work to watch, but none of them went to John's aid. He must be as unpopular with them, I thought, as he was with the bargemen.

"Mr. Pocock . . . " began the ferret man. But John was a powerful man, easily matching the bruiser in weight. He grabbed the man's ankle and pushed him over backwards. He capsized into the ferret and both of them fell to the floor. The bruiser was up in an instant and swung a wild punch at John. But John had evidently boxed before and had his hands up ready to ward off the blow.

The dog, Frank, appeared from somewhere and sensing some fun, planted his jaws firmly on the seat of the trousers of the ferret-man, who was already dabbing at a nose bleed. The two big men circled each other, each looking for an opening.

They were interrupted by Captain Day who ran forrard along the sidedeck hastily cramming cartridges into the breech of the shot-gun.

"Yew two strangers!" he shouted "Git away from this barge, 'less yew want both barrels. Frank, 'eel!"

For once the dog did as he was told and skilfully avoided a kick aimed at him by the ferret man as he and his companion moved off.

"I wouldn't reely 'ave shot 'em," the skipper said to me, "but I wasn't a-'avin' that sort o' thing."

John had recovered his composure.

"Thank you, Captain Day," he said with as much grace as he could muster. "Pity you wont see sense about other things. But what was all that about?" Fortunately he hadn't noticed my part in the scuffle but I honestly hadn't expected violence to erupt.

"Dunno," said the skipper. "Probably aht ter rob yer."

"I'll have a word with the police about them. But there's a lot of odd things connected with this barge and I mean to get to the bottom of them." So saying, he went off to the office to tidy himself up.

"Yew can come aht now, Vic," said the skipper.

Looking very sheepish, Vic emerged from the fo'c'sle.

139

"Them was the bookie's men, weren't they?" said Captain Day. "Got the wrong man, 'appily for yew. Nah, yew git it sorted out, directly minnut."

"If I could a git a decent win, somewhere's else."

"Never yew mind abaht that. Only end up in annuver lot a-cummin' dahn 'ere. Sort it aht, I said!"

He stumped off aft to put the gun away.

"I dunno wot ter do," Vic said pathetically to me.

"Like the skipper says, you'll have to do something," was all I could offer.

CHAPTER 13
ON THE YARD

Ellie came over later that afternoon, ostensibly to see how much cargo remained in our holds, but actually brimming with curiosity about the fight.

"Were they really thieves?" she asked.

"I expect so," I said, "among other things, but it was Vic they were really after, about his gambling debts."

"Well, John's been to the police and they're very interested. They want to talk to those two about several other things."

"Perhaps Vic can relax for a while."

"I doubt that. I know of Pocock. He'll stop at nothing to get back a bad debt. He can soon hire another couple of thugs."

She went on to mention the arrangements for Daisy Maud 'going on the yard.'

"We'll have to split you three up though," she said. "Captain Day will be paid a retainer to stand by the barge. But Vic will be employed at the yard and you in the office. Don't worry, you'll both get the rate of pay for the job. In your case it'll be a lot more than normal. And, don't forget, we'll see each other every day."

"Why the office?" I asked.

"Well, with Mr. Oram away and no office boy, we've got a tremendous backlog of things like filing and sending out invoices. I'm sure you could do it."

Well, it was that or starve, I thought. Much as I disliked the idea of office work it did have its advantages, most of them connected with Ellie.

Discharge was due to be completed the next day and after that we would move round to the yard. Daisy Maud was scheduled to be there for a week at least. That was the message from Captain Day. Rather to my surprise he then said to me:

"Fancy a walk, lad. Yew an' me'll go up ter auld 'Ookers. See how 'e's a-gettin' on wi' them sails."

The sailmaker's loft was situated rather strangely up the hill, opposite St. Michael's Church. The loft itself lay well back from the road with an open space in front of it. Here several of the sailmakers men were applying dressing to a barges mainsail with buckets and brooms.

"Red ochre, linseed oil and sea water," I said.

"So they reckon," said the skipper. "Ould 'Ookers lucky to 'ave this set up. Now Turnidge, what's the sailmaker at Leigh-on-Sea, 'e used ter do 'is sail-dressin' in a field 'longside railway. Only trouble was, the farmer sometimes 'ad 'is bull in the same field. Many's the time the sailmakers ended up on the railway line throwin' flints at the bull ter keep 'im orf of the sails."

The sail-loft itself was raised on stilts leaving a space underneath where sails could be handled in wet weather. We went up a set of wooden stairs into the loft itself. Here a number of men and women were sewing sails, some with sewing machines others working by hand. They were round the edges of the loft, while a yacht sail was pegged out in the middle of the floor.

Wilfred Hooker himself we found in a tiny office in one corner of the floor. There was just about room for him in it, as every surface and a good deal of the floor was piled with paper - invoices, bills, copies of yachting magazines, even several calendars. I thought there must be a system somewhere, otherwise the business just could not function.

"I done yer topsail," said Hooker. "That's dahn below, 'appen yew wants a look."

"I will an' all," said the skipper. "Wot abaht me jibs?"

"Me top 'and's a-workin' on them."

We went down into the area under the loft and the one eyed sailmaker unrolled the new topsail.

Captain Day studied it from many angles.

"Nah!" he said. "That ain't no good."

"Yew ain't seen it up."

"I don't 'ave ter see it up. That ain't no good. Cut far too full."

"An' what am I s'posed ter do wiv it?"

"Well, yew can either alter it, start it agen or git someone else to 'ave a go. I don't care which, but I ain't a-'avin' it."

Sulkily Hooker rolled the sail up.

"See wot I can do," he said grudgingly.

"I dunno whether 'e's a-gettin' past it, or 'is other eyes a-playin' up or wot," said Captain Day as we walked away. "Good job 'is top 'ands doin' the jibs. Might be jus' as well if 'e does the topsail an' all."

Later on I went over to the office to see Ellie. We had, of course, met for a walk the previous evening but that was all.

"Oh! Come to do the filing already?" was her greeting.

"No. Just the pleasure of your company."

"Far too busy. No staff, you see."

"I'll come when I'm good and ready."

"In the meantime, you'd like a cup of tea?" This was the motherly Caroline Murphy.

"Shall I leave you two love-birds together?" she asked when she had placed it in front of me.

"Oh, no!" said Ellie, "I need a chaperone. Besides dear brother John says the work is not to be disrupted."

"Quite right, too" I said.

"Well at least he's back with the Pride out of harm's way."

I asked whether there was any news from the police.

"Oh, yes. Those two thugs have been charged with something unconnected with the fight on the quay. Pocock's also been warned. He's entitled to demand payment but not by those means. Caroline knows all about it, her husband's a policeman in the town."

"And Vic?"

"Well. He was in here this morning. Apparently Rosie's lent him enough to keep Pocock happy for a while."

I told her about the bad sail.

"Yes. Mr. Hooker's sails haven't been too good lately. He'll have to buck up or we'll be looking to Colchester for our sails."

"Well, I'd better get back," I said, finishing my tea.

"Nice chatting to you, lover," she said, "but you've stopped us working long enough. I'll see you later. Usual place."

The next day was a Saturday and our cargo now unloaded we moved round to the yard. Mr. Bliss and one of his men came with us, for the barge was due to go, not on to a slipway, but on a set of barge blocks. These were huge baulks of timber on which a barge could sit, giving access to the bottom for retarring and minor repairs. The two yard men would help us to accurately position Daisy Maud over the blocks. A motor boat was also on hand to assist. To my surprise Ellie arrived as well for the short voyage.

"Anything for a trip on a barge," she said. "Even putting up with that awful third hand. Besides I've got to look after my investment."

I was too busy helping unmoor to query this remark at the time. But later, as we gently sailed down to the yard under topsail and foresail, I returned to it.

"You said investment," I said to her.

"Oh, yes," she said. "All arranged last night. I now own sixteen shares in this barge. Captain Day sold them to me last night, that's why I was late meeting you."

She had been about twenty minutes late, which was not like her.

"I thought I'd surprise you with that this morning. The rest of the skipper's shares have gone to Rupert Dunn. That's the way he wanted it, after Rupert had had a good talk with him. It amounts to Fowler and Dunn owning the barge, but at least it keeps John out of it personally."

"What about the entry for the Match?" I asked.

"Well, Captain Day made that yesterday and one of his conditions was that it stands in his name. The other is that there are no crew changes without his agreement. So I can't pinch you permanently for the office!"

She paused, assessing our nearness to the yard.

"Pride of Upshore remains Fowler's official entry in the bowsprit class and I understand the Resolve is coming from Mistley. There are also entries coming from the Medway and from Goldsmiths at Grays. So there you have it."

She did, of course, have access to the Match Committee and therefore was in a position to know the latest news on entries. I went forward to help Vic drop the topsail and foresail for the motor boat was now ready to help us into position. This was a lengthy process with much shouting between Bliss and his assistant and the men in the motor boat and much running of lines to various points ashore. For Vic and I there was plenty of heaving on winches to fine-tune the positioning.

Eventually Bliss declared himself satisfied and the motor-boat took him and his man ashore. We waited for the barge to ground on the blocks and Ellie waited with us. I thought that this was 'looking after investment' too far, but she had brought a picnic hamper with her and she commenced to share the contents with Captain Day, Vic and myself. She had had the forethought to include some bottles of beer.

"I'll be coming with you on the Match." she announced. The skipper and Vic stopped eating in amazement.

"You can't do that," said Vic.

"Why not?" she demanded.

"Why you're a girl and you don't no nothing about sailin' a barge in a Match. 'Sides skipper's probably got 'is own ideas on a racin' crew."

"I 'ave an' all," Captain Day said.

"Oh no! Not as part of the crew. As part-owner and my young man," she glanced at me, "and I will act as stewards. Keep you supplied with tea and that."

"Yew'd better not get in the way."

"As though we would," she said sweetly.

"Still don't like it," said Captain Day, "but I'll think on it."

Later the barge dried out on the blocks and, by putting a ladder over the side, we were able to walk ashore. Captain Day stayed behind 'to have a look at her bottom'. Ellie and I walked back to the quay through the trees.

"It will be good to have you around for a while," she said. "We should be able to see a lot more of each other."

"Oh yes!" I said, "working in your rotten office."

"It's not a rotten office. You'll love it. Anyway, it's only for a week then you can go back to your rotten barge."

We seemed to be getting close to a lover's tiff, but a distraction arrived in the form of Frank the dog. Scampering along the path through the trees, somehow by some eighth sense, he had realised that his home had moved and was now tracing her. He jumped up at each of us, barking with delight, and then continued in the direction of the boat-yard.

"That's remarkable," I said, "considering he always disappears when we are in port."

"All part of being a barge dog, I suppose," Ellie ventured.

"What are you doing tomorrow?" I asked.

"Chapel in the morning," she said. "Then, if the weather improves, I'll call at the barge and we'll go down to the little beach again."

At the moment it was rather dull and looked as though it might rain.

"And if the weather is no good?"

"I'll think of something."

I walked with her to the car and we paused alongside it for obvious reasons.

"How's about the King's Head tonight?" I asked.

"No," she said. "No, I want to avoid that particular pub for a while. But a walk and then the Jolly Fisherman perhaps."

Odd, why should she be avoiding the bargemen's pub? Possibly because she didn't want to become too familiar with her employees. I put that to one side.

146

"But, of course, it might rain. I tell you what. I'll drive down to the boat-yard, pick you up and then we'll go somewhere."

She got in the car and prepared to drive.

"See yer later," she called as the car began to move.

In the event we went to neither Upshore pub; but instead drove some distance in the country and stopped at a village inn. This was largely because of the weather which had turned drizzly and miserable. Nevertheless we enjoyed the outing and what followed in the car later. However, the weather did not look good for a picnic the next day.

I returned to Daisy Maud to listen to Vic moaning about having to work in the bargeyard.

"Bloody tea-boy, that's all I'll be," he said.

"So will I, in the office." I reminded him.

"At least you'll be wiv yer girl-friend," he said, "able ter git up ter things in the broom cupboard."

I wondered about getting to and from Daisy Maud if the tide was high. Vic said there was usually someone around who could give me a lift off.

"If not Miss Ellie'll allus giv yer a bed fer the night."

There was no reasoning with him in this mood, so I turned in.

Happily during Sunday morning the clouds rolled away to give a hot and sunny afternoon. Ellie duly arrived with her picnic basket and we walked down to the field.

"Who owns the field now?" I asked.

"John does. If he finds out what we get up to here I should think he'll put barbed-wire round it!"

I wondered how his investigations into the mysterious (to him!) events surrounding Daisy Maud were going.

"I think he's worked the bookmaker business out by now. But the receipt and dress, I don't know. I think he's baffled but Captain Day's sale of his shares to me and Rupert Dunn isn't going to improve matters."

We had reached the stile into the field.

"Come on, then," she said. "I'll race you."

We tore across the field, throwing our clothes off as we went and splashed into the river naked.

"Bet you couldn't do it under water," Ellie said when we came to a halt.

"I'll have a darn good try," I said, thrusting myself at her.

We managed after a fashion.

Later as we lay in the sun, I commented on how brown her body was.

"Well I do do some sunbathing..."

"But there's bits turning brown that shouldn't be."

" . . . in the altogether. There's a lovely bit of flat roof at the back of the house. I go up there when I can."

"You're improving it now."

"Yes, when you don't take the light off me."

A bit later she asked: "Looking forward to work tomorrow?"

"Well, there's certain things we wont be able to get up to."

"True. They'll be difficult. By the way, I don't take sugar in tea."

"Oh, no! Not tea-making."

"But you must be an expert after all the tea you drink on barges."

"I'm becoming an expert on other things, too."

"Prove it . . . "

Later as we walked back to the barge-yard, I asked: "Still off the King's Head?"

"I'm not 'off' it, I'm avoiding it."

"Why?"

"Wait and see. I've got my reasons. All will become clear during the week. Daisy Maud won't be clear of the yard until at least next Saturday."

"What's that got to do with it?"

"I said, wait and see. All will become clear during the week."

We had reached the car which was parked at the end of the dirt road which allowed vehicular access to the barge yard. She patted me on the arm.

"Now you be a good boy and have an early night. Busy day tomorrow. First day in a proper job."

My face must have showed my disappointment.

"But first you're coming home for a meal."

Relieved, I climbed into the car and we roared off. This time, when we reached the house, she took me up to see her sunbathing area on the roof. Screened by the kitchen chimneys it was certainly a secluded spot. I could imagine her laid out there in the sun, with no-one likely to disturb her.

"Dinner's too near," she whispered, divining my thoughts. Our kiss was interrupted by a gong announcing the evening meal. When we entered the dining room, Ernie was already seated at the head of the table studying some document while his soup cooled in front of him.

"Have you been up on the roof again, Eleanor?" he asked, looking over his spectacles. Ellie nodded. "Can't see what the attraction is up there," he said and went back to his reading. Ellie raised her eyebrows at me. We consumed the first two courses in virtual silence. But over the treacle pudding Ernie looked up again.

"We're going to make a first class job of Daisy Maud's bowsprit and refit," he said, "and I'm going to chase Mr. Hooker about the sails." He paused and laid down his spoon and fork. "Pride of Upshore is Fowler's official entry but it's Daisy Maud that the locals would like to see do well in the Match. The competitions building up – Resolve's definitely coming from Mistley and the Surrey and Northdown from Kent. Goldsmith and Thames and Medway have both promised entries but haven't named them as yet. There are also rumours of entries from Whitstable and Colchester but Everards at Greenhithe aren't interested. Too worried about war, apparently."

"Do you know anything about the entries, Ernie?" asked Ellie.

Ernest was on the Match Committee and if anyone had good information it would be him. He thought for a minute before replying.

"Only the named ones, naturally. Bully Briggs will sail Resolve to hell and high water, as long as there's some wind about, but hasn't the patience for light weather. That rather applies to John with the Pride of Upshore as well. Surrey's a flyer with a determined racing skipper. Northdown's a barge that deserves better, she's been third in a number of Matches, but never higher, as far as I know. Daisy Maud has the disadvantage of being the oldest barge and of not having been sailed with a bowsprit for a long time. If I was a betting man and I'm not, I would put my money on Resolve or Surrey. Now, if you'll excuse me, I've still got some work to do."

He left the table. I looked at Ellie.

"I didn't think he was interested in anything except building and repairing," I said to her.

"Oh, he knows all about the Upshore Barge Matches. He takes his position on the committee very seriously – I suppose it's his nearest thing to a hobby."

"He doesn't seem to reckon Daisy Maud for the Match."

"Not as a winner, no. But as he said, the locals would like to see her do well. Now why don't we have coffee in the lounge, it's much more comfortable."

So we had our coffee on one of the sofas in the lounge.

"I'm serious about that early night," she said.

"Here?" I asked.

"Oh, no! Nice thought, but I'm not risking it. No, I'll run you back soon for some beauty sleep before you have your big day in the office." She patted my knee like that first time in the office. "But we'll have a night together soon. I'll arrange it, you'll see."

CHAPTER 14
THE VAMP

At quarter to nine the next morning I reported for duty at the office. The red sports car was already parked outside – I had gathered from Ellie that this was now the preferred method of transport to and from the office. She said it was handy if she wished to drive out to see a customer.

Ellie was already there, unlocking various doors. In the alcove, which served as a kitchen, she had already lit a gas-ring under a kettle.

"Come here," she said when she saw me and beckoned me into Isaac's old office, where she held up her lips to be kissed.

"Is that why I'm here?" I asked when we had finished.

"Only partially," she said. "Now let's have a look at you." She stood back. I had done my best with a white shirt and an old dark suit that I had bought from the Salvation Army for a few coppers. But walking or sculling to and from Daisy Maud was not conducive to smartness.

"You'll do," she said. "No worse than Bob anyway." Noises from outside indicated the arrival of Caroline Murphy and Miss Fellows, the typist. The latter I learned would never be known by her Christian name, if she even had one. Ellie had described her as a 'typing machine', for her angular frame seemed a natural extension of her typewriter. There were, however, rumours that she had once been romantically linked with Mr. Oram, which was probably how she got the job of Fowler's typist in the first place.

"Better make the tea as soon as the kettle boils," Ellie said to me and went out into the main office.

Oh no! Not tea-making, but I went through to the alcove and prepared the cups.

Ellie was saying to Caroline Murphy: "First you'd better ring London and see what the latest is on the Hubert." I gathered that the auxiliary-powered barge's engine had failed somewhere in the London Docks.

By the time I had handed the tea round, Ellie was studying a file entitled 'Air-Raid Procedures'. She put it down to take her tea-cup.

"You can have a look at that lot if you like, see what you make of it. But first, I'll ask Caroline to show you the filing system. That will be your first priority. There's an enormous backlog for you to catch up on."

And so I commenced a very boring task of sorting out invoices, receipts and letters and placing them in the correct files. There were some consolations. At lunchtime, Ellie and I sat on a bench outside and ate sandwiches that she had provided. She told me that she had to see a customer in the afternoon, but I could leave the filing for a while and go over to the Alicia, which was alongside the quay. Captain Gascoigne, she said, had hurt his back so Ned, the mate, was supervising the discharge. All I had to do was to enquire how unloading was progressing and report back.

Ned was coping very well and, in any case, had the assistance of Tommy Dolby as Silverfish was moored next astern.

"Make a skipper of 'im yet," Tommy said.

Ike appeared with tea all round. I accepted a mug, as Ellie had said there was no need to hurry back.

"Big booze up, Wednesday night," said Ned. "Special, Rosie sez."

152

"What's special?" asked Tommy.

"Dunno. 'Spec Rosie's got summat lined up."

"As long as the beer flows," said Tommy.

"All gotta be there, she sez."

"No worries, so far as I'm concerned."

"What about yew, Bill?"

This put me in a quandary. What was Ellie likely to be doing? However, I said I would probably be there for at least part of the evening. I then returned to the office to make the afternoon tea and continue the dreaded filing.

When I returned to Daisy Maud at the end of the day I encountered an unusual figure. It was almost entirely covered in sawdust and shavings. Only the protruding ears revealed it to be Vic.

"How did you get in that state?" I asked.

"Bin workin' dahn the sawpit," he answered, "on the end of a bleedin' great two-'anded saw. Sawdust an' that goin' all over the soddin' place."

"You'd better clean yourself up before you go aboard the barge."

"Oh yes an 'ow am I supposed to do that? Jump in the bleedin' tide?"

"Try shaking yourself."

Vic did, and I stood back from the resultant cloud. Then I encouraged him to run up and down Daisy Maud's ladder, jumping from the last rung. After he had done this three or four times and turned his pockets out, he was more or less clear of dust and shavings and we went aboard the barge.

Aboard Daisy Maud progress had already been made. The bowsprit case had already been fitted forward of the windlass and the bottom had already been partially burnt off ready for retarring. Captain Day had already left for home but had left us a note of one or two things requiring attention.

"You seen enuff of that gal fer terday," Vic asked over the evening meal, "or are yew back at it this evening?" I replied that, as a matter of fact, Ellie was staying at home to wash her hair and I would be having an early night.

"Good. Gotta keep yer strength up. 'Ard work in an orfice. Now me, I'm so dry after a day in that bloody saw-pit, I gotta quench me thirst ternight, whether I can afford it or not."

"Dummy run for the big booze up?" I asked

"Could say that. You goin', or won't she let yer?"

"Oh! I'll be there sooner or later. Why is it special?"

"Dunno. But if Rosie sez it's special, it will be orlright."

The next day Ellie created a sensation by turning up for work in shirt and shorts. Caroline Murphy said nothing but Miss Fellows was highly offended and went into her office muttering "not the thing at all" and then firmly closed the door.

"Well, it's a lovely day," said Ellie, "and it's not as though I've got any customers to see and, if something crops up, I've got a change in the car."

But I obtained a certain amount of amusement from watching the expressions of bargemen who called in on business of one sort or the other. One young mate went brick red at the sight of Ellie's legs, but Tommy Dolby's eyes nearly popped out from his head and then we had a job to get rid of him. Old Hoary, Jan's skipper, developed a loud sniff and left the office hurriedly.

As for myself, I was slightly embarrassed by the whole episode. Since I felt at least partially responsible for Ellie's blossoming, I rather believed that she was going too far. But then I didn't know what was about to happen.

By Wednesday I had caught up on the filing and was introduced, by Caroline, to the mysteries of making out invoices. This was only marginally more interesting than the filling.

Ellie was more conventionally dressed, in one of her floral summer dresses, which was just as well since one of our visitors that morning was Captain Day. He gratefully accepted a mug of tea and sat down to report progress on Daisy Maud. The bowsprit was now aboard and shipwrights had given way to riggers, who were fitting the bobstay, shrouds and a new forestay from the topmast head. Most of the retarring was complete but this was a slow process as it could only be done when the tide was out.

"What we need nah is them new sails 'Ooker's draggin' 'is feet over."

"I'll get on to it," said Ellie, picking up the phone and dialling the sailmakers' number.

While she was speaking I asked the skipper whether he would attend the King's Head that evening.

"Nah. Don't like that sort o'thing. Prefer a quiet drink wiv the missus. Leave it ter young terraways like you an' Vic."

Ellie put the phone down.

"One day next week, he says. Seems his top hand who was making the jibs has gone sick. He's willing to finish them himself though."

"Not likely, 'e won't. 'E made a big enough mess of the topsail. Nah, we'll 'ave ter wait till 'is top 'and comes back. Be bloody daft though, borsprit an' nothin' ter put on it."

"Couldn't you borrow from someone else?" Ellie asked.

"'Appen ah could. Tain't the same thing' though. The sails 'Ooker's meant ter be makin' are the ones us'll use in the Match."

"You'll just have to hope for the best," Ellie said and looked at her watch. "Goodness, ten to twelve, I must fly, I've got to see someone. See yer later." And she was out of the door. I hoped she would not be long, for I was looking forward to spending the lunch-hour with her. But it was not to be. Half past twelve came, then one o'clock, and no sign of her.

"I don't know where she's gone," said Caroline when she returned from her own lunch. "But the car's still here, so she can't have gone far."

Ellie eventually returned at half past two, looking very pleased with herself.

"Good meeting?" I asked.

"Yes, very," she said, and immediately changed the subject. I began to feel vaguely jealous of whoever she had been seeing and she did not improve this when I ask about the evening.

"Oh no," she said, "I shan't be around this evening, I've got to go out again. You go to the King's Head with your friends. You know you enjoy that type of evening and Rosie Barnes reckons it will be a special one."

Rather sulkily, I agreed.

"I'll make it up to you," she said softly, "promise."

I ended up looking forward to the evening. Ellie had given me an advance of a whole pound on my office wages, and I felt as though I had never been so affluent. Why, I could even buy a round of my own, and repay some of the hospitality displayed by the bargemen since I had joined them.

It had been agreed by Tommy and Vic that we should arrive at the King's Head early in order to secure a table. Tommy doubted his ability to do this.

"Got ter git the missus in the right frame o' mind first," he said.

So Vic and I made ourselves reasonably presentable (not easy in Vic's case, since he had been involved in finishing the tarring of Daisy Maud's bottom) and set out at half-past seven, picking up Ike and Jan at the quay. Tommy had obviously been successful in placating the missus as he was already in the public bar holding a table for us.

Vic and I went up to the bar to get the drinks, Rosie herself hustled over to serve us, her elaborate gold ringlets swinging. But by the time she had reached us, my mouth was hanging open and I was gazing beyond her. For there, behind the bar, serving a party of farmers in the saloon, was Ellie.

Rosie followed my stare. "Florrie's gorn sick," she said by way of explanation. "She came over lunchtime an' offered ter 'elp so I giv 'er a try on the lunchtime session an' she picked it up quick, so I asked her ter come in this evenin'."

Ellie looked round, saw us and waved, but carried on with what she was doing. She was wearing a rather daringly low-cut blue dress that I had not seen before and higher heels than she normally wore. She also had on more lipstick and make-up than was her habit. Perhaps she believed that this was how a barmaid should look, I thought.

Vic and I took the drinks back to the table.

"You seen wot I seen?" asked Tommy. "Miss Ellie servin' be'ind the bar?" he added for the benefit of Ike and Jan.

"What's she want ter do that fer?" asked Vic. They all looked

156

at me. I shrugged, and said I knew as little as they did.

"Perhaps she needs the money," said Ike. "Expensive boy-friend like." They all laughed.

"I think it is very kind of Miss Ellie," said Jan, "to help Mrs. Barnes when she is so busy."

The bar was really beginning to fill up. Although a number of barges were away, there was a massive turn-out of lumpers, barge yard staff and fishermen.

"Better git another one in quick," said Tommy, whose glass was, as usual, empty. This time Jan went up to buy the drinks. My Polish friend, who appeared to be teetotal when I first met him, had developed a liking for English beer. This I thought might be due to the strain of crewing for the miserly Hoary.

Jan was served by Ellie and when he came back he said: "She is charming, that one. A pleasant smile and nothing too much trouble. That is how your barmaids should be, yes?"

This started a discussion on barmaids in general, but I played no part in it, for I was still thinking about Ellie. What on earth was she up to this time? I disagreed with Jan, whatever her motives were, they were not altruistic. Her lunchtime visit to the pub was obviously pre-arranged and I suspected that some bribery had happened, certainly in the case of Florrie, and possibly Rosie as well. Come to think of it, a number of key personnel were on the sick list, Florrie, Mr. Oram, Hooker's top hand, George Gascoigne. She couldn't have something to do with all of them, could she? Perhaps I was getting paranoid, though.

"I 'eard they eat their young," Tommy was saying.

"Who do?" I asked, coming our of my reverie.

"Barmaids o'course. 'Oo's turn is it? You, young Ike." Ike fought his way to the bar. Men were now standing shoulder to shoulder and a cloud of tobacco smoke was gathering under the rafters of the public bar. Rosie, Ellie and Pat were all serving into the public, and any customers in the other two bars, must, I thought, be getting short shrift.

The cries for Ned to take his place at the piano started up and, after a while, he did so, with his usual show of reluctance. This time he had the accordionist for back-up, but this hardly warranted Rosie's description of 'special'. The usual sing-along items were roared out – 'Daisy-Daisy', 'Me Old Cock Linnet', 'Pack Up Your Troubles' and so on and then it was time for the solo-numbers.

Ned did his jazz item at the piano, the accordionist performed what was believed to be a Scottish number and then there was an awkward pause as we waited for a female soloist. Foot-stamping and table-rapping broke out among the audience. But eventually it was not Pat who appeared to sing, but Ellie.

Instant quiet settled.

"Oh, my gawd," I heard Tommy mutter.

But Ellie had told me she had learnt to sing a bit at her boarding school and she certainly had. She launched into Florrie's favourite, 'The Boy in the Gallery.' True, her voice was not quite up to Florrie's standard but she give a creditable performance and received enthusiastic applause at the end. Then she announced that she would like to sing a song of her own.

It was 'Just a Song at Twilight', and the audience listened, bewitched. She went through it twice and the second time she sang it more slowly and came amongst the audience.

"Just a Song at Twilight".

She lifted the bowler hat of Mr. Bliss, the yard foreman and planted a kiss on the bald pate underneath.

"When the lights are low."

She threw her arms round the neck of a young bargeman and rubbed her cheek against his.

"And the evening shadows . . . "

She sat on the knee of an elderly barge-skipper and it became evident that her skirt was slit up the side, giving a good view of her legs at times. A few of the young spirits dared to wolf-whistle.

". . . Softly come and go."

She tickled a respectable, middle-aged lumper under his chin. And so, she worked her way round the room, until, as the song ended, she came to me, and planted a kiss full on my lips.

The applause was tumultuous, those sitting rising to give what amounted to a standing ovation.

"Ain't she good," a bargeman at the next table to ours shouted to his friend. "Pulls pints for us, sings for us an' all that. Nah that's wot I calls a guv'nor." This was the same man who had once called Ellie "a bloody stuck-up little cow." So that's what it was all about – a public relations exercise to win over her men. If it worked, there would be no more grumbling about Thames & Medway or anything else.

Cries of "encore" were now being taken up all over the bar. Ellie glanced at Rosie, who was leaning on the bar with little to do during the performance. The landlady nodded her approval and Ellie did a shortened version of 'Just a Song at Twilight' once again ending up with me, sitting on my lap and resting her cheek against mine. She stood up to acknowledge thunderous applause and then I saw him.

Brother Ernest was standing at the back of the crowd, a half-pint glass in his hand, surrounded by some of his yard employees. I dreaded to think what his reaction would be. But he was applauding with the rest and as Ellie went back behind the bar there was a slight lull, during which I distinctly heard him call: "Well done, little sister."

So, one Fowler brother at any rate was on our side.

"Well, I'll go ter the foot of our stairs," said Tommy as the applause died down and conversation became rife.

"Better if yer go ter the bar, skipper," said Ike. "That's fair parched me."

Tommy at last decided that it was his turn to buy a round and departed, with Vic to help him with the glasses. There was obviously going to be an interval for the replenishment of glasses and general recovery.

"When are you to be wed?" Jan asked me, surprisingly.

"Er – I hadn't really thought about that."

"She obviously loves you – very much."

Ike nodded agreement. But I was embarrassed by such speculation. I did want, more than anything in the world, to ask Ellie to marry me, but I was held back, partly by my lack of background, partly by fear that Ellie's ambition would lead to her turning me down.

Vic and Tommy returned with two laden trays.

"We got two lots," said Tommy. "Saves time."

Apparently Ned had abandoned any further sing-song. It was probably a case of "follow that." From the conversation around me there was no doubt that the men now thought of her as "Their Miss Ellie." Quite simply, they loved her.

After a while she came round, collecting glasses and smoking one of her cigarettes. As she bent down to pick up the empties, her lowcut dress revealed the top half of her breasts to the delight of the others.

She hissed in my ear: "Stay at closing time."

"'Oo's the best barmaid, then?" shouted Tommy.

"I am," she replied lifting the glasses in the air and moving on. What was she up to, now? Stay at closing time. Perhaps Rosie, as she was entitled to do, was holding some type of after-hours party. But the others hadn't been invited. It was very nearly closing time and the crowd was thinning out. Tommy, in a fit of closing time generosity, decided to buy one more round and we sat around the table drinking it till well after time. Then the party split up. Vic went first, to talk to Rosie who was clearing up in the Saloon. Ike and Jan left together rather unsteadily since they had been trying to match Tommy's capacity for beer. Finally Tommy belched, finished his beer, announced he was going to have a pee and then go home to face the "missus."

This left me alone in an empty bar but Ellie was washing up at the public bar sink so I went over to talk to her.

"Good drink?" she asked. I said it was very good and the entertainment had been marvellous. She, too, seemed a trifle unsteady.

"I'm a bit tipsy," she admitted. "I was bought a lot of drinks, but I haven't had all of them. Got to keep a clear head for later. Look, you can help me by emptying the ashtrays."

I did as I was bid and, for good measure, wiped the table-tops

160

over as well. She carried on the conversation as I worked.

"Rosie's given me a room for the night. Doesn't like the idea of me driving home this late. We'll go up there when we've finished."

So that was why I was to stay on at the pub.

A few minutes later Rosie called through from the saloon: "That'll do you two. You can go up now, me an' the cellarman'll finish up."

Vic, I noticed, was still in the saloon, smoking and drinking what looked like a glass of rum. It seemed that he had switched his affection back to Rosie.

We mounted the narrow stairs that led to the rooms over the pub. It seemed that we were not the only 'guests' that night, for through an open door on the landing we saw a young bargeman hastily disrobing Pat, the other barmaid.

We reached the room allocated to Ellie. Before we went in, she held up her face to be kissed. It was a long and passionate affair.

As she firmly closed the door behind us, she said quite simply, "Undress me."

CHAPTER 15
NIGHTS OF PASSION

What followed can only be described as a night of passion. Several times Ellie woke me, whispering, "Let's do it again." She was fast becoming an accomplished sexual athlete and each time suggested a new position or variation.

At some time in the night I remembered her original worries about precautions and asked her about this. She sleepily murmured what sounded like "Wanna have your babies." Which gave me cause to think.

About half-past seven Ellie had just rolled off me, when the door opened and Rosie bustled in with a tray of tea and toast. She was wearing a dressing gown and curlers and seemed not to be the slightest bit worried by the fact that we were both stark naked.

"'Ave a good night, me dears?" she asked breezily as she put down the dray. We both grinned and nodded.

"Good, I am pleased for yer," she paused at the door and studied us. "Seen a lot worse sights in this ould pub, I can tell yer."

"I expect she's been doing roughly the same as us," Ellie said after she had gone.

"Very likely," I said, pouring the tea.

We ate and drank in silence for a little while.

"Ellie," I said, almost on impulse, "will you marry me?"

She laughed. "I wonder how many proposals are made when the couple have no clothes on." Her eyes sparkled. "Of course I will, silly. I've been waiting for you to ask."

I pulled her over to me and kissed her. But there was more: "But we'll have to find your past, first."

"Why?"

"Well, brother John's head of the family now and he's not going to be keen on me marrying a third hand off a barge, let alone one without a past. But don't worry, I can get a good solicitor on to it, they're very good at ferreting things out. You never know, you might come from a wealthy family. An' if the worst comes to the worst, fuck John, we'll elope."

This was the first time I had heard her use bad language for a long time and it made me sure that she meant what she said.

"So we're engaged then, even if it's unofficial."

"We're engaged. Now, as a token of my love, I'm going to try something different on you before we get dressed."

She knelt down before me . . .

We walked over to the office hand-in-hand and a little late. Ellie was wearing shorts and shirt again rather than the revealing blue dress which was now in a suitcase that she had brought with her.

"We're a bit late, I expect we'll find the others waiting to get in," Ellie said. "How embarrassing!" She grinned at me.

But Caroline and Miss Fellows were already in, for Mr. Oram had turned up and opened the office. He still seemed a little bent from his lumbago. He, too, did not approve of shorts as office wear and looked at Ellie's legs and sniffed.

"Are you sure you should be in?" Ellie asked.

"I'll be orlright if I don't do no lifting," the old man said. Ellie then introduced me as her fiancée. This caused considerable twittering by Caroline and Miss Fellows, who happened to be in the main office. All offered their congratulations and we celebrated with a cup of tea, made, for once, by Caroline. I wondered whether other reactions would be as favourable.

Mr. Oram and I started work on the invoices. The old man had forgotten that he had already told me that he had been the Fowler's coachman. So I heard this again together with plenty of anecdotes about horses and passengers that he had dealt with. He also, although being shore-bound, had a good knowledge of barges and their crews. He reckoned that Captain Day was probably the best skipper in the Fowler & Dunn fleet and said that I was lucky to be his third hand.

"Happen you've been third hand with him," he said, "you'll get a mate's berth anywheres."

George Gascoigne he dismissed as a bladder of wind, Tommy Dolby as too fond of his ale but, surprisingly, he thought a lot of Jan's skipper, Hoary.

"He may be a terrible old miser, but he knows his stuff all right." Zeke, too, came in for praise.

"Great pity that man had his accident, He'd 'ave done well if he'd stayed in barges. Happy Day needs him for this match, cos I reckon Happy may be gettin' out of his depth with it."

At this point the telephone rang. Caroline answered it, then handed it like a hot potato to Ellie.

"John," she hissed, "wants you."

It was a long call with John doing most of the talking. Ellie's contribution was limited to several "I see's" and "if you think so", and "have it your own way". From the way she was frowning and the reddening of her face, I could tell she was becoming angry. Eventually she slammed the phone down and took a deep breath.

"What was that about?" I asked.

"That was John," she said, "He and the Pride are at Mistley. So he's been to see Reuben Fox and, would you believe it, Captain Day is not to sail Daisy Maud in the match. John's putting Reuben in as racing skipper."

"Who's Reuben Fox?" I asked.

"Only the greatest racing-barge skipper ever," said Ellie.

"I thought he must be dead," said Oram, "he retired at sixty-five. Kept making come-backs though. Must be around eighty now. I'm surprised he's still at it. They say he's got a room in his little old cottage at Mistley full of trophies what he's won. Floor to ceiling they stretch. Why there's several what he's won out-right, three times in a row like."

"There's more," said Ellie. "He's coming on Saturday to in-spect Daisy Maud, never mind whether the repairs are finished or the sails ready. He wants her put on a buoy with no other barges so that he can see her afloat with nothing else to get in the way. He wants all the regular crew there with me and Ernest."

"But what's this Reuben like?" I insisted.

"A martinet," said Oram. "Not a pleasant man at all. Makes Bully Briggs look like a school kid. But he gets results. That's why owners ask him to race their barges."

"God knows what John was thinking of," said Ellie. "But we've got a lot to do. There's three barges on the buoy and they've got to go somewhere. Council's got another buoy down in the Home Reach but it's not to be used for a long time. If they can't use it, they'll have to go on anchor. And, oh God, someone's got to break the news to Captain Day." She glanced at me. "That'd better be us two. We'll go down in the car shortly. Mr. Oram, could you get hold of the river bailiff and have him check out the buoy in Home Reach? Caroline, your job's to contact the skippers of the three barges on the buoy and tell them to be ready for a move. We'll sort things out at the yard."

She picked up her car keys and a pad on which she had been making notes.

"Ready, darling?" she said to me.

"There's only one bright spot in this fucking business," said Ellie in the car, "and that's that my fucking brother isn't coming down with Reuben."

She seemed to be taking her anger out on the car, slamming the gears and driving rather too fast for Essex lanes.

If she couldn't work out John's motive in engaging Reuben Fox, I certainly could. It was revenge on Daisy Maud and those aboard her. The torn dress, the mysterious receipt, the unexpected fight

165

with two thugs, his exclusion from the sale of Captain Day's shares – it had all built up inside him and any way of striking back, however petty, would be employed by him. It did not auger well for Ellie and I, especially when it came to marriage.

"We're here," said Ellie, pulling up with a screech of brakes. "Now we'll start rounding people up."

We quickly found Ernest and Mr. Bliss the foreman and, since the tide was in, a boat to take us out to Daisy Maud. Captain Day could be seen, sitting aft on the cabin top, smoking his pipe. Vic, too was aboard, helping a shipwright renew a piece of deck planking.

As we came within earshot, Vic said to his companion, rather too loudly. "The trouble with that Miss Ellie is she's all tit and legs. Now me, I prefer women wi' a bit of meat on 'em." Ellie looked at me and shrugged. I wondered what Vic's reaction to our engagement would be, he was obviously still plagued with jealousy and I had noticed his rather low-key reaction to the previous night's performance.

We boarded the barge via the port-side leeboard and I thought that Ellie's rig of shorts and shirt was very practical for this activity.

Vic, who was in a chirpy mood, seemed delighted to see Mr. Bliss.

"You still got that lipstick on yer bald bit, Blissy?" he asked.

"Yus, keepin' in fer a souvenir," said the yard foreman.

"Bet your missus loves that,"

Ellie quickly restored order and quietly informed Captain Day about Reuben Fox and related matters. The skipper's reaction was not as I expected.

"Reuben Fox, eh. I'm 'onoured. Yus, I am. The best racin' skipper ever an' 'e wants to race my li'le ould barge. Still I wish that John 'ad tole me."

Ellie turned to Ernie and Bliss

"How's the work going?"

"Bottom's finished," said Ernie. "Not much more to do, is there?" he asked Bliss.

166

"Nah!" said the foreman, "Nuffin we can't finish on the buoy."

"So we'll put her out on the buoy tomorrow, ready for Saturday," Ellie decided. "Vic and Bill, you'll be needed for that, so you'll get time off your other jobs."

She made towards the boat.

"Now 'ang on, lass," said Captain Day. "'Ave a rest from dashin' arahnd. There's a cup o' tea. Put the kettle on meself when I saw yer comin'. No third 'and, see."

He went below to deal with the tea. Ernie and Bliss were talking technicalities and Vic had gone forrard again.

"All tit and legs, eh?" Ellie said to Vic's retreating back.

"Not a bad description, really," I said. She kicked me.

Captain Day reappeared and dispensed tea all round. Ernie and Bliss drifted forrard to look at the work on the deck planking, leaving the skipper, Ellie and I together.

"Wot's all this abaht yew gallivantin' arahnd the King's 'Ead larst night?" Captain Day said to Ellie. "Makin' an exhibition o' yerself. Whatever are they goin' to say at chapel?"

"It was something that had to be done," said Ellie, unrepentant. "But I had my man to look after me."

"Yew two – er . . . "

"We have an understanding," I said.

"That's good. Pleased fer yer both. Congratulations."

We shook hands and he gave Ellie a peck on the cheek.

"Mind yew," he went on, addressing himself to me. "She needs a fella ter keep an eye on 'er. Bit wayward like. Last night fer example . . . "

"You wish you'd been there," Ellie rolled her eyes at him. "Don't you, really?" I thought it was as well the skipper didn't know what else had gone on.

"Well . . . " he said and changed the subject. "'E's not goin' ter like it. Yew two, that is. But then tha's 'is 'ard luck." He obviously meant Vic.

Ernie and Bliss were now standing by the boat, looking fidgety.

"We must go," said Ellie. "See how the others have got on. See yer Saturday, Cap'n Day."

We drove back to the office in a much calmer mood.

"I'm glad Captain Day took it so well," said Ellie. "But I got the impression he knows something that we don't didn't you?"

I said that I hadn't noticed anything.

"Call it woman's intuition, then. We'll see. But I think I was right about last night, he would have liked to have been there."

"Yes, all tit and legs," I said.

She smacked my thigh.

"I hope you're going to stop knocking me around once we're married."

Back in the office Oram and Caroline reported success. The river bailiff had been down to the buoy in Home Reach and decided that it wanted re-shackling to it's chain with a new shackle, he and his men had now gone back to deal with this. The crews of the three barges on Fowler's buoy had been contacted and were ready to move when the bailiff gave the word.

One of them had auxiliary power and could tow the others if the wind fell.

"Wells, that's that little panic over," said Ellie. "Now we've just got Saturday to look forward to."

I spent the rest of the afternoon with Mr. Oram, preparing invoices and listening to coachman's tales. By the end of business Ellie and I both felt exhausted after the activities of that day and the previous evening and night and decided that we would both have an early night in our respective homes.

Next day I reported to the office at the usual time of 9am.

"They'll want you at Daisy Maud at about midday" said Ellie, "But we've caught up on the work well, so I'll take some time out and come for the ride. That way I can drive you down there. If that's all right with you." She looked at Oram and Caroline in turn.

"Us'll be fine," said Oram.

So we went down to Daisy Maud by car again. Ellie had obviously planned this trip for she was in shorts and shirt again. By the time we reached Daisy Maud, Captain Day and Vic had her ready to go, with ropes coiled up and loose gear stowed.

Although the shipwrights would probably be back in the afternoon, most traces of their activities had been removed.

The yard motor-boat took the towline, the remaining lines were let go and within a few minutes we were moored to the now empty buoy.

The inevitable cup of tea was suggested for all concerned and, this time, I was elected to make it.

While we were drinking it, the auxiliary barge Hubert appeared round the last bend of the river under power. Her engine had obviously been repaired. As she drew level her skipper throttled the engine down and put his helm over to bring the barge head to tide.

Her mate had come forrard and was getting a mooring line ready to throw.

"He wants to come alongside," said Captain Day.

"We can't have that," said Ellie and shouted. "Go away," at Hubert and pointed downriver.

The rest of us added our voices but Hubert's skipper merely shook his head.

"They can't hear," said Ellie. "The engine's too noisy."

The yard-hand in the motor boat used his initiative and went alongside Hubert aft where he made shouted explanations to the skipper. The auxiliary barge then backed off and went down river to join the others on the Home Reach buoy.

"Someone better say aboard tonight in case anyone else tries that," Ellie decided.

Captain Day and Vic both looked at me.

"We've both got business ashore," Vic said.

"Sorry, looks like you're elected," Ellie said, then came closer and whispered again. "I'll make it up to you, promise."

So I was left alone aboard an empty barge for the night. By around seven o'clock I had finished a list of chores left for my by the skipper and had had something to eat, so I went up on deck to gaze at the shore. So near and yet so far. Ellie was ashore there somewhere and this was the second evening that I had not seen her. I considered taking the barge's boat and going ashore. But that would mean deserting my post and I thought that, knowing I was stuck aboard, Ellie was unlikely to walk among the trees. Nothing was moving on the river except a lug-sail dinghy dropping down on the last of the tide and a light westerly breeze. I decided to go below in search of something to read.

Minutes later, I was alerted by a familiar voice crying "Daisy Maud, ahoy!"

I nipped up on deck to see the smart varnished lugsail dinghy that I had seen earlier, coming alongside. Ellie was at the helm, dressed only in a bathing suit, which emphasized Vic's earlier description of her.

I grabbed the dinghy's painter that she threw to me.

"Why it's all tit and legs" I cried.

Ellie unshipped the dinghy's tiller from the rudder-head.

"Enough!" she cried, "Less you want tiller soup." She waived the tiller in the air.

"Whose dinghy?" I asked, as she lowered the sail and tidied it up.

"Mine, of course, silly," she replied. "But I don't often use it, what with one thing and another. Now take these packages. There's a salad for us to eat, which I made myself and clothes for me, which I might not need, if I'm lucky."

She scrambled aboard. Despite the lateness of the hour she didn't seem worried about being scantily clad.

"How are you going to get back?" I asked. "The tide's nearly done and the wind's dying."

She put her head on one side, "Well, it's like this. I ran out of wind and I drifted into this sailing barge with no-one aboard, so I spent the night on it. You'd be surprised at the yarns I tell Ernie and the servants. Anyway I fancied a really good fuck with my fiancée."

We went down in the cabin and she unwrapped the salad. I had already eaten a tin of stew, but any food prepared by Ellie tended to be delicious, so we both tucked in. She sat opposite me, still in her bathing costume, her golden brown legs crossed in front of her.

"This is lovely," she said. "I could do it for ever. You know, one day we ought to buy our own sailing barge and use it as our yacht."

"It will cost a lot of money."

"Oh! I'll make the money all right. I could always go on the streets as a sideline."

"Not while you're married to me, you won't."

"Well I could try high-level stuff. Seducing millionaires and such."

"You'd be good at that."

We had both finished our meal.

"Talking of which," she said, undoing her bathing costume and revealing her magnificent breasts. "Let's not waste any more time."

We spent the rest of the evening making love. For some reason, possibly the isolation of the barge, she was noisier than usual, calling out things like "Faster – you bastard – faster", as she writhed underneath me.

We finally sprang apart for the last time around nine-thirty, both covered in perspiration.

"Phew!" she said. "That was well worth all the sailing and salad-making. Now, an end to all this. What are the sleeping arrangements, we both need a good night ready for the big day tomorrow."

"Two separate berths in the foc's'le then," I said.

"I don't know about that," she said demurely. "I haven't brought a nightie."

"I'll leave you alone."

"You dare!"

We looked round at the wreckage of our meal and the tangled bedclothes on the spare bunk.

"We'll have to remove all traces of our having been down here," I said.

"Come on, then," she said, gathering up the crockery.

A watcher from the shore, a little later, might have seen two nude figures creep forrard on the barge, carrying their clothes and other bits and pieces.

True to our decision we turned straight in and had a good nights' sleep apart from one short and passionate episode around two in the morning.

FURTHER INTERLUDE 1964 — JACK DOWNING

"Have you ever visited Upshore?" I asked Bill.

We were sitting in the same pub that I had met Inspector Johnson in. He had been telling his story to me since eleven o'clock that morning and we both felt that we deserved a breather.

"No, not at all," he replied. "It's the one east coast port that I've never visited. Probably because it's right up a river."

"And Nether Rushbrook?"

"No, definitely not. I wasn't even aware of its existence."

"And the London Docks?"

"I once met a friend who was a passenger on a ship that came into Royal Docks. But the other docks, no. I've seen pictures of them, of course."

"Well, a lot of us have done that. What about sailing barges? Any family connections?"

He had to think about this one. Then he said slowly. "An uncle by marriage had a part share in one. She was a yacht in the nineteen-twenties. But I never went near her. Again I've seen photos."

I shook my head. "Curiouser and curiouser. And Ellie, did she resemble anyone you've ever met?"

Again he thought and obviously had difficulty with coming out with the words.

"She – she was very like a girl I knew at college. She was kind to me when I was getting over my accident."

"Accident?" He hadn't mentioned this before.

"Yes, I was knocked off my motorbike. I was in a coma for weeks. That's why I wasn't in the war. Medical grounds."

172

"When was this?"

"1939. Summer."

"The same period as your story covers. This could be the answer. Your 'dream' replaces those missing weeks and Ellie is your college friend."

He digested this.

"It's not that easy," he said eventually. "You'll see when I continue."

But I persisted: "And what about the other 1939 characters? Do you feel that you've known any of them before?"

"No. None of them. I don't even think I'd ever heard the Essex accent before I met Captain Day." He began to sound petulant. "You must let me carry on with the story. But not here, let's go back to my place."

I began to feel that I shouldn't cross-question him. But it had to be done if I was ever going to get to the bottom of this. I drank up and followed him as he pushed through the swing-door leading to the pub's car park.

CHAPTER 16

THE EXPERT

Ellie woke me with a kiss around seven o'clock. She was already fully dressed in a Guernesy and slacks, which indicated a cool morning.

"I'm going to take the dinghy back now," she said. "But I'll be back with the others about nine o'clock in the motor boat. There's bacon and eggs on the stove and the tea's made."

I slipped on a pair of trousers and went on deck to see her off. Then I went below to bacon and eggs and tea. How typical of her efficiency, I thought, to see to my needs before she left. The breakfast was well up to her usual standard of catering.

The motor-boat appeared shortly after nine with Ellie, Captain Day, Vic, Ernie and the helmsman aboard but no-one else.

"No sign of Captain Fox," said Ellie, when they were all aboard. "But then John didn't give me an actual time." She turned to the man in charge of the motor-boat. "You'd better go back to the quay and wait for Captain Fox."

We had the inevitable tea and talked among ourselves. Vic seemed very subdued after his perkiness of the previous day.

"'E's 'ad bad news," Captain Day told me. "That bookmakers gettin' 'eavy agen."

Ten o'clock came with so sign of the returning motor-boat.

Whereas the rest of us were happy enough to chat and drink tea, Ernie was getting impatient.

"This is wasting time," he said. "There's work to be done." He hailed the yard boat, which took him ashore. A few minutes later he returned with two shipwrights who re-commenced work on the deck planking.

"It's one thing me having to hang around aboard here," Ernie said, "but another when my men can't get on."

He had earlier proffered polite congratulations to me on my engagement to his sister, but so far Vic had said nothing, seemingly lost in his own misery.

A little while later Captain Day said: "Ain't that the moty-boat a-coming now?"

It was and as the boat drew nearer we could see it had not one, but two passengers. The elderly one was obviously Reuben Fox. He looked very sprightly for his age and was dressed in a suit complete with wing collar and tie, his only nautical concession being a peaked cap. My impression was that rather then a barge skipper, he looked like a lay preacher, which, I found out later, he was in his home town of Mistley. His companion was a younger man, more casually dressed, who was armed with a camera and a notepad.

As the motor-boat drew alongside, Reuben Fox leapt aboard with an agility which belied his age. Without preamble he asked, staring at the shipwrights: "What are those men doing here? I thought I asked for this barge to be uncluttered for a proper inspection."

Ernie, realising his mistake, said to the men: "Come on, boys. You go ashore for a while. You can finish this later."

The two unfortunate shipwrights gathered up their tools and clambered into the motor-boat to go ashore. Reuben stared with distaste at the shavings that they left on the deck.

"Up the rigging," he said to his companion, who had followed him aboard. He seemed oblivious of the reception committee. His assistant put down his gear and went nimbly up the mast towards the bob which fluttered from the top-mast head.

"Looks all right up here, grandfather," the younger man called down. So he was Reuben's grandson.

"We'll see," muttered Reuben.

The younger man came down from aloft and the pair of them proceeded to examine everything on deck, paying particular attention to halliards, brails and other running rigging. I heard a sharp intake of breath from Reuben as he picked up one of the handles for the crab winches and found it to be rather worn. The grandson occasionally took photos. Reuben eventually paused in front of our little group.

"Who is the mate?" he demanded.

Vic reluctantly stepped forward.

"I want you to scull us, very slowly, round the barge in the boat."

The boat, unused for quite a while, was hanging in its davits. Ellie said something about the motor-boat being available.

"No, Miss Fowler. I do not wish to use a motor-boat. The noise of the engine would be a distraction."

So Vic and I put the boat in the water. As he climbed into it, Reuben said: "The rest of you can set the sails."

We did as we were bid. Fortunately Ellie, Ernie and I all had a fair idea how to do this and, with our help, Captain Day made an efficient and quick job of it. Daisy Maud swung slowly head to wind.

Again Reuben Fox made a minute observation, this time of the outside of the hull, even the pintles and gudgeons, from which the rudder was hung, being examined. More photos were taken. Then Vic sculled the boat further away so that the sails could be observed.

"What a horrible man," Ellie said now that the boat was out of earshot. "I'm glad I didn't ask him to stay for lunch or anything."

"That's jist 'is way, Miss Ellie," said Captain Day.

The weather was warming up and just before the Foxes boarded the boat, she had slipped off her Guernsey. She was wearing her swim-suit underneath so this left her shoulders bare and gave a good indication of the contours of her bosom.

Whether she had done this because she was genuinely hot or in an attempt to seduce the formidable Reuben Fox, I was not quite sure. But it had no effect on the old man, although his grandsons' eyes registered interest.

"His grandson fancies you," I said.

"Let him. I expect he's just as nasty as his grandfather."

The boat was returning so we gathered aft to wait a verdict. Once again Reuben Fox sprang aboard in his agile fashion. He addressed himself to Ellie.

"You are, I believe, Miss Fowler, the owners' representative."

Ellie nodded. Reuben glanced at her bare shoulders and shuddered. "Such a young girl too." He drew himself up to his full height.

"It is my belief that there is only one place for a barge to be in a Match and that is first. Every other consideration – gear, crew, sails, everything - should bear that simple theory in mind. To that end I cannot and will not consider sailing an inferior barge. Whose idea was it to fit this barge with a borsprit?"

"Mine, 'spose," said Captain Day.

"That was a mistake and a bad one. This barge might have stood a chance in the staysail class of the Match. As it is her leeboards are hung at least four inches too far aft. You're going into this match not knowing what your sails will be like – very foolish. Her topmast should be raked a lot further forrard and some of the running rigging leaves much to be desired."

He paused. "Remind me of the borsprit entries for this Match." Ellie looked at Ernie who recited the entries, adding that the Thames & Medway entry was expected to be Ardent.

"Forget her," said Reuben Fox. "This barge is not capable of beating Bully Briggs, nor yet Surrey or Pride of Upshore. Miss Fowler, I am sorry but I cannot sail your barge. Kindly summon the motor-boat."

A few minutes later the motor-boat had borne the Foxes away. "Well, that's a relief," said Ellie.

I was surprised to hear Captain Day chortling with laughter.

"The ould fraud," he said when he could manage it. "'E ain't goin' ter sail no more barges. Bully tole me up Lunnon. 'E's got summat wrong wiv 'is innards. Still likes everyone ter think 'e's the king though. 'E's pulled this stunt afore, lookin' at a barge an' a-tellin' the owner it ain't no good. I wager this is Bully's doin'. Got brother John an' Reuben all fired up at Mistley, so as Reuben 'ould come dahn 'ere. Bet ould Bully's laughin' up 'is sleeve." He nudged the sullen Vic who was still smarting about all the sculling he'd had to do. "Picked up a few tips though, didn't we? Can't do nothin' abaht the leeboards, but us'll do the rest. Any chance o' a new winch 'andle?"

"I've got one in the yard," said Ernie. "Nearly new. You can have it with my compliments, might help you win."

"Thank'ee," said the skipper. "Now us 'ad better get these pesky sails dahn."

When the sails were stowed we naturally had another mug of tea. This time Ellie insisted on making it. We sat on the main hatch to drink it.

"Is there much more work to do?" Ellie asked Ernie.

"Only the deck-planking to finish," said her brother. "That reminds me, it's gone midday. Can we leave that till Monday? Otherwise the shipwrights will want overtime."

"Yes, of course," said Ellie. "So Daisy Maud should be able to sail Tuesday or Wednesday?" Ernie nodded.

"So us might as well go up Lunnon an' pick up a freight," said Captain Day.

"Well, that's my point," said Ellie, "with the Match getting close I don't want anyone involved straying too far. Who did you have in mind as Match crew, Captain Day?"

"Zeke as mainsheet-hand, Tommy as mate, an' Vic an' Ike."

"John will have his own mate, plus Brewster and his mate from Voracious and old Hoary. Pride will have to go on the yard anyway, so that's Daisy Maud, Silverfish, Reed Warbler and Voracious I shall have to keep an eye on. Good, I'm glad that's cleared up. Try for a London cargo by all means but I'll have a word with Rupert Dunn to try and make sure it's for here or nearby."

She leant over to me and whispered: "It looks as if we have to part again, my love." There was some embarrassed foot shuffling from the others.

Vic suddenly said: "You go ashore ternight, Bill. I'll stay on the barge."

"That won't be necessary," Ellie said, "the big event's over."

"I know, miss. But I got me reasons. You two got things to celebrate, anyway."

This was the nearest he ever got to congratulating us. Ellie and I drifted forrard for a discussion.

"The motor boat's due any time now," she said. "If you come with us you could come home for tea."

"That sounds a good idea," I said. "And this evening?"

"Oh, the King's Head, of course. Public bar."

"Public bar?"

"Oh, yes. I made a lot of friends there on Wednesday. Remember?"

In the evening, replete after both tea and dinner at Ellie's home, we drove down to the King's Head. We were immediately the centre of attention, for not only had the news of our engagement spread, but the memory of Wednesday night's events was still fresh in everybodys' minds. Congratulations were showered upon us, together with so many offers of drinks that we could both have become drunk quite quickly. However, Rosie Barnes intervened: "The first drink," she announced, "fer this young couple an' their friends, is on the 'ouse."

We immediately found that we had plenty of friends. Eventually we tore ourselves loose and sat down with Tommy, Ike and Jan.

"I am very pleased for you, my friend," said Jan. "May I kiss your so beautiful young lady?" I gave my assent. Jan plucked Ellie's right hand from the table and raised it to his lips.

"Thank you, Jan," said Ellie. "Now this is how we do it in England." She leant across the table and kissed him on the cheek. This, of course, triggered Tommy and Ike into demanding their turn and she duly obliged managing to deal with them almost simultaneously.

"Oy, oy. It's the lipstick brigade," said Mr. Bliss gleefully as he wandered past. All three scrubbed furiously at their cheeks while Ellie and I curled up with laughter.

"Where's Mrs. Dolby?" Ellie asked Tommy, once order was restored.

"We, er – 'ad a disagreement 'bout Wednesday night," said Tommy. "So I'm on me own." He rubbed his cheek again. "Jus' as well reely". He pushed his empty glass over to Ike, who went up to the bar.

Ned was already seated at the piano and played the first few bars of 'Just a Song at Twilight' while looking at Ellie hopefully.

"Oh, no!" she said. "Not tonight, Ned. I'm out to enjoy myself. Let Florrie do the singing."

And enjoy herself she did, laughing at Tommy and Ike's jokes, flirting with Jan, joining in the sing-song, applauding Florrie's performance and insisting on buying a round, although she was only drinking lemonade with a dash of beer.

We left the pub as Tommy started his belching and peeing routine.

"What's your arrangement with Vic?" Ellie asked

"He'll pick me up from the boatyard and he'll be watching out from about closing time onwards."

"I'll run you round there. But no sex tonight. One can have too much of a good thing and we'll be able to have a cuddle while he sculls in."

I'd been half-hoping that Vic had fallen asleep and would miss the rendezvous, so that I could spend the night with Ellie somewhere, but this was not to be. As we sat, arm-in-arm on the bonnet of the car, after flashing the headlights at Daisy Maud, we heard him clatter into the boat.

"That was a lovely evening," said Ellie. "Thank you."

We kissed several times until the sound of sculling drew close.

"See you tomorrow," Ellie whispered and jumped into the car.

CHAPTER 17
THE RING

For the next three days we stayed on the buoy while the ship-wrights finished their work on the deck planking. Of course there was no work on the Sunday and I was able to spend an afternoon at the house with Ellie when she tried to teach me tennis, not very successfully. She said that she had hoped that I would be able to spend the remaining time before we sailed in the office, but that Captain Day had said he had plenty for me to do aboard Daisy Maud.

And indeed he had. We spent the three days doing our best to remedy Captain Fox's criticisms. With the assistance of a rigger from the yard, we pulled the topmast as far forrard as we could. Then we set about the running rigging looking for the faults that he had found and correcting these. Every evening Vic told me to go ashore to be with Ellie. I began to wonder whether this was some sort of engagement present from him. I remarked on his desire to stay aboard to Captain Day.

"'E's layin' low," said the skipper. "Prob'ly from that bookie. But that won't last, I know 'im."

And the evenings with Ellie were pure joy. We visited local hostelries, made further attempts at tennis, and made love whenever possible. And all too soon it was time to go, but there was still no sign of our new sails.

"Bloody good, this is," said Captain Day. "Borsprit barge an' nuffin' to 'ang on the borsprit. That'll jis' stick out the front an' be a nuisance. Talkin' abaht nuisances, anyone seen that daug lately?"

But of course Frank was with us when we sailed on the Thursday and Ellie took time out from the office to wave us out of sight. We need not have worried about the lack of jibs and the new topsail for we had a vile passage with a hard slog to windward to reach the Thames, sailing under mainsail and foresail only with the topsail remaining lashed in position at the main-mast head.

We moored to Starvation Buoys and waited some days for a call from Mrs. Bax. This came on the Tuesday.

"That's good," said Captain Day, on his return from the shore. "Bone meal from a ship at Butler's Wharf back to Upshore. Yew'll be able ter do some sight-seein' young Bill, Tower of Lunnon an' that."

Butler's Wharf was adjacent to Tower Bridge, in the East Side. We sailed gently up there on a light easterly. Captain Day and Vic, who had cheered up considerably now that we were clear of Upshore, pointed out some of the landmarks on the way. Admittedly many of these were public houses. The Town of Ramsgate and the Prospect of Whitby on the north shore and the Dover Castle and the Angel on the South. There was also the Greenwich Naval College with the adjacent Dreadnought, Seaman's Hospital and the site where Brunel's Great Eastern was built at Millwall. Closer to home was the anchorage known as Mudhole where sailing barges used to lower their gear before proceeding up above bridges.

"Useter blow up thro' bridges wiv bridge sails up," said Captain Day, "'fore there was so many tugs arahnd. Don't 'appen much now, though."

Lying at a buoy off St. Saviour's Dock just below Butler's Wharf was one of Thames & Medway's big auxiliary barges.

"We'll lay 'longside 'im 'til we're needed," the skipper decided.

"You sure, skip, you know what us Kentishmen can be like," said Vic.

"Nah! The ould boy what's got that one's orl right."

So we went alongside the Kent barge. The skipper was absolutely right. The crew of the Thames & Medway barge had acquired a bottle of illicit duty-free whisky from one of the crew of the steamer alongside Butler's Wharf and invited us aboard to help them drink it. Although Captain Day said he rarely drank Scotch and thought I shouldn't drink it at all, we accepted and took the concertina and Frank to provide music. A jolly evening ensued, especially for Vic, and after a while, talk turned to the Upshore Barge Match.

Naturally the Medway men were fully behind their entry, Ardent, but, more realistically they thought that Resolve or Surrey was likely to be the winner. They were, however, curious about the two Fowler entries Pride of Upshore and Daisy Maud.

"Well, yer can see we ain't got no sails for our borsprit yet," said Captain Day. "But other than that, I reckon it's abaht crew."

They asked him to explain. He said that none of the younger men wished to crew for the bombastic John. Captain Brewster of Voracious would, as a fellow skipper, no doubt be John's mainsheet-hand.

"But that don't leave 'im much up forrard," the skipper when on. "Ol' Isaac Carney's well past jumpin' arahnd up there an' John's mate's gettin' on. That only leaves Brewster's mate what's reely fit. Now us, we'll 'ave me ould mate Zeke as mainsheetman an' 'e knows 'is stuff, despite 'avin' a peg leg, an' three good blokes up forrard, though there's one what I 'as me doubts abaht sometimes."

He watched the mate of the Medway barge refilling Vic's glass for the umpteenth time. A second bottle of Scotch had been produced.

"Wot abaht this young man?" asked the Medway skipper. "Ain't 'e sailin' wiv yew?" He meant me.

"Well, 'im an' 'is girl, what's more or less owner, 'ave worked their way aboard. S'pose thats orl right provided they don't do no actual sailin'."

The Medway skipper said that he had heard that Goldsmith's of Grays were entering their Ailsa for the borsprit class.

"That makes seven," said Captain Day. "Good number. Be as many as the staysails, I warrant."

And that started a discussion on the staysail class, for which Thames and Medway had an entry but Fowler's did not.

"What abaht some more music?" the Medway mate asked after a while. So we concluded the evening with another sing-song.

The next day we received orders to go alongside the ship and start loading. Our new friends had received a similar request and, since they had auxiliary power, offered us a tow over. This was just as well as Vic was in no fit state for any sailing, however short.

"I'm beginnin' ter think 'e'll 'ave ter go," Skipper Day confided in me.

Once alongside loading proceeded quite rapidly, the Bermondsey dockers having marginally more enthusiasm than their counterparts in the enclosed docks. I had a look round at the other craft loading from the ship. Two of them were canal barges which served the country's network of canals. These craft were highly and prettily decorated. The artwork extended from the slab sides of their cabins to their tillers, to their funnels and even to some of the utensils in use aboard such as buckets and kettles. Much of it depicted roses and other flowers and, strangely, castles. They seemed to be manned by complete families, the bargees' wives and children all being aboard.

Captain Day saw me studying these ornate vessels.

"Them's bargees," he said. "That's summat a lot o' people what don't know git wrong. Bargees are off canal craft, lighterman work the dumb barges on the Thames, but us, on the sailormen, we're bargemen. 'Appen anyone calls us bargees, they can just stand by, that's all."

He changed the subject and nodded at the Bermondsey hinter-land.

"Jacob's Island over there somewhere. That's where ould Bill Sykes got killed and Fagin ran 'is outfit."

This was an obvious reference to Charles Dickens 'Oliver Twist' which, strangely, I remembered well.

"You know Dickens, then?" I asked.

"Oh yus. Allus readin' 'is stuff. Good ould writer 'e is."

Surprising people, sometimes these bargemen.

Next day we finished loading and were able to sail in mid-afternoon. We were only able to reach the Southend anchorage that night, but next day had a good, fast passage to Upshore in a moderate southerly.

As we moored up at the Town Quay, Hooker the sailmaker's van drew up. The one-eyed sailmaker jumped down from the passenger seat.

"Where've yew bin?" he asked Captain Day. "Yer sails 'ave bin ready fer two days."

"Bin earnin' a livin', that's wot. Can't wait arahnd fer no lazy ould sailmaker."

Hooker ignored that. "Where do yer want yer sails?"

"Jibs can go dahn the foc's'le for the minit. 'Appen yew git a move on, yew can change the topsails directly minit. Lumpers won't start till termorrer."

I didn't wait to see the operation of changing topsails, for there was someone I had to see in the office.

"Hallo, come to do some invoices?" was her greeting.

"Never miss a chance, do you? But I've given them up."

I had a job not to kiss her in front of Mr. Oram and the other staff. There was a new office boy, or lad, called Sam. Ellie introduced me, saying mischievously that I was his predecessor who had been sacked for inefficiency.

"I see you've got your new sails," she said. "If you're not too busy admiring them we could have a little walk this evening."

"That's the first sensible thing you've said."

When I returned to Daisy Maud, Hooker and his men were just leaving.

"We'll come back termorrer an' give them jibs a try," said the sailmaker. "Shouldn't git in the way of the lumpers too much."

"'Ave ter watch the weather, though," said Captain Day. "No good tryin' ter do that in a capful o' wind."

Hooker sniffed the air. "Should be orl right," was his weather forecast.

The next morning Daisy Maud was a hive of activity. The lumpers confined their activities to the main hold, leaving the foredeck clear for the testing of the jibs. But first, Voracious, moored immediately ahead of Daisy Maud, had to be hove up the quay to give enough room for us to lower our steeved up borsprit. Once this had been done, Hooker and his top hand bent on the jibs with the assistance of Vic and myself. This operation was carefully watched by Captain Day.

But I became aware of another watcher. A big car had drawn up on the quay opposite and a large, florid man in a loud check suit alighted. As he watched our activities he lit a large cigar with exaggerated care. He was every inch a bookmaker and could only be Vic's persecutor, Mr. Pocock.

Captain Day wet one finger in his mug of tea and held it up to test the wind. It was light and off shore.

"Let's try 'em," said the skipper.

The two jibs were run up and filled gently with the breeze. Daisy Maud stirred against the quay. Captain Day jumped ashore to observe them better. He walked backwards across the quay, studying the sails, and almost collided with the bookmaker, who had moved closer.

"Can us 'elp yew?" asked the skipper.

"You can't, but 'e can," Pocock pointed at Vic with his cigar then raised his voice so that Vic could hear. "Either you pays up, straight away, an' you can stay away from my missus or I'm comin' after you! No fifth-rate London mobsters this time. Me. An' I can be unpleasant, most unpleasant!"

He symbolically dropped the remains of his cigar on the quay and ground it into the surface with his heel.

"An' there's interest ter pay, a lot of interest."

He stalked off to his car and drove away.

"Friend o' yours, Vic?" Captain Day asked sarcastically.

Vic had gone pale. "I'll sort 'im aht, don't worry. 'E's all wind and piss." His expression did not back up this statement.

186

"What abaht the sails?" asked Hooker.

"You done well, there, me ould mate," said the skipper, "or your lads did, rather. Let's jus' 'ope the torps'l's as good."

But I was still thinking of Pocock's words: "Stay away from my missus" he had said. So Vic had been busy there too. This would account for some of the unexplained absences and swings in mood. Perhaps our mate was attracted to another man's wife. By the sound of things Pocock had more than gambling debts to avenge.

Unusually, Captain Day stayed aboard Daisy Maud after Hooker and his assistant had gone. All that had to be done was the supervision of the lumpers, and this could easily have been carried out by Vic or myself. Vic took the opportunity to disappear somewhere.

At lunchtime the skipper produced a box of sandwiches and fruit, no doubt prepared by Mrs. Day, which he shared with me. Ellie called over to enquire how the demonstration of the new sails had gone, but did not stay long. After lunch Captain Day lit his pipe, accepted a mug of tea from me, and showed every sign of settling down for the afternoon.

He began to reminisce about barge matches and particularly of Everard's famous Veronica. She had been known to sail at fourteen knots in one match and the following tugs and viewing vessels had been unable to keep up with her. When she finished a reporter asked her skipper what it was like to sail at such a fast speed.

"Why, I'll tell yer this much, me ould son," replied the skipper, "she was 'eeled over so far I didn't need no two legs, one an' a stump would've done."

Everards were always experimenting with Veronica and for one Match provided her with a Bermudan mizzen instead of the traditional spritsail one. After the match the owners wanted to know what help the new sail had been.

"Oh! I dunno," said the skipper, "that just slatted an' banged be'ind me all the way rahnd. So I jis' went ahead an' won the Match anyway."

While Captain Day had been telling me these stories a group of bargemen had assembled on the quay opposite Daisy Maud. They included Ned who, during the continued absence of Captain Gascoigne, was now being paid a skippers' retainer to stand by Alicia, while she had a thorough refit at the bargeyard. Whatever was going on, I thought, must be important for Ned to desert his post at the yard.

Captain Day stood up and stretched.

"'Appen we'd better go up an' see what's a goin' on," he said.

The tide had now dropped, so the skipper went up the iron ladder on to the quay. By the time I followed him he had joined the group, which was now augmented by the lumpers.

"Stay there, young Bill," he said as I reached the quay side. He was evidently now going to be spokesman for the group, and seemed somewhat embarrassed.

"Well, it's like this . . . " he began, "we reckoned you might 'ave a job findin' the money fer a ring fer Miss Ellie – yew know, engagement, like. So the lads 'ad a bit of a whip-round like . . . "

Ned handed him a small package.

"Us an' those what's away, like Tommy an' Ike, an' we goes ter the blacksmith dahn at the yard – jool'ry a 'obby of 'is like – an' 'e made up this."

He proffered me the package. There was a small ripple of applause.

"Open it," said Ned.

I did so. Inside was a roughly-hewn ring, made of, I thought, brass. A stone of an indefinable nature was set into it. It twinkled in the sunlight.

"Speech," someone called out.

It was my turn to be embarrassed.

"Oh, thank you," I managed to get out. "Thank you all and those that can't be here." There was more applause.

After that the men drifted away and Captain Day, still rather embarrassed announced he was off home.

The temptation was to dash over to the office and present it to Ellie straight away, but I decided that this should be a private ceremony and best left till I met her in the evening. During the afternoon I took the ring out of its box every now and again and gazed at it. The lumpers glanced at each other knowingly.

I thought the ring was the best gift in the world.

And so did Ellie when I slipped it on her engagement finger in the quiet of the trees that evening.

"Oo, Bill!" she said when we had finished kissing. "It's lovely. Thank you. Thank You. I shall wear it always, I promise."

I had already explained about the bargemen's collection, but it made no difference. The ring sealed our relationship and she was delighted with it.

"We must go to the King's Head," she said suddenly.

"Why?"

"To thank people, silly, and buy some drinks. But don't worry, we'll take it slowly. Plenty of time for cuddling and that."

I did not imagine that 'and that' referred to sex. For some reason Ellie, who usually initiated it, had been avoiding this activity since our night on Daisy Maud on the buoy. I assumed that she considered it not something that engaged couples indulged in.

So we made out way to the King's Head pausing now and again for a clinch.

"There's an ominous event, tomorrow," she said between two of these intervals.

"The return of Brother John," I guessed.

"Exactly. The Pride and Silverfish and Reed Warbler are all due tomorrow. The other two have got cargoes but Pride will go straight on the yard so hopefully John will be too busy standing over Ernie and making Mr. Bliss' life hell to bother us. But we'll ignore him anyway, won't we?"

She smiled at me.

"Come here, 'All Tit and Legs'," I said.

It was quite late when we eventually reached the pub. We headed straight for the snug in the hopes that Captain Day would be there. He was, with Mrs. Day. Ellie immediately showed them the ring and in no time at all, Rosie and her two barmaids came out from behind the bar to have a look as well. The air was loud with female excitement.

"Wimmen," Captain Day said to me.

With Mrs. Day offering to make a wedding dress, Florrie and Pat volunteering to be bridesmaids and Rosie suggesting the King's Head as a venue for the reception, our wedding could almost have been arranged on the spot. But Ellie calmed them down, and said it was too early yet, and for the moment, she merely wished to buy some drinks. The bar staff took the hint and returned behind the bar to the delight of some farmers in the saloon who had been waiting to order.

After we had settled the skipper with a pint and Mrs. Day with a stout, we moved on the public bar. Here we found both Ned and the blacksmith. The latter, like many in his profession, was a huge man with an immense capacity for beer. It was hard to imagine his spatulate fingers fashioning anything as delicate as the ring. It fitted exactly, Ellie told him, either he had been lucky or some research had gone on that she did not know about.

"Ah, Miss, trade secret, that," he said.

"I'd like to buy you a gallon," she offered.

"Oh! I'd drink it, Miss, no worries, but I'll settle fer a pint. It was me pleasure ter do the ring."

"Make it two pints."

"Done, Miss."

Freshly supplied with beer, the blacksmith returned to his game of darts. Next, we talked to Ned after Ellie had supplied him, too, with a pint. I was surprised to find that the young mate-cum-pianist was ambitious. He was hoping that George Gascoigne continuing absence might mean that he would become a skipper, if not of Alicia, then of one of the other barges.

"I don't wish the old wind-bag any 'arm miss," he said. "But it can't go on. 'Im being sick all the time."

Ellie was not to be drawn on this subject.

"You ought to go into show business, Ned. Versatile pianist, like you."

"Oh, no miss. That's an 'obby. Bargin's me life. Wish I could crew in this Barge Match, though."

"Well, there could be vacancies, yet."

"I 'ope so."

The blacksmith had finished his darts.

"Fancy a game, Miss? You and your fiancé 'gainst me an' Ned." Now, here, I thought after a while, is something Ellie is not good at. She was fortunate to get all three darts in a throw on the board. I, on the other hand, was lucky obtaining scores like treble sixteen several times. In the end we were left with double twenty to win, while our opponents, who had played a more skilful game, wanted double sixteen. Then it was Ellie's turn, and, closing her eyes in concentration, she threw her first dart straight into the double twenty.

So then the losers had to buy the winners a drink, and then Ellie felt she had to redress the balance and buy them another. Then it was closing time and we went into the night.

"Are you sure you're all right to drive?" I asked Ellie when we reached the car, parked by the Jolly Fisherman.

"Oh, yes," she said. "I only had shandies. Pity Tommy and the others weren't there, but it was still a good engagement party, wasn't it? Now you come here, silly."

CHAPTER 18

VIC'S UNDOING

Both Silverfish and Reed Warbler arrived next morning. Silverfish replacing Voracious ahead of us and Reed Warbler coming in astern of us.

As soon as Silverfish was moored up Tommy came down the quay for a word.

"Your gel get 'er ring orlright?" he asked. I told him that we were delighted with it and thanked him and Ike for their contributions. Then I asked him whether he had seen Pride of Upshore and John Fowler anywhere.

"Oh, yus. We sailed up river wiv 'im. Yew could 'ear 'im shoutin and a-bawlin' at 'is poor mate an' third 'and all over the river. Reckon 'e's gettin' worse."

This did not sound like good news. Jan arrived and reported that the Pride had gone into the bargeyard.

"Say a prayer for them poor buggers dahn at the yard," said Tommy.

"Is it good, the ring?" asked Jan and again I issued thanks. Later Ellie came over and conducted an impromptu quayside meeting with Tommy, Old Hoary and Captain Day, who had just arrived.

"As soon as these three barges are empty," she said. "They'll join Voracious in lighterage work. That will keep them here for the Barge Match."

"What sort o' lighterage, miss?" asked Hoary.

It should be explained that there were two types of lighterage work on the River Whitewater. Both involved the carriage of timber from ships moored lower down in the river. Some of it came up to Fuller's Wharf opposite the Town Quay whilst the rest went to wharves in the Corchester Canal further down river. This latter operation was the preserve of ancient sailing barges which were stripped of their gear and used as pure lighters. For a full-rigged barge to be employed on this work would be a disgrace, and as the skipper of Fowler's oldest sailing barge, Hoary was right to be concerned, as such employment might spell the end for Reed Warbler.

Ellie put his mind at rest, though.

"It's all to Fuller's," she said. "And there's plenty of it fortunately. The only snag is, we'll have to pay skippers and mates a weekly wage while you're on it. You'd cost us a fortune on the freight system, doing a cargo per day!"

There were no arguments with this as it was obviously more reliable than the freight system of shares. But these arrangements would not affect me for I was already on my weekly wage of 2/6d. paid by Captain Day. And this brought me back to something that had been worrying me for sometime. This was no wage on which to support a wife. True Ellie had considerable private means and her salary as Fowler & Dunn's manager. But she might not always be in a position to work and I had no desire to be a 'kept' man. I resolved to seek a mate's berth. Jan had done it without the advantage of first being a third hand. So why shouldn't I? Especially with Ellie behind me, if only I could convince her that I was not interested in office work.

After Ellie had gone, Captain Day said:

"There's summat missin'."

"The dog?" I suggested.

"Nah! 'E always goes ashore in port. I meant the mate. When did you last see 'im?"

I was now so used to Vic's erratic comings and goings in Upshore I had to think about this, although Mrs. Pocock was a likely answer. In the end I said that it was the previous morning before the ring presentation.

"So much for lyin' low," said the skipper succinctly. "'E's gettin' worse."

And that made two of them.

Vic returned that afternoon, as usual offering no explanation as to where he had been. He seemed very depressed again. I could only assume that he had been making another unsuccessful attempt to raise the money to pay Mr. Pocock his remaining outstanding debt. I told him of the lighterage work and, of course, he had a good moan about that and then lapsed into a gloomy silence. I was relieved to depart in the evening to meet Ellie.

As Ellie and I walked amount the trees that evening, I asked her what John's reaction to our engagement had been.

"Amused disbelief sums it up," she said. "For the moment anyway. He cannot believe that I am serious about a third hand off a barge. He says that he's going to find me a proper husband – probably the son of some rich farmer, I expect. Ernie's been telling him what a nice lad you are and how he's sure we're serious but John just told him to get back to his boatbuilding and concentrate on a proper refit for the Pride, 'cos he means to win this Match. I think he's a bit preoccupied with that at the present."

"And when he realises that we mean it?"

"Oh! He'll be angry all right. Probably step up his hunt for a suitor. May even try and stop us seeing each other. But he'll find that impossible, won't he?"

I agreed. I was sure that Ellie would have many ways of getting round any such ban and, in any case, we could still meet in the course of our work and John would not always be at home. Ernie, I was sure, was now on our side.

"Talking of suitors," Ellie went on. "I had a letter from that David Fox. You know, Reuben's grandson."

"Oh, yes."

"He wants to meet me somewhere, Very impressed with me, apparently. That's what comes of me baring my shoulders."

"I dread to think what he would have written if he'd seen what I've seen."

I pulled her towards me.

The next day we commenced lighterage work. Ellie was right, we could do one freight per day if we were lucky. The timber ships, which were too big or of too deeper draught to reach Fuller's Wharf, anchored in a deep spot about two miles down river. Here the stevedores used the ships' own gear to load the cargoes, sometimes of logs and sometimes of sawn timber, into the barges. Whatever the weather the passage to Fuller's Wharf was a fast one. As soon as the tide had flooded sufficiently we would leave the anchorage. If the wind was strong enough, we would sail to Fuller's Wharf. If not a motor-boat would be on hand to tow us up. Naturally Captain Day refused this assistance if at all possible.

Once at Fuller's, discharge was fast as the wharf was well mechanised and the timber was urgently needed for the construction of houses in the Upshore district. So it was possible to do a complete cargo in a day. Sometimes Daisy Maud had to be left down on the anchorage for the night. When this happened we could hitch a lift to Upshore on the stevedores' tug. A bed for the night could either be had on one of the other barges or in the King's Head, where Rosie was quite prepared to let me have a room, free of charge.

Of course, the new sails had plenty of use. On the first occasion, Captain Day surveyed the new topsail critically.

"'E done good in the end, that one-eyed ould bugger," was his verdict. "That's a corker. Match winner that, I'll wager." So we put the lot up, with the bowsprit down, and the new jibs billowing out. The only sour note came from Vic, of course.

"Bloody daft this," he said. "Borsprit barge wiv everything up ter sail two miles."

He had taken to staying aboard the barge again, whether she was at Fuller's or down at the anchorage. He was obviously frightened of something. I was sure it had to do with Pocock's threats but if the bookmaker had made any move, I was not aware of it. Then one day he suddenly took me into his confidence. He produced a tatty piece of paper from his jacket pocket.

"I found this stuck to the foc's'le scuttle jis' before we started on the lighterage."

I took the paper from him. Written on it in crude letters was: "You won't be in the Barge Match. You won't be able to walk by then."

"Pocock?" I asked.

"'Spec so."

"So that's why you're staying aboard."

"I ain't takin' no chances."

I tried to console him. "He's only trying to frighten you into paying. This is Upshore not Chicago."

"Well I ain't got the money, so I'm stayin' aht o' the way."

"Do it your way then."

The lighterage work meant that, not only did I have the evenings free, but also most of the time at weekends and sometimes I was finished fairly early on weekday afternoons, so I was able to see quite a bit of Ellie. We had our evening strolls amount the trees, drives into the country, and times in the King's Head or Jolly Fisherman. We also had another nude swim from our private beach. We played around with each other afterwards, but again no sex, not then or at any other time. Brother John was rarely seen, for both Ellie and I thought it unwise for me to visit the house and, in any case, his time was probably fully taken up with the Pride.

One afternoon Ellie decided to teach me to sail her lugsail dinghy. I met her at the small upstream boatyard where she kept it. By the time I arrived she had the little boat ready and was dressed in what seemed to her normal sailing garb if the weather was not too cool, a one-piece swim-suit. This did everything for her figure, but I couldn't help wondering what she'd look like in a bikini.

It was quite cramped with two people in such a small boat but it was friendly enough. She sailed the boat down clear of the wharves and then said to me:

"You take over."

We swopped places and I took the tiller. After about five minutes she said: "You're a natural. I'm not having to tell you a thing." She gave me a knowing look. "You've done this before, haven't you?"

"Only in much bigger yachts." I answered without realising what I was saying. She gave me a penetrating look.

"You're memory's comin' back, isn't it?"

"What do you mean?"

"You've just said you've sailed bigger yachts."

"I meant the barges and the barge's boat."

"But you wouldn't have called them yachts." But her tone conveyed doubt and she didn't mention the subject again. We didn't let it spoil our afternoon.

But I laid awake worrying that night. I was obviously having odd snippets of recall. I had once mentioned aerodynamics to Captain Day and, more recently and in fairly quick succession I had recalled the works of Charles Dickens, remembered the rules of the game of darts, talked of sailing larger yachts and thought of Ellie in a bikini. And I knew, in my own mind, that a bikini was a brief two piece bathing costume and unheard of in the Essex of 1939. I was afraid – scared that if my memory came back fully, I might lose something precious.

All too quickly we were on our last lighterage voyage. Only two days remained to the barge Match. On our way up to Fuller's we saw Northdown, one of the competitors, arriving. She joined Pride of Upshore, now fully refitted on Fowler's buoy, which was reserved for competitors.

"Look's like John an' 'is crew are still workin'," said Zeke, who had arranged his river bailiff duties so that he could join us for this trip – "ter get the feel o' things."

We could hear John bawling at his mate across the water.

"They'll be tired aht, by the time o' the Match," said Captain Day. "Wi' any sort o' luck. Me, I'm going ter tek it easy. Git me 'ead dahn a lot."

We moored up at Fuller's and, as usual, unloading commenced immediately. But we weren't quite finished that evening. The tide had gone out, leaving our only access to the Town Quay and King's Head side of the river, the long walk round via the bridge. So I was somewhat surprised when Vic announced, after the evening meal, that he was going ashore.

"Isn't that risky?" I asked.

"Don't think so. Bin too long. Anyway I've got an important meetin'."

I was relieved, for Ellie had promised to drive down to Fuller's Wharf in the evening. Shortly after Vic had left she arrived. I had a cup of tea ready and we sat on the cabin top to drink it. Suddenly we became aware of Ike shouting and waving from the Town Quay opposite.

"Tommy sez can yew come to the King's 'Ead quick?" he managed to convey. We swallowed our tea and jumped in the car to drive round there, wondering what this could be about. I hoped that Vic wasn't in trouble.

Ike and Jan came over to the car when we pulled up on the quay.

"It's your brother John, Miss Ellie. 'E's in the saloon bar wiv Vic, We think they ain't up to no good."

"Why not. It's a free country."

"Yes, Miss. But Tommy an' Rosie reckon it's all ter do wiv yew an' young Bill 'ere."

"I'll go in and see what they've got to say," I decided. "You stay here with Ike and Jan." I added to Ellie.

"Oh, no," she said, "I want to know what's going on as well. I'll sit at the back of the public. They won't be able to see me there."

So we went into the public.

"You sit here, lovely lady," said Jan, ushering Ellie to the public's rearmost table. I went up to the bar where Tommy was talking to Rosie.

"See 'em?" asked Tommy. The heads of John and Vic could just be seen over the saloon counter.

"They've bin there some time," said Rosie, "natterin' an'

198

drinkin' whisky like billy-oh. Me an' the girls done our best to over'ear an' they was talkin' 'bout you an' Miss Ellie a lot."

"That's a dangerous combination, them two," said Tommy. "Wot yer goin' ter do?"

"All we can do is wait," I said. "See what happens."

"You go an' sit with Miss Ellie and the others," said Rosie. "I'll let yer know o' any changes."

We took the drinks over to Ellie, Jan and Ike and sat down to await events. The pub was quiet, the only other occupants being a group of old men playing crib. We sat and drank quietly for a while.

After a time Rosie came over and said: "John's gone, but that Vic's still there, drinkin' on 'is own. Seems ter be tryin' ter mek 'is mind up 'bout summat."

I had a sudden alarming thought that John would see Ellie's car outside. But did this matter? She was perfectly entitled to be out and about, whether in the King's Head or not and whether in my company or not and, in any event, there were several routes to wherever John had left his own car.

I went up to the bar to buy some more drinks. Vic saw me and waved but made no attempt to come round to the public. He certainly did seem preoccupied.

"I seen John giv 'im some money, earlier," Rosie whispered as she handed me the drinks. Again I rejoined the others for more quiet conversation.

Suddenly Rosie came out from behind the bar.

"'E's gorn," she said. "Up terwards the 'Igh Street, Florrie saw 'im aht of the winder. Yew oughta keep an eye on 'im, state 'e's in."

"Let's follow him," I said to Jan. "You stay with Tommy and Ike, Ellie."

"No, I'm coming too," she said.

I knew it was no good arguing with her, so the three of us ran out of the bar and into the road leading to the High Street. We could see Vic further up the road, lurching drunkenly along, but we were not the only ones following him. A saloon car was also going up the road very slowly about twenty yards behind him. I suddenly recognised it.

"That's Pocock's car. Vic, look out!"

As I spoke the car accelerated. Vic turned at my shout, saw the car racing at him, and managed to jump out of the way. The driver must have lost control, for the car mounted the pavement and struck a brick wall. Vic limped back and peered through the driver's window. The three of us reached the car and I elbowed Vic out of the way so that I could open the driver's door. Pocock was crouched over the steering wheel, evidently dazed rather than hurt.

"He is gone again," Jan said.

Vic had seized a brick from the broken wall and set off again, running awkwardly, for, alcohol apart, he had evidently hurt a leg in avoiding Pocock's car.

"Stay with Pocock," I told Jan then Ellie and I started running after Vic again.

"What the bloody 'ell is he up to now?" Ellie panted as we turned into the High Street.

"I think we're about to find out," I gasped.

Vic had stopped in front of a shop-front and raised the brick above his head.

"Vic, don't do it!" I yelled.

Too late. With a cry of "Bastard!" Vic heaved the brick into the shop's window. Glass flew in all directions, a sliver catching Vic on his bare forearm. By the time we reached him, he was holding his injured arm with his other hand, blood running through his fingers.

"Let me look," said Ellie, "I've done some first-aid."

"Why did you . . . " I began, then realised the name over the shop was 'Pocock'.

"That's a nasty cut," said Ellie. "It'll need stitches."

"I'm sorry, I'm sorry," said Vic. "It was yer brother, Miss. 'E made me . . . "

We were almost opposite Upshore Police Station, and now two policemen arrived, one a sergeant, the other Caroline's husband.

200

They grabbed both me and Vic, thinking we were both responsible.

Ellie, who was making her headscarf into a tourniquet round Vic's arm, protested that she and I were only witnesses.

"Sarge, this is Miss Eleanor Fowler," said Pc Murphy.

"Sorry, Miss. You an' your boyfriend carry on. We'll let you know if we want statements. I daresay Mr. Pocock will want to bring charges."

This reminded me. I told the sergeant there was a wrecked car around the corner that might be of interest.

"Bleeder tried ter kill me," said the unfortunate Vic.

"You get this one off to the cottage hospital, Murphy. Nasty cut that, need stitches when 'e sobers up. Now you show me this car, young man."

By the time we reached the car, Pocock was sitting on the kerb, being tended to by Jan and a lady from a neighbouring house. Tommy and Ike and several others had arrived out of curiosity.

"This gets better by the minute," said the sergeant. "I 'ear you tried to kill someone, Mr. Pocock."

Pocock shook his head.

"There's three witnesses to that," said Ellie.

"Then we'll definitely want some statements. Let's all go up to the station and sort this out."

We spent the rest of the evening and part of the night at the police station making statements on both incidents.

"I dunno what Pocock will be charged with," said the sergeant as we left. "That's up to the inspector, when 'e comes in. But we've been after 'im for sometime. Attempted murder, would be nice. As for your friend, 'e ain't likely to get off scot-free, 'e'll be charged with summat, as well."

"What are you going to do?" I asked Ellie as she, Jan and I walked back to the waterfront.

"How do you mean?" she asked.

"About going home. We don't know what Vic was telling John and it sounds as though he may have been paying Vic for information. You don't know what sort of reception you'll get at home, especially since it's so late."

"I'm not worried," she said. "With any sort of luck he's in bed and asleep. If not, I'll brazen it out. He can check with the police about tonight."

"Vic. He will not be able to sail in the Match," said Jan.

"That's true," I said, wondering whether my friend had hopes of taking Vic's place.

We had reached Ellie's car.

"Sorry, Jan," I said. "This is turning private. I'll see you in the morning."

CHAPTER 19

CONFRONTATION

Early next morning the last of our timber was lifted out and Captain Day and I moved Daisy Maud over to the Town Quay. As a local competitor we were to lie there for the night before the Match, an honour not accorded to Pride of Upshore, from which I concluded that the river bailiff was another of John's growing band of enemies. Silverfish and Reed Warbler were the other two barges there and Bully's Resolve was to join us later that day. No doubt Bully had pulled some strings to obtain this berth as all other competitors were to lay either on the barge-yard buoy or the Home Reach buoy.

Captain Day was annoyed at Vic's absence, so I gave him a brief resume of the previous nights' events, adding: "He's either at the Cottage Hospital or the police station."

"'E won't be doin' no Barge Match then," said the skipper. "'Appen we'll go over the office when we're moored. Find aht the latest."

So later on we went over to the office. Ellie, rather to my surprise, seemed positively radiant. Yes, she said, she had heard from the police inspector. Pocock was being charged with attempted murder, but the inspector also felt that the bookmaker had clever lawyers and the charge would probably be reduced to something like dangerous driving. In any event, the inspector felt that Pocock was finished in Upshore.

As for Vic, he had spent the night at the Cottage Hospital, where he had had twelve stitches in his arm. He was also suffering from a twisted knee. He was now "assisting the police with their enquiries" and it was probable that he would be charged with malicious damage.

"That's that, then," said Captain Day. "'E won't be doin' no Barge Match. Reckon I'll 'ave to ask young Ned ter tek his place."

I was disappointed and it must have showed, for the skipper went on: "But I'll need a mate arter the Match, so 'appen young Bill be'aves 'imself, 'e might get a promotion – like."

"Oh! But I don't know that I could allow that," said Ellie, but she winked at me as she said it. And, bearing in mind my worries about becoming a married man, it was just what I needed.

Captain Day and I were about to leave when Ellie said: "Bill, can I have a word?" She looked round the office at Mr. Oram, Caroline and the new office boy, Sam. "In private."

We went into Isaac's old office. Whatever was troubling her was not bad news, that at least was obvious.

"Will you be aboard Daisy Maud, tonight?" she asked. "It will be a quiet night. Everybody will rest up before the Match."

I said that I certainly would be aboard as I had nowhere else to go.

"Good," she said. "I've got something important to tell you."

"What's wrong with telling me now?"

"Walls have ears," she said mysteriously.

She obviously wasn't going to tell me until the evening, so I changed the subject.

"How's John been?" I asked.

"Very quiet. But he gave me a lost of dirty looks at breakfast. I wouldn't worry about it. We're engaged and there's nothing he can do to change that."

We risked a quick kiss and then I went to catch up with Captain Day.

By the time we reached Daisy Maud, Resolve had moored

astern of her, containing Bully Briggs and his crew of lusty young Mistleymen. Bully stood on the mainhatch addressing the world.

"Splendid auld wheeze, that," he announced. "Windin' that barstard John up inter sendin' ould Reubin Fox dahn 'ere. Got everyone a-goin' that did. You goin' ter be busy Arthur?"

Captain Day replied that we had a few pre-match adjustments to make to Daisy Maud.

"Oh, yer'll need 'em orl right. Twelve o'clock me an' me crews goin' ter sort yer l'il ould pub aht. King's 'Ead, ain't it?"

Captain Day replied that he didn't drink on the day before a Match.

"Garn! That's evenin'. I don't drink then either, jus' eat ter keep me strength up. This is lunchtime. We gotta 'ave a few, 'cos termorrer, yew'll all be buyin' me drinks for winnin' an' then I'll drink gallons not pints. Twelve o'clock, yew an' yer lad be ready."

This seemed to be an offer we could not refuse, so we finished off the last minute tasks as quickly as decently possible.

In the event we reached the King's Head a little later than Bully and his crew. Naturally Bully had scorned the snug, preferring to drink with his lads in the public. In addition he had rounded up Daisy Maud's racing crew. Tommy, Zeke, Ike and even Ned, who had only just heard of his opportunity, were all there. As soon as he saw me, Bully let out a great shout.

"Young Bill! Rosie's jus' bin tellin' me about yew an' the lovely Ellie. Yew go an' get 'er, lad. Tell 'er ould Bully wants ter buy the 'appy couple a drink!"

Five minutes later I said to Ellie: "It's a sort of royal command."

"Well, I'm happy to obey it. I'd like a word about the Reuben Fox affair, anyway. Won't be long," she added to Mr. Oram.

"Ardent, Ailsa, Northdown, load of rubbish," Bully was saying as we entered the bar. "Yew others stand a l'il ould bit of a chance, but not much – Ah! Bill, Miss Ellie – congraterlations – wot yew goin' to 'ave?" We went up to the bar and ordered. Rather than heave his vast bulk out of his chair, Bully had appointed his mate treasurer of this event. The mate came over to the bar and paid for the drinks.

"Discussin' tactics," he said, jerking his thumb at Bully.

"An' while yer there," Bully bawled. "Ask Rosie 'ow me pies a comin' on. An' get Tommy another pint, 'e reckons 'e can outdrink me."

"Yew ain't a-thinkin' of nobblin' me mate, are you?" asked Captain Day.

"As though I'd do a thing like that," said Bully. "Where's Vic anyway?"

Ellie and I told the story. Rosie came from behind the bar bearing a huge pie for Bully.

"That's the ticket. Thank 'ee luv. Reckon Vic 'ad that a-comin' sooner or later." He took an enormous mouthful of pie. "Good, steak and kidney. Nah, that John, 'e needs 'is come-uppance an' all, nasty bit o' work. Beggin' yer pardon, Miss Ellie. Know 'e's yer bruver, but 'e ain't no good ter us bargemen."

"I'm not arguing," said Ellie. "You were behind that Reuben Fox business, weren't you?"

"Yeh! Good laugh that," He looked at his mate. "What abaht some more beer, then?"

"Well, it had us worried," Ellie persisted as glasses were re-filled.

"Yew worry too much, l'il lass. Ould Bully knew what'd 'appen. Reuben's an old fraud. Ain't that right, Arthur?"

After that the party went into top gear. Ned was persuaded to play the piano. Considerable quantities of beer were drunk. Bully led a raucous version of 'Alouette'. Tommy, feeling that he was being upstaged by Bully, then gave a truly terrible rendering of 'Danny Boy'. Bully ate two more pies and Ellie, who had been trying to go back to the office for some time, was made to pay a forfeit and sing a couple of verses of 'Just a Song at Twilight' before she was allowed to leave. Finally, Rosie drew the event to an end by announcing closing time.

We adjourned to the barges, where Captain Day and I finished off what we had been doing, to the strains of raucous singing from Resolve.

"Good job us took it easy on the beer," said the skipper. "Wouldn't 'ave got nuffin' done else."

Not that we did much other than drink tea anyway. Captain Day had just gone and the noise from Resolve was dying down when Jan arrived. He was sorry to have missed the lunchtime party, but Hoary had kept him busy aboard Reed Warbler.

"I came to wish you luck for tomorrow, my friend," he said. I explained that my position aboard Daisy Maud was purely as a tea-maker. I could take no active part in the race.

"Ah! But at least you will be there. I only watch."

A pleasure boat from Clacton had been chartered by the Match Committee for interested parties to follow the race. Jan had purchased a place aboard it.

"But, perhaps next year I will be able to sail," Jan went on, "but I fear not. Herr Hitler will make war." I said that I doubted that this would happen.

"Oh. But it will, my friend. I feel it here." He tapped himself in the breast area. He shook me rather formally by the hand.

"But I wish you luck once more. You and your beautiful lady both." He turned and walked away.

This was strange behaviour, even allowing for his European ways. It was almost as though he was saying goodbye.

After Jan had gone, I had nothing further to do but wait for Ellie to arrive with her mysterious news. Whatever it was, it didn't sound like bad news, neither did it seem to involve John.

I sat on the main-hatch speculating on what her announcement would be, until a shower drove me below to continue my thoughts lying on my bunk. I had no means of telling the time, but the clock on St. Michael's had read six-thirty when I had come below. I guessed that Ellie would not appear until about eight o'clock, after the evening meal at the house. I must have dozed off, for I was awakened by the sound of her footsteps on deck.

"Wake up, sleepy head," she said as she ran down the companionway. "Be a dear and make a cup of tea."

I busied myself with kettle, teapot, cups and tea for a while.

207

When I looked up, she had stripped to the waist. I was annoyed. Didn't she realise that there were people on the barges around us, who might drop in at any moment?

"Yes, dear," she replied demurely, "but you didn't see me shoot the inside bolt on the scuttle, because you were half-asleep. Now, this is important. Tell me, are my breasts any bigger?"

"That's not possible."

"I'm deadly serious."

"Well," I studded them. "You're probably nearer a thirty-eight than a thirty-six, now."

"I thought so, even allowin' for your exaggeration," she was getting excited. "An' I missed last month an' I've bin a bit sick some mornin's. Darling, we're goin' to have a baby, isn't it marvellous?"

I had to sit down. This I had not expected. She was still talking excitedly.

"We'll have to bring the wedding forward, of course. I don't want to be too big when I go up the aisle. I should be able to book St. Michael's quite quickly. The vicar's an old friend. Aren't you pleased?"

I was, indeed, pleased, but at the same time somewhat apprehensive about the future. I just hoped that Captain Day was serious about making me mate of Daisy Maud. Ellie sensed what I was thinking.

"I shan't give up my job," she said. "Not for long anyway. I can easily afford a nurse-maid."

I walked over and kissed her. There was a long pause.

"I can't get pregnant all over again," she whispered. My hands were already loosening the rest of her clothing. "Let's do it." Her clothes slid to the floor. Then I was throwing off my clothing.

Naked, we fell on to one of the bunks and I mounted her. Such was the intensity of our passion that we failed to hear angry footsteps on the deck overhead. The first we knew of the intruder was a splintering crash as the foc's'le scuttle was forced from the outside. We sprang apart as John charged down the companion ladder.

208

"I knew it!" he shouted. "Fornicating!"

Ellie sprang from the bunk.

"John! It's not as you think!"

"Shut up, you slut!" And he slapped her round the face with such force that she was sent sprawling across the other bunk, legs spread indecently. I threw myself upon him pummelling his body with all the force I could muster. But I quickly found that a naked man is at a distinct disadvantage when attacking a clothed one. John's huge left hand closed on my genitals and squeezed. The pain was incredible and as my resistance ceased his right hand pinioned my throat. He began to bend me backwards towards the deck. Through the red mist that swam before my eyes, I began to wonder which would happen first, would he break my back, strangle me or would the pain in my private parts carry me away? Suddenly there was a far off clang and John's grip loosened. We both fell to the floor, John landing across my legs. The mist cleared for an instant and I was aware of Ellie standing over John holding the shovel that was used for feeding the stove.

"I've killed him, Bill," she keened. "I've killed him."

Somehow I managed to pull my legs from under John and get on my hands and knees to examine him.

"He hit his head on the stove," Ellie sobbed.

"Still breathing," I managed to rasp and fell back to let the pains subside. After a while I felt as though I might live. "Better get dressed," I said in a horrible whisper. This was easy enough for Ellie, but for me it was obviously going to be a long and painful business. At last I managed to pull my trousers up.

"Get some help," I hissed at Ellie, who was now not only fully dressed, but had managed to stop crying. John was beginning to groan and stir. As Ellie ran up the companionway I pulled the shovel to me, ready for use again.

Ellie was soon back with Bully and his mate. Ike, too appeared from Silverfish, wondering what the commotion was.

"What the 'ell's been a-goin' on 'ere," Bully demanded, looking at the somewhat disturbed foc's'le.

"He broke in and assaulted us," I wheezed, judging that this was all he needed know.

"Yew want us to remove 'im?"

I nodded, for speaking was painful.

"It'll be a pleasure. Perfectly good 'orse trough back o' the quay. A drink in that'll bring 'im rahnd proper."

Ike and Bully's mate carried the still comatose John on deck. Bully was reduced to supervising as his bulk would have got in the way. We listened to the sounds of their departure.

"What if he comes back?" Ellie asked fearfully.

"Not yet, he won't," I managed. I thought for a minute.

"Will you be all right on your own for a minute?"

She nodded, but her eyes were full of fear and she pulled the shovel closer for protection.

I staggered aft to the cabin, every step setting my groin throbbing. If only I knew where the skipper hid the gun and its cartridges, I thought. But I didn't like to ransack the cabin looking for it. However, in the locker where we kept the cooking utensils was a carving knife, which I knew to be very sharp. I armed myself with it and staggered forrard again.

Back in the foc's'le I added it o the existing armoury of one stove shovel.

"What are we goin' to do?" asked Ellie. The incident seemed to have completely drained her. For the first time since I had first met her she was bereft of initiative, and seemed to be leaning on me. All of a sudden I had the roll of leader.

"Well, you can't go home tonight," I said. "You'll have to stay here."

"But he might come back," she said again. She now seemed truly terrified of her brother. I patted our weapons.

"He wouldn't dare," I said with more conviction than I felt.

At this point Ike returned. He had the good sense to announce himself, but nevertheless, I took no chances and had my weapons ready for use.

"We giv 'im a duckin' in the 'orse trough," said Ike. "That brought 'im rahnd orl right. Then Bully got a taxi to tek 'im

210

'ome." That was a relief, he was unlikely to return easily from there.

"Did he say anything?" I asked.

"Plenty, once 'e 'ad a taste o' the trough. Summat abaht we'll settle this on the water termorrer."

It was beginning to sound as though the 1939 Upshore Barge Match could become a grudge match. John had good reason to dislike most of those who would be aboard Daisy Maud – Captain Day for selling his shares, Zeke for the sacking episode which had led to Isaac's death, Ike for his role tonight, me for deflowering his sister, Ellie for several reasons and Tommy and Ned just because they supported the rest of us. It didn't take much effort on my part to work out that Vic had given John, possibly for money, a lurid account of the antics of me and Ellie. John, I suspected, had become slightly unhinged by his various humiliations, most of which involved Daisy Maud and her crew. Vic's news had been the final straw and he had followed Ellie to the barge this evening. Catching Ellie and I having sex had sent him over the edge and it was possible that he sexually desired his own sister. I shuddered as I thought that he might have killed both of us.

Ike saw the shudder and said: "Are yew two goin' ter be orl right? Yer welcome aboard Silverfish, Tommy'll be dahn later."

I declined his kind offer, as I felt Ellie and I had further plans to discuss, if she was up to it.

"Well, us'll be lookin' aht fer yew an' so will Bully an' 'is lads. Yer needn't be fearful ternight."

After that he left, with my profuse thanks.

"What are we going to do?" asked Ellie for the second time. I was becoming really worried about her. Was she having some sort of breakdown?

"You're staying here," I said, with an effort.

"Long term, silly," I glanced at her and she gave me a wicked grin. Thank God for that, she was recovering!

"Elopement is on the cards," I said. "After the Match while they're all celebrating, would be a good time. We could get married somewhere else."

"But, it will mean leavin' all this," she gestured around. "Our jobs and everythin'"

"We can come back as a married couple."

"We'll be together," she said, brightening. "That's the main thing."

I explained my views about John. She agreed with them, especially when I hinted that John himself desired her.

"I've wondered about that," she said. "Sometimes when I've sunbathed on the roof in the – you know – I've felt that someone's been watching. And he's barged into the bathroom when I've been in there. Fuckin' sauce!"

Now that was more like the old Ellie.

We had one more visitor that night. This time it was Ernie and he, too, had the sense to announce himself so that we relaxed our grip on our weapons. He had a small suitcase with him.

"I've brought you some clothes and things," he said to Ellie. "Mainly warm clothes. You'll probably need them tomorrow for the Match." Ellie was only clad in a summer dress and sandals. "Best you stay here tonight. The way John is talking, I'd fear for your safety at home."

I told him we had come to the same conclusion. He then asked what would we do after the Match. I told him we intended to go away for a while and get married.

"Pity," he said. "I was looking forward to giving my little sister away. Still it's wise." He gave Ellie a searching look. "You're expecting, aren't you?" Ellie nodded.

"I'll put some more of your things in your car tomorrow when I come down for the Match." We'd forgotten the car parked on the quay. Ernie went on: "But you needn't stay away for long. John hasn't many friends left – only his own crew and a few cronies like Captain Brewster. I'm sure Rupert Dunn and I can keep him away from Upshore until you are settled. As for your job Eleanor, Oram and Caroline should be able to hold the fort until you get back, even if it means the old boy postponing his retirement." He looked at me. "And you, young man, are dependent on Captain Day, if he wants you as mate. But I'll have a word with him, perhaps he'll sail with temporary mates until you return."

I thought that under Ernie's vague and quiet exterior, there lived a much shrewder person. He was, by a long way, the best of Ellie's relations.

Shortly after that he left and we took the opportunity to shift into the cabin aft. If Captain Day didn't like this, too bad, I thought. The cabin with its hatch intact was more secure and I took additional comfort from the fact that the gun was somewhere in this area.

We slept in each others arms that night, but not for sexual reasons. My crotch was far too sore for that sort of thing. And we did not sleep well. My various injuries kept me awake and Ellie evidently had nightmares and woke up crying several times. I eventually drifted off to sleep, hoping that the next day would not bring any more unpleasant dramas

CHAPTER 20
THE MATCH

We were up early on the morning of the match, partly to tidy the cabin and partly to start the breakfast that we were sure the racing crew would want when they arrived between seven o'clock and half-past. Ellie now had quite a good bruise on the side of her face, but at least the pain of my own injuries had eased and I was able to move around better. We were just sorting out bacon and eggs when I heard footsteps on deck. Automatically I reached for the carving knife, but I caught a whiff of pipe tobacco and realised it was Captain Day.

We both went on deck and found him studying the damage to the foc's'le scuttle.

"What 'appened 'ere?" he asked, and then saw our bruises. "'An what 'appened to yew two?"

We gave him an edited version of the previous night's events.

"Ah, see," he said when we had finished. "I 'opes us sails that bugger John inter the ground, terday."

Zeke arrived next.

"Yew look the part, Miss Ellie," he said. Ellie was sensibly dressed in Guernsey, trousers and plimsolls. Ernie had also provided her with an oilskin similar to Vic's. "Nasty ould bruise, though," Zeke went on.

"John did that," said Captain Day grimly.

"Did 'e now. 'Appen I sees 'im ashore ternight 'ell 'ave a worse'n, even if I 'as ter tek me leg orf ter do it."

It struck me that John's actions had actually done much for the fighting spirit of Daisy Maud's crew, at least as far as Pride of Upshore was concerned.

Tommy and Ike arrived from Silverfish and Ned from Alicia in the barge yard. Captain Day sniffed the wind and addressed all of us.

"Light westerly, we'll sail dahn ter the start. No moty boats. So let's get 'er ready." The rest of the crew dispersed and he then addressed himself particularly to Ellie and I.

"Yew two, are 'ere official like, jus ter do the caterin'. That don't mean yer can't keep yer eyes open an' let me or Zeke know what's a-goin' on. Nah – breakfast. Jus' bring some bacon an' eggs in sandwiches-like an' send 'em on deck. We'll all be busy."

This was most unusual for the skipper, breakfast was normally eaten at the cabin table or at least off a plate on the cabin-top. Even the sail down to the start was being taken seriously.

The start was off Hibbert's Island. Or rather two starts, for the staysail class would start at eight-forty-five with our class, the bowsprits, a quarter of an hour later at nine o'clock. The course would take us to the outer reaches of the River Whitewater, round the Bench Buoy and back up to Hibbert's Island to finish more or less where we started. In the event of persistent light winds the course would be shortened and we would be instructed to round a buoy not so far downriver.

By the time I took the first serving of egg and bacon sandwiches on deck, we were ghosting slowly down river and were off the barge yard buoy. Only one barge remained there - Pride of Upshore. All hands were studying her.

"Perhaps she ain't goin'," said Tommy.

"But they're gettin' the sails ready," said Ned.

"No sign o' John aboard," Ike added.

"'Appen the mates goin' ter sail 'er or Brewster," was Zeke's opinion.

215

"There's that John now," said Captain Day. "'E's a-goin' orf ter 'er in the yard moty-boat."

"They'll be late," said Tommy.

"That's good."

I went below to where Ellie was slaving over the stove to produce the rest of the breakfasts and told her about her brother.

"I hope the bloody Pride sinks," she said.

I took the rest of the sandwiches on deck and this time went forrard to where Tommy and Ike were now studying Ardent and Resolve who were about one hundred yards ahead of us.

"Nice day for it," said Tommy, taking his sandwich.

"Skipper sez that'll blow later," said Ike gloomily.

Across the saltings we could see the high ground of Hibbert's Island and the sails of the staysail barges as they waited for their start.

"We'll be able ter see 'em when we gets rahnd the next bend," said Tommy. "Mebbe pick up some tips for our start."

Ike was still thinking about Captain Day's weather forecast.

"Won't need no jibs if it blows," he said dolefully.

The crew arrangement was that Tommy would be in charge forrard with Ike and Ned to help him. The headsails would be their responsibility and also the topsail, if need be. They would largely operate from the mast deck between the two holds. Captain Day, would, of course, be steering and he and Zeke would also look after the mainsheet, mizzen, the two leeboard winches and the two vangs which controlled the end of the sprit. Zeke, in his capacity as mainsheet hand, would also be tactical adviser to Captain Day. With so much depending on the two men aft, Tommy would send one of his men aft to help them if necessary. This would probably be Ned, who would also be the one to go out on the borsprit if required. In this respect Ned was a useful addition to the official crew, for he was the youngest and fittest member.

Her stint at the stove finished, Ellie had come on deck and had gone to sit on the cabin-top aft. I went and joined her. She was staring astern at Pride of Upshore which was now setting full sail

216

for her run down to the start. Ellie's lips were moving and I though that she must be putting a curse on the Pride and her brother.

"Sorry," she said. "I was miles away."

"'E'll be late fer the start," said Captain Day, referring to the Pride.

"Does that mean he's out?" Ellie asked hopefully.

"Nah! Jist be'ind the rest o' us. It's bein' too early fer the start yew gotta watch."

"What happens then?" I asked.

"Yew teks a time penalty."

"No recalls, as in yacht-racing?"

Captain Day gave me a strange look. "Nah, we ain't yachts."

There it was again. I was remembering yacht racing. Could this Barge Match bring my memory back?

Now we could see the starting area off the island. The staysail barges were milling about in anticipation of their five minute warning gun. There were six of them. That meant the combined entry of the two classes in the Match was thirteen. I hoped that this reputedly unlucky number was not an omen.

Nearer at hand Surrey, Ailsa and Northdown were tacking too and fro, waiting for the staysails to start and for the other bowsprit barges to join them.

"Gun!" said Zeke, as a puff of smoke appeared from the open bridge of the tug that was acting as Committee Boat. The report of the discharge arrived seconds later.

"Allus go on the smoke. Yer see that, afore yer hears the bang." Zeke added, winding a large alarm clock which was to be our timepiece. "They've borrowed cannons from a yacht club. Mek a much better sound than an 'ooter".

"They ain't tekin' no chances," said Captain Day. All the staysails were staying well up-tide of the Committee boat.

"They're goin' fer it, now," said Zeke, as his alarm clock said one minute to the starting time. "That leadin' one'll get a penalty if 'e ain't careful."

And as the starting gun went it was obvious that one barge was over the line. We heard a massed groan from Ardent.

"Gotta be the Thames & Medway entry," Zeke guessed. "Make them lads on Ardent try 'arder."

Now it was the bowsprit barges' turn to manoeuvre for their start.

"That clock was right at the staysail's start," said Zeke.

"Let's 'ope it don't bloody stop, then," Captain Day said with a glance at Ellie, who giggled.

Ardent and Resolve had both sailed across the starting line. Captain Day felt that this was risky as, if the wind dropped, the ebb tide might prevent them getting back in time. The ten minute gun was fired.

"Surrey's comin' across, skipper," Tommy shouted from forrard. "'E's got right o' way."

"That's orl right, we'll tack."

It was noticeable that, whereas Vic and Captain Day had normally sailed in silence, each knowing roughly when to expect a tack, Captain Day was now punctilious in announcing his intentions with "Ready abaht, lee-oh," and "Leggo" when he judged that the bowline had done its job of backing the foresail to spin the barge's bows round.

The five minute gun went.

"Anyone near us?" the skipper demanded.

Zeke, Ellie and I looked round. Resolve and Ardent had gone inshore of the committee boat, intending to tack and just clear the tug on the side nearest wind and tide - a dangerous tactic but one that could pay well. Surrey was level with us but on the opposite side of the river about one hundred yards upstream of the start. Northdown and Ailsa, both nervous of the Whitewater tide, were further upstream, while Pride still had about seven minutes sailing to reach the start. We reported all this to Captain Day. I suddenly had a vision of large yachts starting a race.

"Go, skipper," I said. "Go."

"Go?" he said.

"Go for the starting line. You'll be just right."

"An' what if the wind freshens?"

218

"Spill some."

"That ain't easy in a barge. Anyhow let's giv 'er a try."

We bore away for the line. Zeke adjusted the vangs and Ned ran aft to help with the leeboard winches. Somewhere, seemingly right over the borsprit, the cannon went off.

"We're over!" shouted Zeke. His alarm clock read nine o'clock and five seconds.

"Well, that's the cup for fastest start under our belts," said Captain Day. "Well done, all. Get 'er up Tommy."

But Tommy was already hoisting the topmast staysail which had been dropped while we gibed for the start, and Zeke was already turning the boat into a little wind-scoop for the run downriver. This last struck me as rather a futile exercise, since all the competitors would do it. But no doubt whoever did it fastest would gain the most from it.

While the foredeck crew boomed out the jibs to Captain Day's satisfaction Ellie and I looked round to see how the others had fared. Surrey must have crossed the line about ten seconds behind us, but was to leeward near the far shore. Resolve and Ardent had failed to weather the tug and had both had to make a short tack to clear her. Ailsa and Northdown were still only just nearing the line and almost overtaken by Pride. Ellie related all this faithfully to Captain Day.

"Ol' Bully'll be 'oppin mad," was his comment.

"That's my department," said Zeke, balancing on his peg-leg.

The skipper was not satisfied with the arrangements up forrard.

"Git that ould fores'l dahn, Tom, it ain't doin' no good." The foresail rattled down, the skipper turned his attention to Surrey. "Reckon she's holdin' us."

"She is, too," said Zeke. "'Appen she's too far in. Could touch bottom in there."

"We'll see," said Captain Day philosophically. I gave Ellie's thigh an affectionate squeeze.

Things were sorting themselves out astern. Resolve had got the better of Ardent and crossed the line third. The other three were in a group and it was difficult to tell which one was leading. Again we reported to the skipper.

"That Bully'll try 'eaven an' earth ter catch up nah," said Captain Day. "We gotta think o' sommat ter keep us ahead."

"'Ow abaht us all spreadin' our coats," Zeke suggested. "Like the lightermen do ter blow across a dock."

"Nah, what we need is a watersail from the truck o' the mizzen ter the foot o' the mainmast. That ould jib still dahn the fo'c'sle?"

Here we missed Vic who was the expert on what was in the fo'c'sle. I said I thought it was.

"Get Ned an' go dahn the fo'c'sle an' git it then."

"Look at Surrey!" Ellie exclaimed.

Surrey was sailing away from the shore, screwing up towards the wind, and losing drive from her jibs.

"I thought 'e was too far in," said Captain Day. "Lay 'e's knocked up 'is leeboard on the bank over there." He saw me still standing there. "Go on then."

I collected Ned and we went down to examine the sails in the fo'c'sle. We found the old jib all right and as we carried it on deck I explained to Ned what it was for.

"That's orl very well," he said. "But we need sheets as well as a sail."

"Moorin' ropes?" suggested Tommy, who was nearby.

"Too thick," said Ned. "Won't go through the cringles." He shouted aft. "Anythin' we can use for sheets, skipper? An 'alliard, mebbe?"

Captain Day thought. "Nuffin' that ain't in use. Fergit it. We're doin' orl right." We took the jib back again.

By the time I returned aft, it was evident that we were indeed 'doin' orl right'. Surrey's encounter with the mudbank had done her no good at all and she had fallen back considerably. Resolve looked as though Bully was trying hard but with no noticeable result as yet. Ardent was gamely chasing Resolve and Pride seemed to have drawn clear of the other two. Ahead of us the last two staysail barges were within a few hundred yards.

At this point the chartered motor-boat from Clacton went past.

As she came alongside us she slowed down. Whether this was to save us being disturbed by her wash or whether it was to give the photographers aboard a chance, I was not sure. But plenty of Upshore people were aboard. There was Jan, of course, and Caroline Murphy and her husband, Mr. Oram, Ernest in his official capacity as a member of the Match Committee, Mr. Bliss and Wilfred Hooker, Barney Thornton and his family and Mrs. Day, with the dog Frank on a lead, for he and the other barge dogs were not allowed aboard for the Match. This must be very galling for such a free spirit as Frank, I thought. Finally there was Vic, standing aft on his own. He raised his good arm in salute as the boat accelerated away.

"D'ye think us'll make it dahn ter the Bench?" Zeke was asking Captain Day.

"Don't see why not, 'appen this wind 'olds."

"Ah! But do the Committee think that? Strange ol' lot they are. Yachtsmen, solicitors an' the like."

"And Ernie," said Ellie.

"Well, 'e at least knows wot 'e's doin'."

We sailed on for an hour in the order Daisy Maud, Surrey , Resolve, Ardent, Pride of Upshore, Northdown and Ailsa. But there were changes. Resolve began to gain on both Surrey and ourselves while Northdown offered a strong challenge to Pride. One by one we overhauled the staysail entries. Captain Day forecast that the fleet would arrive at the Bench Buoy as a mixture of borsprit and staysail barges.

The skipper decided that it would be a good idea to have lunch before reaching the turning mark, so Ellie and I went below to prepare it. This was quite simple as it was to be another sandwich affair, Mrs. Day having provided bread, butter, ham, pickles and bottled beer. This last would provide a welcome break from the everlasting mugs of tea that the crew demanded. Ellie had evolved a system of having two kettles on the go to constantly top up teapots to meet this demand.

For no apparent reason, Ellie and I fell into each others arms while preparing lunch. She clung to me for a long time until a shout of "Where's the grub?" broke us apart. Somehow, as with Jan the night before, there seemed a strange degree of finality about this clinch. As we went on deck with the meal there was a slatting and banging of sails.

"Git the foresail up, Tom. We need orl we can git," Captain Day was shouting.

"Wind's gorn," said Zeke as we laid out food and beer for him and the skipper.

"Not fer long, it ain't," said Captain Day. "Can yew manage the vittles on yer own, Miss Ellie? I want Bill as look-out aft."

I had a look round. We were nearly up with the first stay-sail barge – a Leigh-on-Sea entry, Maid of Leinster. Another stay-sail separated us from Surrey and two more hid Resolve from view, then there was Ardent, the other two staysails, Northdown, Pride and Ailsa.

"What am I looking for, skipper?" I asked.

"A change in the weather."

There were fast-moving, ragged clouds astern, which looked as though they bore rain. Astern of the fleet a fishing smack was beating to windward and making heavy weather of it. As I watched her topsail came down. I drew Captain Day's attention to it. As I spoke Ailsa, at the tail of the fleet, sprang to life, surging forward with her headsails flogging.

"I reckoned so," said Captain Day.

"Tom! Jib staysail dahn nah!"

Tommy put down his beer bottle.

"What?"

"Don't argue, jus' do it an' a 'and on the tops'l 'alliard in case!"

Pride, Northdown and the last two staysails were all affected now, their bow-waves building up and their jibs hastily being dropped. Jib topsails were coming down aboard Surrey and Resolve as well, Their skippers had spotted the squall also.

"Christ," Zeke exclaimed, "Ardent's lost her topmast."

The Rochester barge's topsail, jib and staysail were falling as the mast collapsed. Ellie came running aft.

"Will they be all right?" she asked.

"Never known a fallin' topmast 'urt no-one yet, Miss," said Zeke.

"Stand by!" yelled Captain Day.

The squall reached us. Sails that had been drooping filled with wind, and a wail came from the rigging. We seemed to rise up on our own bow-wave our bowsprit pointed straight at Maid of Leinster's mizzen. Then the staysail barge was away as well, her sails bulging with wind.

I glanced astern. Surrey and Resolve, which had had the wind before us, had both closed up. Aboard Ardent tiny figures were already aloft, clearing the debris. One of the staysail barges had pulled out of line, her sails flogging. Damage of some sort, I surmised.

"Great sailin', this," said Captain Day, without looking round. Ellie was perched on the cabin-top, the wind ruffling her hair, looking as though she was born to this type of thing. Zeke stood grasping one of the boat davits, he too, relishing this wild sail. The three men forward, who had earlier been lounging on the mast-deck, now stood alert, ready for any emergency. The Bench Buoy, a dot on the horizon before the squall, now loomed larger.

"'E'll be in our way, when we go rahnd," said Captain Day, referring to Maid of Leinster. I had another vision of yachts racing.

"Get between him and the buoy, skipper. He'll have to give you room if you get an overlap."

"Dunno what yer on abaht. Worth a try though."

We ranged up on the Leigh barge's quarter, gradually over-hauling her. Her skipper took no notice, no doubt concentrating on staying at the head of his own class.

"Wot's John think 'e's a doin' of," said Zeke suddenly. He'd looked up from his task of returning the boat to its normal position. Pride of Upshore was now sailing to windward away from the fleet and back towards Upshore. Captain Day risked a glance.

"Retired, I 'spect," he said.

"Don't look damaged," said Zeke.

223

"Probably annoyed, 'cos only Ailsa's be'ind 'im. Sod 'im anyways." The end of our borsprit was now level with Maid of Leinster's mast.

"Sheetin' in, Tommy. We're goin' fer the mark."

The barge became a hive of activity as vangs, sheets and leeboards were adjusted for the beat to windward. Maid of Leinster, not as efficient, sagged away to leeward. On our other side, the Bench Buoy flashed past, a few yards clear.

Only Pride of Upshore occupied the broad stretch of river ahead of us. Retired, the skipper and Zeke thought. That was what John had almost certainly told his crew but I had a feeling that she and John were waiting to settle scores with us.

CHAPTER 21
THE WAY BACK

So now we were round the Bench Buoy and beating to windward back towards the finishing line and whatever fate awaited Ellie and I at Upshore. This was very different to the run down to the buoy, especially now the wind had freshened. We were butting into the seas which were quite steep outside the protecting banks of the River Whitewater. It was becoming a wet ride for the men up on the mast deck and they had donned their raincoats which they considered sufficient protection against the spray. Without the topmast staysail less was required to be done up forrard and Ike was sent aft to help with the leeboards, which would be in constant use during the beat upriver.

The chartered Clacton motor boat went past throwing spray high over her bows as she butted into the seas. Some of her passengers must be feeling pretty grim, I imagined. The wind must be a good force five on the Beaufort scale - Beaufort scale? Was this another memory? I had never heard the bargemen refer to it.

I joined Ellie on the cabin top. She seemed to be thoroughly enjoying herself, her depression of the previous night completely gone, but she kept glancing towards Pride of Upshore. I felt that she had the same sense of foreboding that I did.

"Do you think he's waiting for us?" she asked.

John had dropped both Pride's jib topsail and jib and appeared to be sailing very slackly, with sheets eased off. But then he had apparently retired from the race, and had no need to press on, sailing hard. In fact, he and his crew were probably watching the remainder of the fleet battle it out.

To reassure Ellie, I said: "No, he's just watching the race."

"I've got a nasty feeling about it, though," said Ellie

"There's not much he can do out here, and we're surrounded by friends."

"But he could follow us, see where we go when we get to Upshore."

"Then I'll ask some of the others to create a diversion. Once we're in the car, we're away."

This seemed to allay her fears and we turned our attention to the Match. Although a beat to windward was Daisy Maud's best point of sailing, we were not doing so well. A strong challenge had developed from both Resolve and Surrey. Both were nearly up with us and aboard Resolve we could clearly see Bully, sitting on his packing case to steer, and wearing a new straw hat. How he kept it on in the wind was a mystery. As we watched he raised one arm in salute. Northdown was rounding the Bench Buoy. One bad mistake by one of the three leaders and she would be assured of her customary third position. Astern of Ailsa, plucky Ardent was continuing with the race, rigged as a stumpy, without topsail and jibs, but determined to complete the course.

"That's goin' ter be a three-way tackin' duel, directly minute," said Zeke to Captain Day.

"Wish I could do sommat ter pull clear," said the skipper. "Tryin' all I know now."

We sailed on in silence for a while. The rain arrived and Ellie slipped on her oilskin.

"Wot's Bully up ter?" Captain Day asked. He evidently couldn't see the other barges now for the mainsail was hiding them from him. Ike went down to leeward.

"'E's got Surrey right alongside 'im," he reported. "She's tryin' ter go thro' 'im ter windward. No she ain't, 'e's luffin' 'er!"

"Ready abaht! Lee oh," Captain Day shouted. "I'm steerin' clear o' that. Let 'em get on wiv it," he added, by way of explanation.

"Leggo" and Tommy released the bowline, letting the foresail crash over on its iron horse. We were round sailing away from the duel between Resolve and Surrey but towards Pride of Upshore. Once we had settled down on the new course and the leeboards had been adjusted for the new tack, all eyes, except Captain Day's, were on Resolve and Surrey again.

"'E's doin' it agen," said Zeke.

Once again Surrey tried to pass Resolve and Bully luffed until both barges were almost head to wind, their headsails fluttering.

"Think 'e's doin' it ter let us git away?" Ike asked.

"Nah!" said Captain Day, "That ain't Bully. 'E's goin' ter sort Surrey aht, then 'e'll come after us."

"'Appen we gives 'im the chance," said Zeke.

Again Surrey tried to pass and was luffed.

"Why doesn't Surrey tack?" asked Ellie.

"Bully'ld only cover 'im on the other tack," said Zeke. "There ain't no way aht, Surrey's goin' to 'ave ter let him go."

All the afterguard with the exception of Captain Day had been watching the contest between Surrey and Resolve. Now Tommy called from forrard. "Pride's gettin' awful close, skipper."

"That's all right. I'm watchin' 'im," Captain Day shouted back. "'E's retired. So 'e ain't got right o'way over a barge racin', whatever tack 'e's on."

"'Ope he know that, skipper. Looks like 'e's 'oldin' on."

"Nah, 'e's clear ahead, 'e'll be orlright."

Indeed, Pride was going to pass clear ahead of us on the opposite tack. Then suddenly things changed.

"Christ. 'E's bearin' away on ter us," shouted Zeke.

"Everyone 'old on," shouted the skipper, frantically spinning the wheel to minimise the collision.

But I didn't hold on. I started forrard to see what was happening. Aboard Pride, Captain Bristow, the mainsheet hand, was

227

fighting John for possession of the wheel, while old Hoary ran aft, shouting. Behind me, Ellie screamed. The two barges met in a grinding, glancing blow.

But in my excitement, I had forgotten the mainsheet and stepped athwart its horse and the mainsheet block hit me at knee level propelling me over the side.

I caught a glimpse of Ellie's agonised face, then the seas swept me away from the two barges. Someone aboard Daisy Maud flung a life buoy and I tried to swim to it. But there was a strange feeling in my legs where they had been hit by the block, and they would not function.

Two of the crew were lowering Daisy Maud's boat, but they were going to be too late . . . far too late. I was calling Ellie's name as I went under for the last time.

EPILOGUE (1)

NARRATIVE OF JACK DOWNING
1964

"Then you woke up in hospital?" I said.

"No, I remember briefly coming to on the beach with a dog sniffing me – I thought it was Frank."

I sighed. Whatever this was it was very real to him and, now to me, also.

"But if it wasn't a dream, what was it?" he persisted.

"How old are you, Bill?" I asked.

"Forty-seven."

"It can't be that, then."

"Can't be what?"

"A previous existence. As Bill, the barge-hand, you drowned in 1939. If your spirit had been taken over by Bill, the architect, as he was born he would now be twenty-five. That theory just doesn't tie up. And, another funny thing, as Bill the barge-hand, your memory began to return – your 1960's memory - yacht racing, bikinis, darts matches and so on. Moreover, and I'll tell you more in a minute, research proves that you were dealing with real events, real sailing barges and, most important of all, real people."

"Tell me more of your research."

"Well, first of all, during one of the breaks in your narrative I visited Upshore and Nether Rushbrook, where Barney is still remembered with affection, although his family have left the village. Neither place was changed very much, although I understand that there are big plans for Upshore. Everything was much as you described it, the quay, the two pubs, the bargeyard, the trees and so on. But, naturally, twenty-five years has caused some changes. What you describe as Fowler & Dunn's office is now Upshore Cruising Club, obviously a fairly recent change as the name 'Fowler & Dunn' can still be made out over the door. The only barges using Upshore are now yachts apart from the odd motor-barge at Fuller's Timber Wharf on the far bank.

"But I didn't spend long looking round for my main reason for the visit, naturally enough for a journalist, was to see the local paper, Upshore Gazette, to look at their archives. They were helpful enough, but I didn't really get a lot. In the 1939 section I found an obituary for Isaac Fowler, which tied in with your tale and mention of the members of his family. I then looked for a report on the Barge Match but only found a brief paragraph which stated that it was abandoned after a crew-member on one of the barges was lost overboard and believed drowned. Then I found a report of the trial of Pocock, the bookmaker. The charge was reduced to dangerous driving and Pocock got off lightly with a fine, for, as was said in court, one important witness had died since the incident and another was too distraught to appear." He blanched at that.

"I also checked several minor things. For example, the score in the football match that Vic attended was as you say."

"But what about the researcher who was looking into the barge angle?"

"I'm coming to that. Her letter does say a great deal more, so I'd like you to read it in full."

I passed him the letter which read as follows:-

230

Maple Cottage,
Faversham,
Kent.

Dear Jack,

I'm sorry that time has not permitted me to delve into your friend's tale as thoroughly as I would have liked to have done. For instance, I have not, so far, interviewed any of the surviving participants.

Yes, the good news, is that all the people, places, barges and events that you have mentioned did exist. But there is one important exception and that is Bill Furlong, your third hand, himself. I will try, however, to bring you and Bill up to date.

After the 1939 Upshore Barge Match, Vic Halliday left Upshore and worked briefly for the Thames & Medway Barge Co., in his native Kent. He spent his war service in the Royal Engineers, and after the war, returned to Thames & Medway and has now risen to be captain of one of their largest motor coasters.

Shortly after the events in Bills' tale, the war engulfed everybody, and the bargemen probably more than many others. Several barges went to Dunkirk – not Daisy Maud, she was on the yard having some damage put right – but Tommy Dolby, by then commanding the auxiliary barge Hubert, was there and bought back 270 troops from the beaches. John Fowler and the Pride also went, loaded with ammunition for the rearguard. Pride took a direct hit from a German bomb and there were no survivors.

Bill's friend Jan was something of a war hero. He was still with Horace Carney on Reed Warbler when she set off a German mine in the Thames. She did not sink at once, but was obviously going fast. Horace and Jan had got the boat in the water, ready to abandon, when the old man insisted on going below for his wallet. The barge then started to go down fast. Jan cut the boat free and then managed to rescue the old man from the fast-flooding cabin and swam with him to the boat. Although they landed safely, Old Hoary died a few days later, officially

231

of pneumonia, but some say of heartbreak for his lost money. After this, Jan joined the Polish Navy, and, after the war, transferred to their Merchant Navy. He is now chief officer of a Polish cargo passenger liner, which often calls at Tilbury Docks, when he takes the opportunity to look up his old barging friends.

Bully Briggs did not survive the war either. Bargemen were forbidden to use the Swin Spitway during the war, for it was part of a British minefield. Bully maintained, however, that the mines were set too deep to affect a barge and continued to use the Spitway. Several mates deserted him because of this. Eventually the inevitable happened and Resolve set off a mine. Again there were no survivors and Resolve's remains drifted on to the Buxey Sand where they lay for the rest of the was as a grim warning to other bargemen.

However, there were those that did well out of the war. One was Rosie Barnes, landlady of the King's Head. She made a fortune from quenching the thirsts of airmen from nearby bases, especially once the Americans came into the war. Shortly after the end of hostilities she retired to live with her sister in Brighton – although there are rumours that this was not immediately the case and that she lived with Vic for a while. The new landlord was George Gascoigne, by then retired from barging, but he hadn't the right attitude for running a pub and trade declined. Subsequent landlords were not interested in the maritime customers, but recently Ned Harris, once a part-time pianist at the pub, and his wife, the former Florrie Hooker, who had been a barmaid at the pub, have taken over and are restoring the inn to its former condition and attracting the crews of the yacht and charter barges that use the quay.

The barge trade has altered immensely since 1939. The only barge still genuinely trading under sail is Bob Robert's Cambria. A few others eke out an existence as power vessels, but practically all their former trade is now hauled by road transport or motor coasters. The only barges to use the Town Quay are yachts or charter vessels and this is something that the Town Council is encouraging as a tourist attraction. Upshores' maritime trade is

232

now almost entirely yachts. Fowler's former bargeyard, still managed by Ernest Fowler, concentrates on this activity but still has the facilities to deal with a sailing barge.

The firm of Fowler and Dunn still exists as Fowler Motorships Ltd. As the name implies they have had the foresight to concentrate on motor vessels, selling their last sailing barge in 1953. They now operate from London, not Upshore, a commercial decision taken by Eleanor Fowler when they absorbed the shipbroking business of Rupert Dunn. The firm also has interests in shipping, forwarding and air freight. Miss Fowler has been chairman of the company since Rupert Dunn's retirement.

Tommy Dolby and his mate Ike have had to leave commercial barging and are now partners in a fishing vessel. They are still active in the barging scene giving advise on the re-rigging of barge hulls. They also skipper yacht barges when this can be arranged between fishing. Zeke Brown still "unofficially" helps the Upshsore river bailiff, although he must be nearly eighty now.

Captain 'Happy' Day died only last year. He retired from barging in 1948 – not something he wished to do, but he was informed that Daisy Maud was too small to be economic and was to be sold. He was offered command of the big auxiliary powered barge Balthazar but declined because he "didn't 'old with no injuns". For some years he tended his garden and forgot his barging days. However, after Mrs. Day died in 1960, Tommy Dolby felt that Captain Day needed something more to occupy himself and involved him on the re-rigging of Alicia which had been a motor-barge for some years and was converting to a yacht. Happy really took to this task and was eventually asked to sail as skipper by the young couple who owned Alicia. He had a couple of happy years doing this, but last year collapsed aboard the barge and was rushed to hospital. Alas, he died the same night.

And Daisy Maud? Well she's still afloat. She was sold out of trade and became a houseboat on the upper reaches of the Thames. Fortunately her various owners looked after her and she was recently surveyed and declared fit to be re-rigged as a yacht. Her most recent owner dearly wished this to happen but unhappily died before much was done. However his will provides sufficient funds to do most of the work if a suitable owner can be found. Now, don't think I'm dropping a hint to your friend Bill, but . . .

Yours sincerely,
Julia Newman.

P.S. I've just had a quick try to get in touch with two of the participants in Bill's story. I chose Vic Halliday and Eleanor Fowler, these being the nearest two to where I live in Kent. But unfortunately Vic was with his ship in Bristol and Miss Fowler's secretary said she was far too busy to see me at short notice. Sorry. J.

There was a pause while Bill digested all this. After a while, he said. "It's good to know what happened to them all and I'm sorry that some of them are dead, especially Captain Day and Bully. But she doesn't say much about Ellie, does she?"

Feeling rather like a fairy god-father, I reached for my briefcase and produced an envelope.

"I've saved the best till last," I said. "The Upshore Gazette came up with a recent photo of your fiancée."

I placed the photo in front of him and stood up to have another look myself. The caption read: "Miss Eleanor Fowler opening the village fete at Little Nissenden." The lady in the photo wore a cream suit with a picture hat. I thought that she looked very well preserved for her age, which must be 43 or 44. Without her glasses, she would be considered pretty if not beautiful. She was reaching out with a pair of scissors to cut a tape. She was not wearing gloves and her hands could be seen plainly.

"She's still wearing our ring!" Bill exclaimed. "The one that the blacksmith made!"

I looked where he was pointing. The ring on the engagement finger was clearly visible.

"I must see her! Straight away."

234

"Hold on," I said. "You can't get hold of her this time of night and from what Julia says an appointment isn't easy."

"She'll see me all right. But you're correct. It would be best if I start in the morning."

"Be very careful," I warned. "It will be a great shock for her and she could be married or anything."

"She still calls herself 'Miss'. But I suppose that could just be for business purposes. You're right, I'll have to be careful."

"I'll leave the rest to you, then," I said, gathering up my papers. He thanked me profusely. I felt that he had recovered from any trauma caused by his near drowning and his transition from one time to another. Whatever his 'experience' had been, I could see no point in probing further. He didn't need a psychiatrist and he didn't need me any further. He would take this affair to its conclusion himself now.

Poor Ellie, I reflected as I drove away, she had lost mother, father, lover and brother in quick succession. Poor Bill, too, for whatever reason, he had lived an interesting and varied life and then had had it, and his true love, snatched away. I felt that his visit to the past did not warrant further explanation and should be accepted for what it was.

It occurred to me that, whatever I had told Bill earlier, as a humble local newspaper hack, I was turning down what could be the 'scoop' of my career, in the hopes of bringing two deserving people some happiness.

EPILOGUE (2)

NARRATIVE OF BILL FURLONG - 1964

Naturally I felt apprehensive as I walked from Tower Hill tube station. The offices of Fowler Motorships were on the first floor of a building in Leadenhall Street. They were, I suspected, formerly the headquarters of Rupert Dunn's shipbroking business, which had been expanded and modernised when Fowler's moved in.

I had fixed the appointment with a secretary, who had been doubtful whether Miss Fowler would see me.

"She'll see *me* all right," I said.

She went away and returned to say would two o'clock the next afternoon do. I suspected that she had consulted Ellie in between. No doubt Ellie was intrigued with a name from the past, but probably believed it was a coincidence, or an imposter.

So there I was pushing open the glass doors of Fowler's offices. A pert blonde receptionist received me. It was the second door on the left, she said, and I could go straight in. I knocked and entered. She was just coming from behind her desk, a file under her arm. She was wearing a tight black top and a rather short floral skirt.

I blurted out a greeting which I had been considering but had discarded as rather too rude:

"Why, it's all tits and legs!"

"I beg your pardon," she said.

Then I realised that this girl was far too young to be the present day Ellie. Moreover her eyes were blue like mine, whereas Ellie's were brown and she had a wider mouth – again like mine, otherwise the resemblance to the younger Ellie was uncanny.

"It was . . . Ellie . . . that I came to see," I gulped.

"Oh, you want my mother. Please take a seat, she'll only be a moment. I just came in to get this," She patted the file. Absorbed, I subsided into a comfortable chair in front of the desk. Ellie's daughter? She must be . . .

The girl went out and closed the door. I heard her talking to someone in the corridor.

"He's weird, mum. He just called me 'all tits and legs'."

The door flew open and she was there. The real Ellie. The Ellie who had poked at the barges coaming with a bare foot, the Ellie who had driven a fast sports car, the Ellie who had run naked into the sea, the Ellie who had laid her brother out with a shovel. My Ellie, the mother of my child.

Her hair was longer than I remembered and she was back to a severe business suit and glasses, but otherwise she was little changed.

"It *is* you," she exclaimed. "But . . . you're dead...you drowned." She tottered on her high heels and I thought she was going to faint. I rushed forward and guided her to my chair, then sat myself down on a settee that ran down one side of the office.

She took a few deep breaths then reached for the intercom on her desk and depressed a button.

"Cancel my appointments for the rest of the day, and please see that we are not disturbed."

"Very good, Miss Ellie," the box replied dutifully.

So her staff still called her that, I thought. She took a cigarette from a box on the desk and lit it with a desk lighter in the shape of a sailing barge.

"I haven't had one of these for years," she said, proffering me the box. I shook my head. "It must be your effect on me."

That was like the old Ellie. This interview was going rather well, I thought.

"I'll have you drinking in pubs and turning up for work in shorts soon," I said.

"And having sex all sorts of ways," she added. Not well, extremely well. "Oh, Bill. I have missed you. Where have you been?" That would need a lot of explaining I felt. For the moment, I said that I had survived, but lost my memory for a long time. Which was near enough.

"Your body was never found," she said thoughtfully. "And, I dunno, call it woman's intuition, I had a feeling I'd see you again."

I changed the subject. "I'm afraid I insulted your daughter just now. I called her 'all tits and legs'."

"Our daughter," she corrected me and then laughed. "I expect she's been called a lot worse. She's Ruth. A clever girl, though I say it myself. She's got a degree in economics and she should become a Chartered Shipbroker soon. I expect she'll take my place one day."

I asked her what happened after I went overboard from Daisy Maud.

"I was in a terrible state for a long time. Just couldn't stop crying. I was off work for ages. But then war broke out and the firm came under all sorts of pressure so I managed to pull myself together and went back even though I was quite pregnant.

"John became some sort of pariah. No-one wanted to know him. He took the Pride, which he regarded as his personal property, to Mistley and no one raised any objections but Bully made sure he didn't stay at Mistley long and he drifted around, picking up freights where he could with a variety of crews, since the old ones soon deserted him. Then he was killed at Dunkirk and I can't say it affected me much, because by then I was dealing with a little baby and still trying to run the firm."

Then she told me more of her struggle to turn Fowler's into the

238

modern, progressive business it was now. She said that she had a very good manager, Sam Turner.

"You must remember him. He'd just started as office boy when you left."

Then I told her of my lucrative career as an architect, designing buildings to replace those destroyed by enemy action in London, Plymouth and many more cities.

After that the floodgates really opened and we talked of many people and things.

Of Captain Day. Ellie said sadly: "He was such a lovely old man, Do you know when he was in hospital, he was still talking to the young couple who owned Alicia about work that needed doing. They said that he could help with it himself when he came out of hospital." Her eyes filled with tears. "But he told them he wouldn't be coming out. It was that night that he died."

Of Vic: "I haven't seen him for ages. But he does stay in touch. I get letters now and again. Did you know it was me that bailed him out and bought his ticket to watch the Match?"

I said that I had had no idea.

"I think he learnt his lesson. He gave up gambling and hardly drinks at all."

Of Tommy and Ike: "They're great fun those two. Real double-act. They've got worse since the've been fishing. I've met up with them a few times. Always ends up with what Tommy calls a few beers."

Of others we had known: Time had taken some - Mr. Oram, Wilfred Hooker and George Gascoigne. Mr. Bliss, with his now old-fashioned bowler hat, was a well-known character around Upshore and Miss Fellows, Fowler's old typist, also retired, still gossiped about the 'goings-on' in 1939. The blacksmith now had his own business in a village outside Upshore. but still came in to play darts at the King's Head.

And of the King's Head itself: "I haven't been there since Florrie and Ned took over," she said. "We must do that some-time. I believe Pat still serves there and if Tommy, Ike and a few others turn up it will be quite like old times."

239

'We' must do that, I noted hopefully.

Of the alterations to Upshore waterfront: "The warehouses will be pulled down next year. They're not much used now and the council believes it will open up the quay to the public. Cynics say it will create another car park. We sold our old offices to a yacht club, but we still have a small depot in one of the warehouses. Caroline manages it, but she'll retire next year when the demolition starts. Did you know her husband made it to superintendent?"

I asked what involvement she still had with Upshore. She told me that the family home had been sold and was now an old peoples' home. Ernie lived in a cottage in the town and still ran the boatyard. But Ellie stabled horses in the area and rode with the local hunt. And she still had her sailing dinghy - the same one – which was kept at one of the local yacht clubs.

"Do you still sail it in a bathing costume?" I asked.

She laughed: "No, a bikini these days."

That led me to ask about the sports car.

"Oh, no! I sold that during the war, to a young pilot. No, I drive a Rover saloon now. Very sedate. But I'd love to drive a sports car again. Feel the wind in my hair and all that."

Maybe I could do something about this, I thought.

"You were good for me, Bill," she said suddenly. "I was in danger of becoming a work-dominated old maid when we first met."

And that led to a discussion of our sex lives.

"I haven't exactly been a nun since you left, Bill," she admitted. "Jan was very sweet and kind after you went, and I think he was more than a little in love with me, but he joined the Polish navy and that was that. He has a family of his own in Poland now. Then that Dave Fox made a pest of himself for a while."

"Dave Fox?"

"Reuben's grandson."

"I remember."

"But then he was called up into the Army and was killed in the D-Day landings. More recently there's been a shipbroker I was doing business with and a guy I met on holiday in Marbella. I slept with both of them several times. But the shipbroker was married with a family and the other was – well, just a holiday romance."

And that led me to tell her of my disastrous marriage which was shortly coming to an end.

There were three interruptions to all this. The first occurred when Ellie insisted on fetching us cups of coffee. While she was out I had a look round the office. There were several pictures on the walls, mainly of the coasters and motor barges that the company now owned. But there was a solitary sailing barge - which proved to be me aboard Daisy Maud and I had no idea who had taken it or when. Probably Ellie herself, I thought, when I wasn't looking. But it was a good sign that she had kept it in a prominent position for so long.

The second interruption was when her - our - daughter, Ruth put her head round the door.

"I'm off home, mum," she said. "See you later."

"Come in Ruth," Ellie commanded. "You've met Bill haven't you?"

"I have, indeed." Ruth said, shaking hands rather formerly. "Pleased to meet you, father. I've heard so much about you."

I thought I detected a sardonic tone. I could have trouble with this one. Then she said: "Must rush. Got a date. I'm sure you two have got a lot to talk about. I'll see you both later." Now that sounded a lot better.

The third was from a cleaning lady who put her head round the door and asked when she could 'do' the office.

"Good Lord," said Ellie. "Is it that late? I'm sorry we won't be much longer."

I realised that time was running out. I took Ellie's hand in mine.

"Ellie," I said slowly. "I realise that ours must be the longest engagement on record, but can we extend it? Please."

She thought for a moment.

"I'll do better than that," she answered. "Before John interfered we were going to be married in St. Michael's, right? That can be re-arranged very quickly, just as soon as your divorce is final. And Ernie can give me away. He's always wanted to do that an' he's not a well man – heart trouble – he may not be with us much longer."

She took my other hand and gazed into my eyes.

"Things won't be the same," she went on. "But they'll be good. Very good. I promise."

And Ellie always kept her promises.

POSTSCRIPT

FROM THE UPSHORE GAZETTE
16th JUNE, 1965.

Today, Miss Eleanor Fowler, Chairman of Fowler Motorships Ltd., launched their new motorship, 'Arthur Day', at Great Yarmouth. Fowler Motorships, Formerly Fowler & Dunn Ltd., was once a well-known employer in this town, operating a large fleet of sailing barges. In naming the ship, Miss Fowler, explained that it was named after one of the company's former barge skippers, a man who she still held in great esteem, several years after his death.

At a press conference after the launch, Miss Fowler announced that, with immediate effect, she was retiring as Chairman of the Company. She would become the firm's first president, while her place as Chairman would be taken by the firm's present manager, Samuel Turner, who himself would be replaced by Miss Fowler's daughter, Ruth.

Miss Eleanor has recently married the well-known architect and yachtsman, Mr. William Furlong. The couple intended to concentrate on refitting, with the help of friends, their recently acquired sailing barge, Daisy Maud.

THE END